Zet – Alien

Species Unknown

By Cherime MacFarlane

Table of Contents

Prologue

You are Zet for two reasons. The laughter in the voice turned Zet into a quivering lump of flesh and scales. The being he couldn't see in the darkness always did more damage to him when playful.

You are the first of this generation—and you may be the last—unless there have been changes. Which means you will do better this time.

Not again. Not so soon after the last session. His wounds would surely open when the thing had him immobilized so it could test the speed with which his body regenerated. The pain would be that much greater.

He could not take another session so soon. **No!** Zet knew better than to ask for a respite. It would count as a mental weakness. All his being must be strong, must measure up. If he didn't, there would be more treatments, time spent detached from his mind and body.

A noise down the hall told him they were coming. The last words of the thing which called itself a "researcher" replayed in his head. He could not do better. Better than the being that said it would recreate him, make him more able to resist pain and the rigors of warfare. He would fail, and this time he would never rise again.

Fear flooded him, the taste acidic in his mouth. The two half-formed teeth barely through the skin of his jaw ached. Zet's fear intensified. His legs felt wet and a sound he'd never made before spilled from his throat.

The door opened, and he charged, using his tail to propel him forward. The creature that had opened the cage sailed backward as the door hit it when the cart flew into the bars. Metal screeched as Zet gripped the cart and rammed it into the shadows where the voice had come from. A scream sounded when the cart encountered something softer than the wall. It died as abruptly as it began.

Zet used the cart to ram it once more. There were noises like those he'd heard when his frame snapped in places. Snarling, he shoved the metal into that softness again. A clanging sounded... and Zet's need to destroy the researcher fled.

He must leave or they would find and kill him as he hoped he had killed the researcher. He didn't turn up the corridor. That led to the room where they tested him. The other direction was a mystery. He took it, feeling he had no choice.

Zet didn't stop to investigate the rooms he fled through. A taste of something in the air led him forward, the smell different from the rest of the corridor. Following the scent, which grew stronger, he came to a door. He launched his body against it, and the metal buckled. Gathering his strength, he tried again with greater desperation. The locking mechanism fell apart and Zet ripped the panel aside to find... a world he'd never seen before.

Sliding into the shadows, he stayed at the edges of something he couldn't name. What could it be? In the distance, over the roofs of the squat buildings he hurried away from, lights lit the vastness. Different colors of lights he had no name for pulsed, sparkled, and vanished only to return brighter.

Cooler air drifted across his face and he turned that way. Still in the shadows, he eased his aching body toward the smell of... water? There it was. The most water he'd ever seen in his short life. Flipping through the educational images in his head, he found a name for it. Because he could see the other side and water above and below where he stood, Zet thought it must be a river.

They had taught him to navigate water.

Gently lowering himself into the liquid, he hushed the gasp that tried to escape when the water touched his wounds. He must be silent. They had taught him that skill—he'd no trouble mastering it.

He could let the force of the water take him where it wished, but decided against that. They would look for him in that direction. They would look in both. For now, making his way against the flow seemed a sounder choice.

A short time later, he came on a conveyance floating in the water. Immobile, it sat near another building, much like the one he'd escaped. After filling his lungs and the other cavity, he dove under the thing, looking for a hiding spot. He found one.

The conveyance had a notch where the steering apparatus went up into the main body of the structure. A small spot where the bottom met the upper part had a place where he could wedge himself above the housing. There was air there. Although most of his body would be in the water, his nostrils would be in the air pocket. It would do.

When the water surrounding him lightened, the thing moved. He didn't know what exactly was going on and didn't care. If it took him away from the place where they had held him for as long as he could remember, he would be content.

Chapter 1

He woke with a jerk, the tip of his tail held in his mouth to stifle any outcry. All his musk glands had opened. Zet pushed his tail aside with his tongue and pulled the covers back around him. No need to move just yet.

He remembered where he was now. Safe on the *Demon Lair*, no one would take him captive again. Free from Calius, he had nothing to fear. Zet, an alien of species unknown, was a valued member of the crew.

Camat ran the gang he'd eventually joined, and Camat made sure they monitored everything. It would not do to have the government raid the Demons. He had been a member one full SUN year when Camat said there had been no outcry for a killer. No news broadcast over the two major news entities telling a tale of an escapee who had killed to free himself. They would continue to check, but it seemed he had made it out with no repercussions.

Camat didn't know all of it, but he knew enough.

Zet turned on the gelbed and relaxed. During talks with Camat about what had happened to him, they both agreed that what had been going on was likely experimental and off the books. He was an engineered being. An entity that shouldn't exist. Someone had been trying to build the ultimate warrior and lost their subject. Such was life.

On his stomach so as not to cramp his tail, he smiled. Slavery was against the law in SUN territory and not allowed on Estevan, their home port. To get him back, they would need to take on all the Demons. His brothers and sisters would allow no one to take him. They protected each other.

It had been a while since that terrifying nightmare had stolen his peace. Only a dream, he refused to let it bother him.

On the way to the galley, he got stopped by Itty. Zet grunted a greeting, and she smiled at him.

Bunde walked out of the entry to the galley and grinned at them both. "How are my strays this happy cycle?"

"Good," Itty chirped.

"Hungry." The word rumbled out of him, causing both females to laugh.

"When are you not hungry?" Bunde asked.

Having finally perfected Trund's shrug, he executed it. A useful move, it kept him from having to answer either female.

Itty's small fingers touched his hand and Zet froze. The tiny Human Houser's thin skin could suffer damage too easily. A few rough patches of scales that hadn't healed properly might do damage to the little female. Fond of her, he would go to great lengths to keep that from happening. "Yesss?"

Because he'd answered too quickly, the word came out in a slight hiss. As disparaged as snakes were, it irritated him to make that sound. He must take greater care.

"You are due a physical. After your next shift, be sure to come to the med unit."

For an instant, he contemplated disobeying her edict and gave a curt nod instead. "I will."

Feeling eyes trained on him in an unfriendly manner, he took a quick glance in the mirror of Bunde's eyes and saw the pilot behind him. The female stood to the side in the corridor and glared at Itty's fingers on his skin.

Zet snorted. He'd seen the pilot's gaze locked on Itty before when they'd had Relda confined in that cell. If Itty didn't want to be claimed, the Ellaerian would take on the entire crew of the *Demon Lair*. To use Brown's phrase—"not happening".

Deliberately, without turning around, Zet intended to address the pilot using her last name only. It would cast a dark spirit over the ship if she continued to behave in that proprietary manner toward their med tech. He shrugged again. *So be it*. "Pilot Relda."

She took a step closer. "Zet."

Had she been a snake, his name would have hissed out between clenched teeth. Her irritation amused him. To drive the claw deeper, he took Itty's hand in his, dipped his head and made a bow good enough for any Messerian at court. "Until after shift."

The female beside him stiffened while Itty and Bunde laughed at his histrionics as Zet suspected they would.

"You've been paying attention to those holos, haven't you?" Itty asked.

"You made an excellent suggestion. My thanks, Itty. If I ever find myself in a situation where extreme manners are called for, I suspect Messerian rules won't be remiss. They certainly know how to do formal."

"I haven't watched that. I'll need to check it out." Bunde slid between the pilot and where he and Itty stood. "Please." The Human-Gossican half-breed female gave Zet's shoulder a pat as she walked past.

Bunde's message of solidarity received, he backed off. "Do you think there are any of those rolls left?" he asked Itty.

She nodded. "Neither Enkel nor Brown have turned up yet. If you hurry, you should be able to catch one or two now. Caran has started a fresh batch, but it will be a couple of hours before they're ready."

She turned to go by Zet and nearly ran into Xigant Relda. "Oh, sorry Xigant. I didn't realize you were so close."

"No! No, my fault. Sorry." The female sputtered like an engine with a problem as she backed farther away. She glanced at Zet and he gave her what he considered his touch-me-and-I'll-take-your-arm-off smile.

The slight turn of her lips Xigant had worn when talking with Itty vanished and her red eyes flashed flames his way.

That had him huffing out a breath, pleased with his effect on her. Opening his mouth slightly wider, he sent a thought her way. His implants were off, though. He'd not bothered to turn them on. A good thing at this moment in time.

The pilot, not a telepath, as was the male from the Life Foundation, she wouldn't get the full force of it. But she might feel a shade. *If I hit you with my tail, I'll break all your ribs and put you in Itty's medbed for days. I know you'd love that. Not now. Maybe later.* A brief nod in her direction and he entered the kitchen where he went directly to the Selvian sweet rolls. That and a cup of the tea stuff from Nippon on the planet of Haakonlan and he'd be ready for his shift.

Which brought Zet to the problem he'd been trying to work out. Unsure of his own being, was he real or a partial construct? A fully animate being or part machine? Zet felt a certain kinship with the ship's AI. Because of his meticulous adherence to procedure and careful handling of the ship, he had its trust enough for it to confide in him.

Hours and hours of squirming into places no one other than Itty could go, he built a map in his mind of the *Demon Lair*. He'd asked the AI during his last shift to explain why the dimensions of the transport tubes seemed off somehow. Zet recognized an attempt at obfuscation when he heard it.

What makes you think there is something off? I've no knowledge of any difference. There's no discrepancy.

With what passed for a smile with him, Zet finished the remaining bite of the roll and tossed down the last of the tea. In the corridor, well away from the kitchen, he turned on his implants and addressed the ship. Zet made sure they had a secure channel and no one else could hear what went on between him and the AI. He stationed himself in vacant quarters on the frame where the gelbed would be. *Did you recheck the plans?*

Ah. Well. You could be correct.

What might be the purpose of the extra width? It isn't much, perhaps 30 millimeters total.

I could not say.

Are there more of those Olta gems hidden away? Come now. You know how dangerous those are to this crew and to your existence. Think of the horror of being ripped apart. All your frame exposed.

No, no. Not those. I am positive they are all gone now.

Demon Lair, talk to me. If you truly don't know what may be in those cavities, how do I get in to look?

That I know.

How? Explain.

The side panels of the tube, on the side facing the bow. They lift, but one must be on the floor to accomplish it. The mechanics are difficult for only one being. One gets only a second after tripping the latch to lift the panel. If not immediately braced, it will settle down and relatch. You only get three tries, then it will lock permanently.

How do you trip the latch?

Seven millimeters from the floor are two slight bulges, one must push in on them at the same time. How will you do that alone?

Zet chuckled, the rumble of sound filling the room. *I have a tail. I will push the tip in when the panel lifts.*

You can wield your tail independently?

Assuredly. I suspect this is best done during the evening watch. I will wait and try it. Are you positive you do not know what might hide in those spaces?

I am. There were times the captain put me offline. I've no knowledge of what he did during those intervals. But I suspect whatever it was, his second-in-command helped.

So be it. If I need your assistance to open the cavities, I'll contact you. Now for the other matter. There is a vent partially blocked in the stern. Do you know what is in there? It's too small for me to crawl through and I will not ask Itty.

Dust and some detritus picked up on Greenhouse 2. All the crawler bots are disabled or I would have seen to it myself.

All of them?

Affirmative. All ten are in various states of disrepair and need parts. I don't have a one I can put through the vent. It's somewhat functional now. Not fully, but enough for us to get to port.

I will rely on your assessment of the problem. We can't open the system and look either.

Both Zet and the AI knew the damage that would cause if they opened the vent to space while they traveled through it. They could seal that section off and put someone properly clad in the area. Still, if it would do to get them home—caution dictated waiting.

Zet shut the private channel he used with the AI off and opened to the wider crew. Time to report. In the control room, he tapped Oolden on the shoulder. "Your relief is here."

The Yadaxian rubbed one orange-colored seven-fingered hand over his face. "Glad you're here. I didn't sleep well. Don't know why."

Zet gave his shoulder a squeeze. "Go straight to bed. There aren't any rolls left, and Caran will be a couple of hours getting the new batch ready."

Oolden sighed. "I wish the things would come out right if she replicated them."

With a laugh, Zet slipped into the contoured seat before the com unit. "We all wish the same. It doesn't work, so we live with having to wait. Get some rest before you head to the galley. Anything going on here?"

"Not a blip of sound from anyone close. There have been a few odd pings, but I suspect SUN may be holding war games somewhere. At least, I hope they're nothing but games."

"As do we all. Say a prayer to Saint Michael for us all that nothing is brewing. We don't need war to break out."

"Certainly. May your watch be supremely boring."

They weren't that far from Estevan and a well-deserved rest. He needed to deal with that vent problem, easier done on the hard. He grinned as he thought about Captain Camat's need to get home to his female.

Still, for all the entire crew knew how much their captain wanted to be home, he never pushed the *Demon Lair* too hard. Having purchased the ex-pirate ship at auction, they had no idea how rough it had been used in the past.

No log existed. Nor did the AI have the information. Someone had wiped a good portion of the AI's records away. They needed a good long stay in Greenhouse 2's shipyard. That took credits they didn't have. Not yet.

Camat was working on it. He and Trund, the second-in-command, said four or perhaps three more good contracts, and the ship would go in for an overhaul. Zet looked forward to it. The rest of the crew could take that time and go wherever they wished. Zet wanted to explore Estevan. He liked the scorching desert far better than the humid and hot jungle that was Greenhouse 2.

Chapter 2

Head in her hands, Xigant sat on her bunk and cursed. She had to stop acting as if she owned Itty. That could get her thrown off the *Demon Lair,* which would see her back in a bar. Without Itty, she might well lose her sanity.

Then there was the coming meeting with Captain Camat's father. The father he didn't know and might well reject. If he discovered she had a hand in bringing the meeting about... Xigant moaned. Why had she ever contacted C'entala? This could well cost her not only Itty, but her position as the head pilot on the ship.

Her addiction to liquor had nearly taken her life and Itty had helped her regain everything. The crew of the *Demon Lair* had welcomed her for her knowledge and Camat now trusted her to teach the rest of the crew how to pilot the ship. Would he turn her away when he learned... That is, if C'entala divulged how the information came to him.

Her mentor swore by Saint Michael to keep her secret. His last email said he'd contacted Shussha on Calius. The Kazzemian had retired and lived on a boat far from either of the two big cities. She verified Camat was indeed the son of C'entala.

C'entala seemed grateful and she hoped that gratitude would keep him from blurting out who connected them. Camat would ask. He had to. She'd jeopardized everything because of her duty to her mentor. Xigant had agonized over contacting him for weeks, but in the end, she told the male who had taught her how to be a pilot because she saw no honorable way to keep it from him.

Two of SUN's twenty-four-hour cycles and she would have an answer.

Meanwhile, she must keep it together better. She already had a demonstration of Zet's strength. He'd had no trouble controlling her in that cell.

He had no emotional interest in Itty other than as a member of the Demons. She knew their history. They had been only a youth gang on Calius. While living in a deserted basement beneath a warehouse, they had developed a collective goal—the ship she now acted as pilot for.

Xigant could only imagine how they had managed it. A partial record existed, the holo recording made when the ship got put up for auction. She'd not witnessed it live as addiction already had taken control of her by then.

Had C'entala seen it? It would be smart to watch the holo. Digging it out of the vast amount of news which had been recorded by now would give her something to do other than sitting on her bed and worrying about the disaster her life could well become in the next forty-eight SUN hours.

It would be best to attempt that from her quarters. Going into the library would leave her too exposed. She would consider it as research. Her goal was to find out all she could about the male whose command she served under.

It took Xigant a little longer than she had thought because she didn't have the proper search terms. Not having the prior name of the ship, it wasn't as easy as she'd hoped. In the end, using Greenhouse 2 and auction in conjunction helped.

Not only did she find that holo, but a related one that sparked her interest. The pirates who forfeited the ship had tried to murder two of the *Long Sword's* crew.

"There was a fool's errand if ever I heard of one," she muttered as she watched the pirates left alive being taken into custody. "Holo off."

Xigant leaned back against the wall behind her bed. Camat had done well for nothing more than a youth. Thinking on it, she realized how young the *Demon Lair's* captain was in SUN years. As they counted it, Camat was still in his second decade. Even for an Ellaerian, this was a laudable achievement.

Personal time drawing to a close, Xigant left the bed and went into the cleaning unit to prepare for her shift. Working with Trund would keep her mind occupied for the next four hours. Off shift, she had hoped to pay a visit to Itty.

A growl left her as she realized how her behavior in the hall had canceled that plan. She must now back off, perhaps for the entire time before they made port. Zet would be watching. Something he was far too adept at.

Xigant scrubbed a hand over her head. Her fault. Had she not reacted as she had, he would have said nothing. Too many times before, she had blamed her faults on others. That was not the way to keep her sanity. Her actions caused Zet's. Blaming him for her stupidity would only push her over the edge again.

No more dishonor. If she wanted her family to think well of her, she must prove herself on this ship.

She danced in the light of the blue moon. Twirled and dipped beneath the glow of the stars that played court to the small asteroid held captive by Estevan's gravity. The mechanics of it were something every Watcher child knew.

Being no ordinary Watcher, she knew more of this planet than did the others.

The land had been alone too long. On the arrival of the colonists, Estevan welcomed the newcomers. They set about making the planet livable for Humans having no idea they were not the first species to call it home.

Then, one of their number, a woman sought the lonely spaces when her mate died unexpectedly. And she found far more than a lonely passing in the wasteland. A civilization long dead left records. Captured by her discovery, she stayed.

A male, a worker instead of one of the administration cadre, got delegated to see if he could find her. A scientist and a female still of breeding age, she would be sorely missed. Her knowledge and her physical attributes were necessary to the colony.

The male they sent to find her found more than he expected. She refused to return and told him he could go back without her or stay and they would become a couple. He knew his prospects in the colony didn't include breeding with a woman of her intellect. Taylor stayed.

Two more joined them, dissatisfied with the administration of the colony.

LaDonna discovered the key to deciphering the information left behind by the old ones. They left maps showing the places where water from deep under the sand and rock bubbled to the surface. LaDonna read them and passed the information down to her daughter.

Four more fled into the wilderness for various reasons. The women controlled matters, and the males agreed this to be for the best. They became Watchers, those who kept track of the colonists and kept them from finding the wonders left behind by the old ones.

Many generations later, the pirates came. When SUN sealed them in the cavern, the Watchers made note of it. With no way to get food, all the water on Estevan would not help the trapped pirates. The Watchers waited. When the new LaDonna felt the time right, they entered the cavern and found the pirates dead.

A pit was dug and their bodies placed inside. Once again, the spaces Watchers had used were their own.

Joun Tay went to town and purchased books and manuals, used of course, so they might learn to use what now belonged to them. What the pirates left behind got parceled out to the kindred. The secret of the caves would remain the Watchers' treasure.

Not in the direct line of LaDonna, Malada Tay Culat, trained as a healer, would not become mate to any of the Watcher males. Held apart, her destiny was to care for the others. She danced because her spirit needed to learn something only the night and the land could tell her.

For many turns of Estevan, something swirled around, pacing her every move. A miasma which hadn't dissipated no matter what she tried. Not material, none saw what she felt. Joun Tay sensed nothing, and his ability to perceive those things had reached legendary proportions in the Watchers.

Malada took to the land, to the blue light of the larger of the two moons circling Estevan. Offering the dance to the spirits of the blue light and the dusty land, she moved to an inner rhythm she sensed. Alone on the headland that had once overlooked a deep harbor, the female danced until unable to move.

On sinking down, she put her cheek on the dusty rock and waited. And waited. Nearly asleep, in that half-aware state between the little death of sleep and the consciousness of the living, something touched her. Another wanted the position she held.

Then she would relinquish it. If another wanted it so much, they would send vast amounts of negative energy her way, then she would yield. Nothing was worth that aggravation. The unknown entity had only to ask. Since the female could not bring herself to do so, Malada would freely give it up.

The LaDonna would be made aware of her intent to step down before the next rising of the lesser moon. What she would do from there was easy enough to decide. Joun Tay always needed help. Loathe to mingle with the entities from the city, the other Watchers refused to step forward.

She would and could help the man responsible for her birth. The ground beneath her seemed to warm slightly. The female took that as a positive response to her situation. She would work to learn the machines. More warmth enveloped her.

Not a bad thing on nights in the wasteland. The end of the light always brought a cooling of the land. It could get quite cold when the planet reached the aphelion of its circuit around their star.

Content, and ready to let herself slip into the land of dreams, something—a vision perhaps—caught her attention. An upright figure wavered as if the heat of the day played with its image. The figure resembled a tryanot in skin tone and composition—possibly. There, all similarity ended.

Not one of the four-legged creatures of the desert, the Watcher's breeding program had enhanced to provide animals that could travel the sands easily. The creature resembled nothing she knew. Sensing it to be male, she wanted a closer look. The image faded, though, denying her wish.

In the morning, Joun would come for her. They would talk and she would ask if he had ever seen such a creature in the city. A spark of interest flared in her mind before she emptied it of all things that might keep her awake. No matter what her father had to say, she had decided.

The spirit of the land had determined it to be time for a change. Malada smiled as sleep took over her body, moving upward from toes to her head. Nothing remained certain but change. Her entire childhood had been spent readying her for this position. In an instant, she surrendered it to the other, whoever she might be.

Chapter 3

"Itty!"

Itty turned to find Camat in the door of her med unit.

"Captain?"

"Door, close and lock," he commanded before taking the patient chair in front of her desk. "You got any clue in seven hells as to what's wrong with my pilot?"

"No. But you're right. Something is."

"Other than being insanely jealous over you. Since she is that."

Itty felt her face get hot. "I've never given her…"

Camat waved a hand in front of her. "I didn't say you had. Still, she leans in that direction. How about you?"

The hair on the back of her neck tingled. "That's a bit personal."

"So it is. And since I'm the captain of this paranoid tub, I've a legitimate need to know. The health and safety of the crew is my first responsibility."

Itty sighed and leaned back in her chair. "I can't tell you…"

He opened his mouth, and she reached out and waggled a finger in his face. "Let me finish. I don't know. I've never been drawn to another Demon. Not sexually, anyhow."

"I wondered. You and Zet were spending a lot of time together for a while."

"Yes. But he was helping me with Xigant. Zet worried if she got too physical that I might get hurt."

"Remains a valid concern. So, you're still untouched?"

"Yes. In mind and body. I simply haven't felt the push. I think I'm still young for a Houser. Since I know nothing about my family, I can't tell you if I'm one of the sort who requires more time to mature. You know there are differences? Depending on where a family is from, some take longer than others."

"I didn't know that." Still staring at her, he nodded. "Fucking Guente! We shouldn't be in this situation."

"Let him go, Camat. He can't do a thing to us now. It's been many revolutions of Sol as SUN counts them. Forget him. This twenty-four-hour turn is where we are now and we must deal with it."

The red in his eyes, which had flared like an eruption from a star, settled to a pinkish color. "You know there isn't any of us who could fill this position a quarter as well as you do. Don't you dare get some crazy idea to leave and become a med tech on another ship."

"As if. I'm self-taught. What captain in his right mind hires a self-taught youth as a med tech? Don't lose any sleep over it."

"Yeah? Well... how about falling in love with some merc or planet dweller and leaving us entirely? That could happen."

"Sure. And we're going to enter Estevan's atmosphere and discover her huge ocean simply appeared overnight. There's about the same chance. You're my family now, all the Demons, including Brown. Family sticks together. Otherwise, you'd be trying to find a job on Estevan so you could stay with Eldara."

He grimaced, then a big grin spread across his face. "Siblings. We are, aren't we?"

"Yes. Otherwise, you'd have given Trund the captain's cabin and stayed behind with Eldara. As Brown says, 'not happening.'"

"Okay. You've convinced me. But if there is any way you can find out what's going on with that nutcase of a pilot of ours, try it. If she get's any more morose, only Saint Michael knows what she might do. Xigant tried death by liquor before. I don't want her trying that again or graduating to another form of self-termination."

"If I suspected anything remotely close to that was going through that female's brain, she'd already be in that med bed. Zet and Enkel can put her in there, no problem. Fact is, either one of them could do so without help. I'm not afraid to enlist assistance when needed. I can do it myself with a mask and mister. *Poof!* One burst of meds and she's down for the count."

Camat stood, reached out and patted her on the head.

"Stop that!"

"But I'm so happy with you."

Itty left the chair and ran around to slam into Camat. She tickled him under his left arm.

He backed away. "Stop! I won't do it again. I promise."

"Sure you do. You big tease, that's what you said last time."

"Oh, did I? I don't remember."

"Get out of my med unit and go bother someone else."

"I'm gone. And thanks."

Arms across her chest, Itty glowered at the door when Camat went through it.

"Itty?" A soft voice coming from the old speakers asked.

"Demon Lair? What do you want?"

"Promise you won't let her hurt me."

The little Houser female rubbed her forehead. "That's what you get for listening in to private conversations. Why do you think Camat came in here and shut the door? It was so we could speak privately."

"But she's the head pilot. Xigant Relda can hurt me if she chooses."

"Now why in the seven hells would she do that?"

"If she's unstable, thinking about self-termination..."

"By the pit and every serpent in the fucking thing. Listen here, ship, your paranoia is going to hurt you more than anyone on board. Stop inserting yourself where you shouldn't be. If I had a way to get you into that med bed, you'd be in it before you knew what was what."

"I didn't mean to make you angry..."

"I'm not angry, you bunch of jumped-up code. Your paranoia worries me. I want a promise from you, no unilateral action. Not ever. I don't get that and I'm going to recommend we replace you with a newer, less irritating AI."

"Sorry! Really, I'm sorry. It's just that all that time as a pirate..."

"I do not care a snake's tail about that. It's all over and done with. I want a response from you. You swear never to take unilateral action regarding this ship or any crew member. Swear it now. No trying to wiggle out. A firm commitment. Otherwise, I'm going straight to the captain."

"Agreed. I promise. You know I can't break my word once given."

"Exactly why I wanted you to promise. If you were any normal crewmember, I'd give you something to knock you out for a few hours. Go meditate or something."

"Meditate? How does one do that?"

"You're the AI and can access any document you want in the library. Go do some research and find out. That should give you something to do for a while."

Itty made sure her connection to the AI was off and left the med unit to find Camat. The captain was going over something in GalDocs in his ready room. After getting him on a secure person-to-person channel using their implants, she told him everything that went on between her and the ship after he left.

Fucking paranoid AI. You may be correct. We may need to replace it at some point.

No, not yet. I have it under control. I gave it a direct command, and it agreed. We're fine for now.

Camat shook his head. *You're the med tech. I'll defer to you—but if anything more happens...*

Itty turned to go and stopped at the door. *New AIs cost a fortune. So, this one's a little paranoid. Which is irritating, but might not be bad.*

Camat shrugged. *It's all yours. Do the best you can. But if it cuts out on us...*

It won't. I'll keep it in line. She gave her captain a sharp salute and left.

Chapter 4

Eldara eyed the big Ellaerian male seated at the back of the room. He'd been in two nights in a row, taking the same seat at the small table in the far corner of the room. Not so much what he wore, although it looked to be excellent quality and well tailored, but his attitude drew her attention.

One set done; she went off to find Lady Pia. She had questions. The male had asked if they had Spodahn whiskey and Eldara's eyebrows rose at that bit of information. "He's got expensive tastes to go with that clothing."

The female in her fourth decade nodded. The sparkling gem she wore on a thick chain, a Luster Orb, glinted in the bright lights of the office. Pia's fingers stoked it. "I'm sorry I wore this tonight. That Ellaerian recognized it. I could tell by the way his eyes flashed red fire at me. He wanted to ask where I got it and didn't."

Eldara wondered as well, but felt it would be impolite to ask.

"I suspect he's meeting someone here. I wonder who." Pia speculated.

"There's the new pilot on the *Demon Lair*. Perhaps he's waiting for the ship to get here. She's an Ellaerian."

Pia pushed the spreadsheet she'd been using to calculate their next order to the side. "She is. I suppose that is a possibility. Still, something about the male bothers me."

"Me as well. It's as if he's jittery about something. That Ellaerian has a bad case of nerves."

"Why do you say that?"

"He's always moving; his fingers never stop. That one is never still." Eldara twisted her fingers together and positioned them in different ways. "He does this a lot. Wait, I can't quite make my joints bend as his do."

"They are far more flexible than we are." Lady Pia grabbed her hands. "Don't try it. You might hurt yourself."

"You're right. Don't know what I was thinking. Has that male ever been in here before?"

"Not that I'm aware of. I wonder if he does business with CNY. If he's buying or selling anything to Lute?"

"Why don't you contact Lute and ask? I seriously doubt Keem sent him here."

"That piece of space junk doesn't have the resources. Those females, Captain Effie and Captain Sundara, took every last credit he had. Keem couldn't afford to buy the dust off the Ellaerian's shoe when they trundled his hide off planet."

Eldara couldn't contain a giggle. "Couldn't happen to a worse entity. He deserves all he gets."

"I agree. Now, before you need to go on again, go to the kitchen and get a cup of that warm atta fruit drink Tonio made for you. I don't want your throat seizing up."

"Aye, boss." Eldara left the chair and went into the hall. In the kitchen, she got a mug of the warm liquid and took it to the darkened stage. The songbird peered around the edge of the long drapes and watched the big male until she finished her drink. She had a bad feeling about the Ellaerian.

The Human female entertaining the diners was his son's mate. Or so said Xigant Relda. Her first contact made him wonder. She was not the first of his former students to come to him with a dubious proposition.

What stopped him from dismissing Relda's without a second thought was she asked for nothing. That fact foremost in his mind, C'entala C'Camat felt it prudent to research the matter. The female he'd once mentored had fallen on very hard times.

Her first and greatest mistake, perhaps the trigger to her downfall, had been the Gossican female she became entangled with after winning her section's highest honors. The Gossican had worked her way through the more amenable staff.

With her willingness to fulfill any sexual fantasy and with that Gossican ability to satiate her prey beyond anything previously experienced, the Gossican's credit account on Royal Joloa swelled. But nothing satisfied the female's lust for more.

With no more staff or instructors willing to be cut from the herd, she started on the best of the graduates. Relda became the next and last victim on the Ellaeria Republic's home world. The pilot's fall took not only herself but a part of her immediate family along for the descent.

The remainder of her kin gathered their evidence and mounted a campaign to have the Gossican declared a danger to the youth of Ellaeria and expelled forthwith. He had wiped her name from his memory, but recalled her attempt to ensnare him.

It failed miserably. Zatha had already taken possession of his emotions.

The songbird started a haunting melody that took C'entala back to the first time he'd wandered into the pleasure palace in search of the youth, W'iecnten. Another victim of the Gossican ability to fascinate other races emotionally, the youth needed to be rescued.

Addicted to the drug Blue Dream, the male hadn't been cooperative, leading to a prolonged and protracted stay on Calius. Which led him to an emotional entanglement with Zatha. He tried to buy the only female he'd ever loved, but Guente refused any offer he made.

When he could delay no longer, he bundled a drugged W'iecnten into a blanket. Shussha, an operative for the Kazzemians working in the pleasure house, helped him remove the youth to his ship. They left before Guente could file a formal complaint for amounts owed him by W'iecnten.

Shussha confirmed Relda's claim that Zatha had somehow given him a son. He'd always thought it an impossibility. There had been claims over the years of half-breed infants on Calius. He and others he knew declared it a myth. Nothing more.

Now he waited for his son to return to his home port with the ship he and the other members of his youth gang on Calius had somehow managed to obtain. He'd watched both the Galaxy Wide News and GalDocs holos of the auction for the pirate ship. It had been a masterful move by Camat and his second-in-command.

But where had they acquired the funds? A question asked by both news organizations and never answered. Since taking to the void, they had somehow gained the attention of both the *Poignard* and the *Long Sword*. If this was indeed his son, he could not ask for a brighter, more determined offspring.

He would proudly claim the youth, if allowed. Would Camat think he abandoned him? Hoping to avoid that accusation, he'd brought along a holo Shussha willingly recorded for him. It told of his attempts to free Zatha and Guente's refusal to part with the female. Would it be enough to allow him to become part of his son's life? C'entala C'Camat twisted his fingers together under cover of the tabletop. He had asked every god he knew of and offered a donation to the local chapel of Saint Michael that all hinderances would be wiped away. The only offshoot he had, C'Camat prayed all would go well.

Chapter 5

"You aren't going back too early, are you?" Malada asked as she helped Joun load the cart.

"No amount of deflection on your part will deter me from the answers I need." The man who paired with her mother to form her turned from the back of the cart. "For what reason do you give up what you have trained to do your entire life?"

She acknowledged Joun to be the source of her bent toward determination strong enough to be declared as tough as Estevan's mountains. Perhaps his being older strengthened it. He would not let his question go unanswered. If they would have a pleasant journey, he must be told. "The one who wants what I have has a desire so great, I felt her need. To heal her, I must give her this. It is not what she perceives. In learning, she will heal."

A tall figure, clad in the long robes of a Watcher, this man whom her mother picked to supply the other portion of her genetic code remained a handsome male. Malada knew they still had a relationship after all these years.

"When she is healed, you will reclaim what is yours?" A calm demeanor hid his irritation inside. She knew the man well.

Malada pulled the scarf over her mouth and nose. There would be a breeze cooling the great flats and lifting the fine grit into the air. The next six hours would be a slog through the plumes raised. At the end, they would find the safety of the caverns closest to the port and the domed city.

"We should go."

He folded his arms over his chest. "I request the courtesy of a reply. An honest one."

Anger had to be suppressed. He would not take her along if she irritated the man beyond reason. The respect Malada owed him outweighed what he owed her by many turns of Estevan. "I have many years between me and the little one who told you a falsehood to get her way."

Joun's arms dropped to his sides. "True. I misspoke. Still, I would have your answer."

"Once she is fully healed, she will have earned the position. It seems I have another path to follow."

"Come." He held out a hand and led her to the half-empty cart. "There are many hours between here and our destination."

Seated beside him on the bench, she watched as he used a long rod to tap the tryanot twice at the base of its tail. She knew that tapping in the middle would have the beast pulling the cart straight ahead. Tapping it on either side signaled a turn in that direction.

They began a journey that had her insides crawling with anticipation. She'd never seen either the port or the domed city close up. Nor had she been in the vast yard filled with the detritus of many planets. First, they must gather the pieces Joun planned to take to the youth who managed the CNY facility for used items.

After mounting to the head of one ancient shelf that marked the place where a current had roiled the water enough to carve away land, the next descent proved steeper. She clutched the bench for balance as they followed a worn trail down the side of what had been a seamount in the distant past.

Malada waited for another hour to voice the question she wished him to answer. They were too far into the journey for him to turn back and leave her. "Joun?"

"Yes."

"Have you ever seen a creature somewhat like the tryanot, but taller? One that walks on two legs?"

"I have. How do you know of it?"

"A dream. Tell me, if you will."

"The one I know of is part of the crew of a ship which recently claimed Estevan as its home port. He is taller than I and has a tail."

"Can you tell me about the ship? Do you think it will be in port when we are there? Also, you didn't answer my question. Are we taking a chance by venturing into the city so soon?"

He tapped the beast four times on the tail in rapid succession. It halted. He picked up his special contrivance which allowed him to see the land at night and looked to the right. "We turn here."

"How do you know?"

The device that allowed him to see in a low light appeared before her face. "Look straight ahead. Now turn, keeping level. A few more degrees. Stop. Do you see a mound of rocks?"

"I do."

"The first of us who came into the wasteland searching for LaDonna thought he might need to find his way back. Those of us who follow him know of the cairns and have added to them over the years. You see a white bump near the top?"

"Yes."

"It is on the left side. That means to go to the caverns, we must stay to the left of the mound. If we intended to travel to the oasis of Neddi, we would bear right."

"We don't need to go to Neddi?"

He chuckled. "No, those pirates died only a short distance from the sustenance they needed. I know how to find it. They didn't. Nor do I have any sympathy for those who murder for gain. SUN needed to stop them."

She handed the gadget back to Joun. "It's a sad thing when life forms, no matter their origin, kill for profit."

"Sing me a song. I've not heard your voice in a long while."

Malada did as Joun asked. The melody floated away on the breeze, which had diminished to a shadow of itself.

Thin to the point of emaciation, Keem felt his legs quiver. He braced himself against the wall that held the door. The Liderian captain of the slaver might look like a cross between a rodent and an amphibian, but his appearance didn't make him stupid. They were known to have immense cognitive ability.

"What is this information you will trade for your freedom?"

Keem pulled up a laugh. "Something quite worth it. But to blurt it out would be to lose the lever."

The captain tilted his head to one side. Whiskers which looked ludicrous on his face twitched. "Give me something or back you go."

"A long dead race. A near dead planet colonized by Humans. Only one entity, a small group, knows of the location of artifacts. You know how ancient things from dead civilizations draw in those with credits to burn."

"I can ask the females who sold you to tell me where you were apprehended. Thinking about it, I'm not too sure I want to give up the reward for you. What you are talking is a uurk in the reeds. The amount posted for your capture is a sure thing. Unless... a Yodoran funeral boat is what we are discussing."

"I know nothing of a funeral boat. That might be too much to ask for. I am aware of other treasures. Surely you recall that SUN trapped a pirate cell inside caverns in a mountain range and sealed them in?"

The Liderian nodded. "I've heard the rumors. Of course, nothing's been verified."

"I know which world it happened on and I know who to get all the information from. The planet's admin knows nothing. They are ignorant of nearly everything."

"How do you know?"

"Credits grease tongues. I had a need to know because I had and still have a need for credits." He raised his arms and rattled the chains they had put on him for a meeting with the captain. "I always have a need. Surely, you do as well. Wouldn't you like to retire with a fat Royal Joloa bank balance someplace amenable to entertainment? Illsdl or Calius? You haven't informed General Shung that you have me..." he let the words sink in.

The captain grinned. "Take a seat. Let us see what we can devise. Surely, we can come to some agreement."

Chapter 6

Xigant's hands shook. Jamming them into the pockets of her lower covering, she shuffled along behind the excited crew on the way to Lady Pia's restaurant. Not only were they home, but Camat had informed the crew he had a request to contact the *Poignard* regarding the *Demon Lair* taking a run. Commander Eirson had a family matter arise she must attend to.

After a quick check of their schedule, Camat agreed and asked the commander to forward the name of the contact to him. Two calls, and the contract sat in Sebe's office. Their attorney would vet it and if he felt no revisions were necessary, Camat would sign.

The projected funds would go a long way toward a stay in the Greenhouse 2 shipyard the *Demon Lair* needed. She felt as good about that unexpected windfall as the rest of the crew. What... rather *who* waited in Lady Pia's had her sending prayers to every god she knew of.

Camat entered first. The squeal that flew around inside the building let her know Eldara had been singing when she spotted him. The last one in, she lingered against the outside wall. Camat and Eldara shared a heated kiss while the guests teased them with various words of encouragement.

Her gaze traveled around the room and spotted him in the far corner at what was usually the help's table. Xigant swallowed hard to keep from spewing what little lodged in her stomach. She'd known this was coming and had eaten sparingly in preparation, but hurling proved to be a near thing. She barely kept the tea and roll down.

C'entala C'Camat's flaming gaze caught hers and he acknowledged Xigant with a brief nod. The male looked older. As he should. It had been over twenty SUN turns since she'd last seen him. Still, the resemblance between C'entala and Camat had her staring at them each in quick succession.

There were differences because of Camat's mixed race. She knew Camat's eyes only got light red, not the flame-laced color of C'entala's. A blazing gaze C'entala turned on his sole descendant.

She'd asked a cousin to check, so Xigant knew this male to be her mentor's only offshoot. A thing she knew for a fact because she'd been the only one with him cognizant. The youth they contracted to fetch being too drugged to notice. C'entala mated with the woman in the pleasure palace and wouldn't touch another.

Lady Pia put on some other music, and the diners returned to their meals. Eldara whispered in Camat's ear, and then led him over to C'entala. Xigant sidled closer.

"... needs to speak with you alone..." The last words Eldara spoke had Camat staring at C'entala.

To Xigant, alone meant in the comfort of Camat's ship and she slipped out the door ahead of the two males. It seemed Eldara meant to stay behind and finish out the evening's songs. Sliding around the corner of the building, Xigant planned to make herself absent somehow. Decision made, she waited until the two males were out of sight and found an available transport. The city and a hotel room seemed like the safest option.

Later, in the hotel room, she realized running had been a grave mistake. Camat hadn't censored his implants. His agitation came banging through unfiltered. The crew, with Itty first, rallied around him. She had to say something. "Sir," was all she could manage.

Hurrying down to the lobby, she asked the half-asleep clerk to find her a transport. Something had come up, and she had to get back to her ship immediately.

Riding high on the flush of the new contract, Camat felt the same exhilaration as he had when the gang pulled off a tough job. He liked this one better because it was all legal. True, legal didn't have the zing of deliciousness for having put one over on the very people who tossed them aside. Still, it meant they would soon have the ship in the yard for much needed work.

Eldara greeting him as she had only increased his elation. Her introduction to the Ellaerian was a slight surprise. His first thought being the male might want to hire the ship didn't change until they entered his office.

When offered a seat, the male shook his head, turned a swirling red gaze on him, then lowered his head and paced from one side of the room to the other. "This is a delicate and difficult task."

"How so?"

"I suppose there is no other way than to state my case." The male stopped and gripped the back of the chair he neglected to sit in. "You are from Calius. Your mother, may those who gather the souls of the oppressed comfort her, was a pleasure slave to that licker of snake cock, Guente. You were born in that place. Shussha, may all gods bless that life form, took over your care when Zatha left this realm of misery. Shussha got you away from Guente and his plans for you. Relocating you to another city was all she could do to help."

Each word drove cold chills deeper into Camat's heart. "How do you know? Why are you here? What do you want?"

The Ellaerian leaned forward. "I know because I'm the male who placed the seed for you in Zatha. I'm here because I didn't know about you until recently. All I want is to get to know you. You are the only product of my seed. There is no other."

Camat shut his eyes and let his head hit the back of the chair.

Camat? Itty's voice called through his implants. *What's wrong? Do we need to help?*

Am I broadcasting? I suppose I must be. No. Stand down. It's a personal…the male I left with says he's my father. We need to work this out.

Ah. Zet's deeper tone. *Then shall we stay here and give you time?*

Bunde came next. *We'll creep on board.*

Eldara wants to come with. What do I…

He interrupted Caran. *By all the seven hells, yes!*

Brother, we are at your command. Oolden said.

Agreed, Enkel added.

Trund's *whatever you need* came next.

Behind you all the way. Brown.

Sir. That came from Xigant.

The last comment, totally unexpected, came from the ship. *Cell ready, if necessary, Captain.*

His paranoid and slightly off-center AI was behind him. The thought alone lifted his spirit.

A smug little *told you* came from Itty.

He silently fought for control.

You're the negotiator. All the points are in your favor here. Trund's words steadied him.

Camat pushed the chair upright. With no intention of cutting his family off from the discussion, he left all the channels open. Camat waved a hand at the chair. "Sit. Let's talk about this. What you want and what I need may be too far apart."

The Ellaerian stepped out from behind the chair and slid into the seat. "I hope not. I only ask to be allowed to stay on the ship in whatever capacity you choose. Paying my way isn't a problem."

"I don't know that we need to go that far. What proof can you give me of your claims?"

"You can verify everything with Shussha and I have a holo where she explains all. She is still on Calius. The Kazzemian says she's retired. I suspect she only left Guente's employ and still helps where she can. And there is Xigant Relda. She was with me on Calius when I met Zatha. We had contracted to bring an Ellaerian youth home who got tangled up with Guente. The Pacifican got him addicted to a drug."

Xigant!

Sir?

My office. Noon Estevan time.

Understood.

Camat stared at the man who must be his father. "What are your qualifications?"

"I'm a pilot and an excellent navigator."

"Any experience as deck crew?"

The Ellaerian male smiled at him. "As a youth. If it's what you require, yes."

"It isn't. What you can do is work in the training section of our library. See what we are lacking and when we have the funds, get what you can. Used holos are far cheaper. Xigant has been working with Trund, my second, on his piloting skills. Perhaps you would take over?"

A tiny little mental groan from Xigant put a grin on his face. That female had a great deal to explain come noon.

"Happily. Then you'll let me stay?" C'entala asked.

"What choice do I have? But don't expect me to fall into a father-son camaraderie here. Like our engineer says — "not happening."

Camat rose. "We need to find you quarters. Since we're a short crew, that won't be difficult."

"I have implants. Can your med tech assist me in recalibrating to you and the ship?"

"Yes. Now, come along. My mate wants time with me. I assume you have baggage to bring on board?"

"Your mate doesn't stay with you on the ship. I noted that."

Camat shook his head. "She doesn't. My songbird has too much talent to be tucked away. It doesn't make our lives easy, but it works."

The male following him made no further comment. Camat thought that prudent on his part. He needed time to digest it all. Any more information might prove too overwhelming.

Chapter 7

Joun waited before setting off from the cavern to make sure they would enter Estevan's port near the close of day. Malada saw the lights in the distance and wondered what the city had to show her. The spirit that governed all had something for her. She had no doubts.

As they reached the base of the ancient river which had once helped fill the ocean, the extent of the habitation became clear. "How do they supply water to all this?"

"They have various methods." Joun exited the cart and went around to help her down. "At least they are very good at reclaiming every drop of what they use. Nothing is wasted. We must walk from here. This climb is too steep for one tryanot to pull if we are inside."

"There is so much light! The star hasn't gone below the horizon yet. Why do they use all those lights?"

Joun chuckled. "To keep the desert at bay? To pretend nothing can wipe them off the planet in an instant? Who can say?"

"You disapprove of them?"

They walked together up the steep slope toward the light and growing sounds. "No. Not really. Wait. It's time for an essential tool if we are to go further."

A hand on her arm stopped her. Beside him, the cart and the tryanot came to a halt. Joun reached for the bag that he wore with the strap over one shoulder and across his body. He pulled a smaller bag from it and opened the closure.

"Here, insert these into your ears. It will cut down on the noise. So much sound all at once can give those of us unaccustomed to it a blasting headache if we don't take measures."

In his open palm lay what appeared to be small balls with slight extensions. "How do I do this?"

"Like so." He lifted his head covering, took one by its tail and inserted it into one ear. "Turn it gently until it seats comfortably. It will cut down on the sound, not eliminate it." Joun grinned. "You still need to hear things. We will talk more of this when settled for the night."

As they came out of the cut that led to the spaceport and onto the plain, the cacophony grew. Malada thanked Joun for the plugs in her ears. The lights all around were enough to confuse and disorient anyone. If the noise blasted her ears as the rest did her sight, she might have run back down to the desert. "What a confusion of things. How do you even know where to go?"

"I have done this many times. The CNY compound they so generously allow us to stay in is a safe place. The high walls cut down on much of this, although not all." He gripped her shoulder as they reached the level land above the ancient dead sea. "Not far now. Our creature will be happy to relinquish his burden. He is an excellent animal and needs to rest. It is up to us to see him settled."

Malada noted the way back to the cut in the event she might find it necessary to leave on her own. One never knew what might happen. As she took precautions in the great dry, she would do the same here.

Calming her spirit, she looked around her as they came closer to the port itself. Beyond, down the long dusty road, the huge dome rose into the sky. Inside it was the city. Safe from the blowing sand and heat, those within knew nothing of the Waste.

Estevan might be a harsh planet, but it had beauty. A magnificence those inside, cushioned in the dome, would never see. The space farers were another matter. She wondered at the things they experienced in that dark void. There must be marvels out in the vastness. Would they meet anyone she could ask?

Too soon for her, they came to the high walls and the inset gate of the yard. They stepped into the alcove holding the huge doors and lights came on.

"Joun? I didn't expect to see you so soon." The voice of a young man floated in the surrounding space.

"I had no plans to make this trip. But I have some needs and have brought you things I hope will provide the credits to obtain them. May we spend the night?"

"Certainly. I suppose it has been a long trip and you will settle in for the night before we can talk?"

"Please. But I have someone with me. My daughter. We need to ask your permission to tap your water storage."

"Certainly. I will meet you in the area you camped in last time." A chuckle filled the air. "We'd had some things come in and I've yet to inventory them. Everything is a gigantic pile that I need to go through. It's on the far edge of that area, but the only actual space I have open."

"Have I inconvenienced you by my early arrival?"

"No."

The gates swung open, and Malada got her first look at a person who lived on the plain. This young man was a Human. Joun had told her not everyone was. The Humans and the aliens who lived and visited Estevan used the term "life form" for everyone, Humans and aliens alike. Often shortening it to "form." That made sense to her.

As tall as Joun, the smiling young man walked with them as Joun guided the tryanot to the area where they would camp. Lute, the manager of the CNY yard, offered the old dwelling to them since Joun had brought a female along.

They both declined the offer.

The tryanot released from its harness and turned loose to forage on the vermin in the yard, Lute excused himself. He had matters to attend to. Tomorrow, they would discuss what brought Joun back so soon.

Malada liked him. Respectful and generous, she thought his employer must be happy with the youth. They set up the small shelter, tying off the two back sides to the cart. Joun explained it made it easier to restrict access to the things he had within. Not that he didn't trust Lute, but others had scaled the wall and attempted to steal.

She felt comfortable surrounded by the walls, and with Joun for company. Malada knew without this safe place and Joun, she would have turned and left for the sanctuary of the desert. The high CNY yard's walls restricted the myriad lights and the things in her ears reduced the noise to a bearable level.

Seated on a cushion in the tent with the sides rolled to allow what little breeze might come their way to enter, she relaxed with a few sips of sweetfruit liquor in a mug. She recognized the clay work as that of her mother. Emara had turned her hand to many things over the years.

Potter, maker of liquor, weaver of rugs, she did most of them well. Except for motherhood. Malada smiled as she sipped the potent brew. As a girl, she had run wild through the oasis and the desert lands beyond.

More than once, Joun and Emara had argued about her lackadaisical attitude toward childcare. Joun had taken her older sibling, Stapen, away with him the summer she saw twelve turns of travels between the various oases and the three dead cities.

Stapen a traveler now, like Joun, she saw him now and again. Her older brother swung between his kin and that of his mate. He had chosen an Ide girl. Malada hadn't met her cousin yet. Watchers kept their families small. Resources in the vast waste were few. Too many births and they might run out of places to camp and the water that seeped up to sustain them.

As the blue moon rose, a pleasing sound made its way over the wall. "Joun? Is that the sound we heard that night when we were leaving the first city?"

"It is. There is a Human girl who sings for others in a restaurant. That is a place where they serve food and drink. If you think you can be in close quarters with a crowd of people, we can go listen to her."

"That would be pleasant."

He laughed. "The others are somewhat smelly, and the air becomes fusty with so many entities in one place."

She wrinkled her nose, which caused him to chuckle.

"It's not as awful as a breeding clutch of tryanots. But it will get strong after some time in a building as tightly closed as that."

Malada gave careful thought to what he proposed before replying. "I would like to hear her in person. When can we go?"

Chapter 8

The small Houser female had him sit while she worked to realign his implants with the ship.

"The newer ships are easier to sync with." C'entala hoped to engage the youngest med tech he'd ever encountered in conversation. He so wanted to learn more about Camat's past.

"It's an older ship." Itty shrugged and went back to her work.

Nothing about the young female invited conversation, unlike most Housers. His implants being of the best credits could buy, he'd researched to refresh his memory of the various species on the ship. Her kind, the females in particular, were said to be quite open and adept conversationalists.

C'entala. Her voice whispered in his thoughts. *You are now tuned to the ship and everyone else in the ship's private network.*

My thanks for a job well done.

She gave a delicate snort. Then, *you want information about Camat, ask him. I am not a pump to be primed. Go, we have finished.*

He rose from the chair which made it slightly difficult for him to do so. C'entala understood they had deliberately made it lower so she could treat patients with no difficulty. The female was tiny.

And fierce. He stepped through the door, which closed behind him.

As am I in defense of the crew, which includes the captain.

Ah, you are the ship's AI.

I am the ship. Camat's ship. He rescued me; they all did. I will do anything to keep them secure.

Standing alone in the hall, C'entala glanced around him. The walls showed large scratches and a badly scuffed floor.

I mean neither you nor the crew harm. Camat is of my line, the only one I have ever produced.

You will not take him away.

That is not my aim. I only wish to get to know the youth as he will gain much on the day of my dissolution. From what I see, you need to spend some time in a shipyard. It appears your previous crew used you a great deal without proper maintenance.

They did. Camat plans to give me a good long time in the yard at Greenhouse 2 as soon as the credits are available.

He walked to the aft transport tube.

You can't take this one.

Why not? C'entala asked.

Zet is busy with maintenance on it. Go to the midsection transport.

With a shrug, he complied. Perhaps, if he worded his queries well, the ship would give him the information Itty refused to divulge. An incentive couldn't hurt.

You realize it isn't necessary to wait any longer. As Camat is my seed, he has the credits to get that matter seen to.

You must discuss it with my captain.

The ship's AI seemed far more aware than any other AI he had worked with. Inside the tube, C'entala mentally expressed his need to find Captain Camat. He stressed Camat's title. The *Demon Lair* complied without the usual response.

As he left the tube and walked down the hall, he knew he needed to get Camat out of the ship where they could talk without the worry of the AI listening in. The last AI war never truly left any rational being's mind.

Sentient life forms might not win the next one.

Camat sat bent over a tablet, staring at something. C'entala tapped the door frame with his boot causing his legacy's head to come up. The brown hair tinged with green proved an intriguing mix. How their races mixed to produce the male amazed him. In the light, the green made a fuzzy nimbus around Camat's head. His eyes flashed a pinkish hue for a moment and returned to a brown iris with a faint red ring.

The mixture had turned out well. His legacy's shoulders were broad, and he moved with Zatha's grace, something the female had in abundance. An ache for his lost love and the need for vengeance against Guente for his refusal to sell her rippled through his soul. He would have set the female free before doing anything else. The second action would have been to ask her to enter a formal mating contract with him.

Now, he had their legacy to see to. The young male would not make it easy. "Would you consider going to Lady Pia's for a short time? I understand you are busy..." He let it sit in the silence of Camat's office for a minute.

"A moment. I need to initial my lawyer's changes in the contract and get them back to him." Those broad shoulders lifted and fell again. "If the other party agrees, we will be on the move in a few days. Are you sure you still want to go along?"

He gave a slight nod. "I am. Shall I wait for you shore-side?"

"Shore-side?" Camat's glance appeared to question his terminology.

"Ah. A short time with the SUN fleet left its mark. The commander I served under always called planets the 'shore.'"

"If you would. I only need to transmit this to Sebe, and I'll meet you outside the aft bay."

"As you say, Captain."

Outside the ship, C'entala pointed to his head and made a cutting motion. Camat didn't respond as C'entala had hoped.

Demon Lair. Camat called to the ship via his implants.

Captain?

We are addressing some possible problems and may be offline for a short time. Don't get paranoid on me.

Thank you for the warning, Captain. I will await your return to the network. Demon Lair out.

Inside the small bar, off the restaurant, Camat asked for a glass of Caleta wine and C'entala followed his lead. Alone, each with a glass in hand, C'entala took a sip before speaking. "That AI of yours worries me. It seems to be far more aware than others I've dealt with over the years."

"It's paranoid. I suspect that comes from having been a pirate. It fears SUN far more than it should. It will do nothing to come to the fleet's attention. That doesn't bother me."

"You think that's all of it? Remember the AI wars..."

"I've researched them. We've nothing to fear from the ship. Its issues with SUN mean it won't do anything stupid. I'm convinced of that."

"Well... on a related matter, I understand you need to get the ship into a yard and get it gone over. If you allow me to turn over what should be your portion, what you should have attained on reaching adulthood, you will have enough to see that job taken care of."

"Really? Is that an Ellaerian tradition?"

"It is. I suspect you will have more available than you understand."

Camat silently sipped at his wine. Then he looked at C'entala. "We need to take a walk."

Tilting his head, he stared at the youth he never expected to have. "It's hotter than the seven hells out there."

With a grin for him, the young captain swirled the liquid around in the glass and tossed the rest down. "Come along, old one. We won't go far. The other side of the CNY yard. We can hide in the shadow of its walls."

A sigh escaped C'entala. One he deliberately pushed out. That this youth held his legacy caused him to smile inside.

Zet checked all four of the voids he found. Only one yielded a find—several money cards with no name attached. He tucked them into a pocket and tried to reach Camat with his implants.

He is not available, the ship informed him. *Some matter he and the other one, C'entala, are looking into at the port and they have silenced communication.*

The comment he might have made, Zet pushed to the back of his personal channel, out of reach of the ship.

What did you find? the AI asked.

Ah, money cards, Zet replied.

Thank Saint Michael it isn't more of those...

Hush. Not another word of what we found before. Be silent. Are there more of these pockets anywhere else on board?

The ship didn't answer immediately.

I thought you said these are the last of them. A low growl came from him. It echoed in the tube.

You specified on board. Does that mean inside the ship only? Anything on the outside of the ship is considered outboard, isn't it?

"If you were sentient, I'd shove you against the wall and batter you with my tail!" Zet hissed out. "It means anywhere on or in the framework. Now, tell me."

Outside, two plates down from the port escape pod bay. It looks like a patch—maybe. Since I've never seen it, I can't be sure. I only overheard them talking, the ship responded in his implants.

"Why didn't you give me this information earlier?" Zet knew the ship was listening and thought to keep their interaction off the log. "Unless you want the rest of this official, I suggest you stop using my implants. Ship's audio only."

"I've done nothing wrong or unethical." The AI's whisper filtered through the speakers. "The pirates..."

"Indeed. They controlled all. You're just a poor AI, doing what you're told."

"True. Sorry, I still worry about SUN. They could destroy me."

"You are legitimate now with a legal crew and captain. As Camat says, you're paranoid."

"I'm not lying in a yard like CNY, reduced to pieces. I'm flying and, as you said, legal. I do not know what is in that patch on the hull. If it's more of the other things, I don't know and don't want to know. The patch was something I suspect he thought he could peel off after launching an escape pod."

"How in the seven hells did he plan to pull that off?" Zet asked.

"I've no idea. I'm just the AI."

"Since we're on the hard, getting to it won't be a problem. Just keep quiet and let me get this 'inspection' done. Everyone knows I'm a safety nut. I'm just checking."

"Yes."

Zet returned the transport tube to functionality and went to find the boots needed for walking on the plates. Time to find out exactly what the pirate captain was trying to conceal. He needed to put together a grid and walk it afterward. Saint Michael only knew what the fool had concealed out on the hull.

He would wait until the larger moon rose. Although he enjoyed the heat, what radiated off the metal plates during the hours of light would be too much for even his warmth-loving body. Duty would cause him to miss an evening at Lady Pia's.

A situation Xigant would take full advantage of. Again, he wrestled with the matter, turning it first one way, then the other in his private thoughts. How much did Camat know about Xigant's obsession with Itty? Should he speak? Continue to keep silent?

The ship had only the bare minimum of crew needed to keep her maintained and space-worthy. They needed both Xigant and Itty. The addition of the pilot to the crew had lessened the strain on Trund. Itty kept them healthy. The loss of either of them would cripple the *Demon Lair*. Losing both pilot and med tech would keep them planet-bound until replacements could be found.

With a shake of his head, he pulled the boots off the shelf. With no obvious reason to say something and no genuine conflict—yet—he would keep his thoughts to himself. Working alone on the ship suited his mood. Worry over Itty needed to be worked off.

Chapter 9

Malada removed her outer robe and washed her scalp. A decision as to continuing to shave her head or not would come later. She had an evening out to enjoy and all concerns would wait.

Her fine inner robe would serve for the evening. Joun explained that some in the town thought female watchers hid their bodies from the sight of others for religious reasons and they shared a good laugh over that. Both men and women used the coverings to keep the sand and fine dust of the vast waste away from delicate skin. The constant rubbing could irritate tissue, causing lesions.

Sand in the eyes could scratch the delicate membrane and eventually render a person blind. A sightless Human in the vast waste without another to guide them was a dead person.

Hidden in their bubble with climate conditioning, the city dwellers were even less informed than those who lived in the port area. Those entities understood how the storms could damage flesh.

Tonight, she would forego the protective covering. Malada felt, as did Joun, they would be safe enough in the building. She wanted to hear the songbird without having to bother with excess layers of protection.

Joun's arm went around her shoulders as they stood watching the blue light of the larger moon creep up over the edge of the land.

"Will you discuss trading with the boy tomorrow?"

"Yes. He has agreed to carve out some private time to have a look at the things in the cart. Lute is always fair. He knows I don't care for an audience. There would be questions, ones I refuse to answer for anyone. Lute is discreet. We have done business for over two turnings now."

"A good thing for us."

"It is. You may well expect some penetrating glances in the restaurant. Few females of any species shave their heads. They'll not ask, though. Those who work in the greater vastness out there"—Joun lifted his chin toward the sky—"have better social skills with different classes of life forms than those shut up in the bubble."

"I understand the first LaDonna's urge to get clear of that."

Joun gave her a quick hug and lifted the whistle to his lips. He would call the tryanot in and have it remain with the cart until they returned from the place he called a restaurant. She found it all quite interesting.

A casual thief would hesitate to bother the large creature. Harmless for the most part, they could give the impression of being dangerous when they began hissing. A mouthful of teeth was enough to discourage any entity surprised by the creature.

They could be killed. Removal from the here and now happened to all creatures. Still, when a puffed-up tryanot suddenly erupted from the sand and dust of the vastness, hissing and showing a mouthful of teeth, unless one had prepared, flight usually seemed the best solution.

It responded to the whistle only it could hear with a bit of fur hanging from the side of its mouth.

"I think it has had a snack," she observed.

"Good." Joun reached out to scratch between its eyes. "Then it is time for a nap."

A beam of blue light came over the top of a piece of equipment she couldn't name and touched the three of them. Two Humans and the beast.

"Come. I believe we should leave now if we wish to get a seat. We will eat there. The cook makes these things he calls 'sausages' and we can have one split on bread with condiments. I think we will get a bottle of Caleta wine to go with it. Another thing you've not tried."

The man who bred her mother put out a hand for hers. "This shall be a night of firsts for you. Let's see what you think of it all afterward."

"I am ready." Malada put her hand in his and they made for the big gate in the high wall that guarded the yard and its treasures from the casual traveler.

She marveled when the gate opened for Joun and silently closed behind them. The youth, Lute, had made sure the AI which had charge of security accepted them. A kind gesture on his part. Lute knew Joun well. There were two Estevan turnings between them. More than enough time for Lute to be sure of Joun's honesty and for Joun to be sure of Lute.

The first strains of music floated out over the port as the moon lifted above the vast waste. They walked toward the restaurant and as they passed the spaceport itself, a slight thump caused her to look up.

Malada gasped. The figure she had envisioned walked on the skin of the spaceship sitting behind two smaller transports.

Her fingers tightened on Joun's. "It's the creature I saw."

"Ah. That is Zet. He is one of the crew of that ship. The *Demon Lair*. Camat is the captain and Eldara's mate. Those two don't have it easy. She won't go with him on jobs. Too much the songbird."

"What species is he? Zet? I've seen nothing like him before."

"A good question. One I cannot answer as neither have I seen his like."

Zet looked down from the upper level of the ship directly at her. Her skin felt as if someone had touched her. Malada tugged on Joun's hand. "We need to go. He's staring at me."

Taking a step to her left, Joun put his body between Malada and Zet. "It seems he is busy tonight with the ship. Usually, he joins the crew at Lady Pia's. Good. You won't need to be concerned this time."

"There won't be another. I don't think I want to meet him. He is terrifying."

"Zet is a good sort, but I'll not have you feeling upset no matter how nice that life form is."

Why am I frightened of him? The thought left her with much to consider. Malada put that away for now. She meant to enjoy the evening with Joun. She would return to contemplation of her fear later.

A fitful breeze cooled the air. The night would be fine. Her first foray into the settled world, Malada planned to experience all she could.

The back of her neck itched. Almost as if fingers played across her skin.

Zet! He stared at her still. The large building that guarded the entrance to the spaceport on her left and others on her right were like a wall of cliffs, funneling his gaze on her. Malada ducked her head and sighed when they reached the corner, turned it, and Joun directed her to a door.

Once inside, she shrugged off the wariness. In here, the life form couldn't see her. She had come for a night of entertainment and wouldn't allow anyone to dampen her pleasure. Not even the form she had somehow seen before. How had that happened?

Ruthlessly, the young woman put it to the back of her mind. This night was for her and Joun. They'd had little enough contact over the years. First, she had been too little to go anywhere with him. Then had come her healer training.

The music swirled around them. The young woman's voice balm to her ears. A plump woman smiled at them and led them to a table. Malada relaxed into the comfortable chair and let the song flow over her.

When Joun asked what she would like, she smiled and told him to choose. With her chair turned toward the young woman, Malada put her attention on the songbird. She would remember this night until she could no longer breathe.

Chapter 10

Cooler temperatures eased his way onto the skin of the *Demon Lair.* Before running the grid he'd laid out, Zet went hunting the "patch." Out of reach to anyone on the ground, the boots kept his feet attached to the hull. His tail provided the additional balance needed to allow him to walk parallel to the ship.

Zet made good use of his tail. A helpful appendage, he wondered why only a few races held on to that limb. Since he suspected someone had engineered him, he applauded their good sense in giving him a tail.

After finding the spot in question, he had difficulty removing it from the skin—which made sense to him. Keeping it in place meant securing it properly. How the pirate captain thought he could easily remove the thing while trying to flee for his life had Zet shaking his head. That life form didn't have the reasoning power of a fungus on Greenhouse 2.

Someone had the forethought to make sure the money cards, four, were all stuck to the inside of the patch. He laughed at the mental picture of the pirate captain trying to pry the money cards off the hull and the four cards drifting away in different directions.

Securing the cards in a pocket, he turned to glance behind him at the ground. With no one close, he allowed the piece of metal to fall. Later, he would retrieve it. He wanted to inspect it before stowing it in case of future need. He didn't trust the membrane to not have something concealed inside.

The lesser moon barely bridged the gap between starset and the arrival of the blue light of the larger moon. In the first rays of blue, Zet made his way to the top of the ship. Before beginning his chore, he stopped and enjoyed the panorama.

None of the buildings close by impeded Zet's gaze. All were two stories or fewer above ground level, allowing a sand or dust storm to pass over them with little or no damage.

The tallest thing in sight was the big bubble dome of Estevanana. Inside the city, several buildings rose to a height of four stories. Protected by the bubble, the wind and blowing debris flowed up, over, and around the slick dome.

On his right, the vast rolling dry ocean bed butted against distant mountains. The same ones that the blue moon slid clear of as it rose. Faint smudges against the sky, several sharp peaks stood like small teeth outlined in blue.

This wasn't the easiest world in the universe to live on, but Zet preferred it to the constant wet heat of Greenhouse 2. He'd already asked Camat for leave to stay on Estevan when the ship went to Greenhouse 2 for refitting.

For a while, he'd been considering a trip to the closest of the mountain ranges that ringed the dead ocean. Rumor had it that the SUN fleet had found a cell of pirates hiding in caves in those peaks and entombed them inside.

He had no interest in the pirates or what they may have hidden. Finding traces of an old civilization within those mountains piqued his curiosity. Unlike exploring the vast darkness of space, here he could touch what he found.

Being alone didn't bother him. Often, he craved silence. The lack of other forms. Having grown somewhat immune to the sidelong glances from other species as they tried to define him, Zet still felt more comfortable with his family.

The members of the *Demons* didn't care that no one could pinpoint his species or the combination thereof from which he originated. So if he wasn't in company with them, he wanted to be alone.

Which brought him to the problem of Itty.

The evening breeze that always accompanied the rising of the larger moon blew a small dust cloud in his direction. His inner eyelids closed, protecting tender flesh.

Zet could still see. It was a little blurred, but he could navigate if necessary. Another thing he had to thank his creator for. Long ago, he'd deduced what they were looking for. A warrior for use on a planet much like this one. He wished them and their backers to the lowest of the levels of the Pit of Shealin, may the seventh hell and all the serpents in it feast on them while they still lived.

Back to Itty. She didn't want to stay on Greenhouse 2 any more than he did. The little Houser never took leave on Greenhouse 2. One or both of her parents had come from that world. It certainly couldn't have been much further back in her ancestry.

No one asked her about it. If Itty wished to divulge data, she would. Not one Demon pressured another for information. They all had secrets. Stories kept hidden in the deepest recesses of their hearts.

Whatever kept Itty from Greenhouse 2 was her business. Still, the results of her disinclination to be on her home world brought a few concerns to his mind. Where would she want to be when the ship docked for what could well be many turns of the SUN clock?

He intended to bring up the subject when the actual yard stay became a real possibility. Since neither of them had any interest in spending downtime on Greenhouse 2, she might want to spend it with him. He would make the offer and see what she said.

The blue light of Billie created an atmosphere of mystery in the port. It hid the scruffy look of the buildings and the harsh land. Never having had quite this view of Estevanana's port before, Zet grinned.

Another small cloud of dust floated before the breeze. This one had a life form cause. One gate of the large salvage yard belonging to CNY swung open as music drifted up from Lady Pia's. Eldara would soon be performing.

His gaze on the gate, he observed as Joun ushered another form through the opening. Shorter and slimmer than the Watcher, she—Zet decided the form had to be female—joined Joun in the dusty street.

She had neither the second gown that Joun usually wore when first coming out of the wasteland nor another covering. Something far lighter clung to her body. A feeling he'd not encountered before started in the back of his head and slid down his spine to pool in his groin.

Who was the female? What was she to Joun?

They got closer and Zet's gaze stayed on her. Head uncovered; she had no hair. She had a form so slim, he could almost count every rib that rippled the cloth as she moved. Her gaunt face, with shadows beneath sharp cheekbones, lifted.

Their eyes locked. Her steps hesitated for an instant before the female glanced away. She leaned into Joun. The other male looked upward to where he stood on the ship before putting his body between Zet and the female, removing her from sight.

What was that about? Had he done something wrong? It wasn't Zet's fault she went bareheaded and without the flowing robe that Joun usually wore. That had to be her choice. Or did it?

Nothing about the encounter relaxed him. Zet felt as if a charge had been applied to his body. His normally flaccid male organs buzzed, and his entire body felt on fire. He willed it to stop. There was the ship to walk. He needed to know if that idiot pirate had tried to hide anything else on the skin of the ship. Only the warrior saint knew what the fools were capable of.

He did his job, as planned. Zet stifled the urge to go down to the restaurant and find the female when he finished. Instead, he went to his quarters. Implants off, he lay on his side and couldn't keep his hand from touching himself. The urge to find out what would happen was too strong.

The result left him breathless. Panting. He'd never expected the pure pleasure of the act. He would do this again. How would it be with a partner? A picture of the female popped into his head. Zet again toyed with his body all the while picturing the female's hands on him instead.

Chapter 11

She wanted to hide. Malada corrected herself. She didn't want to avoid everyone and miss the female who sang, a pleasure she would deny herself for no good reason if she turned back now. It was the alien she wanted to stay away from. The feeling of being the tryanot-like thing's prey, if she correctly interpreted what had shaken her to her soul, caused her response. But only regarding the creature who watched her so intently.

Not a Human by any stretch of her imagination, alien in every way, he somehow captured her attention. Capture felt more than appropriate as she continued to shuffle through her impressions of the figure and the feelings it engendered.

Joun, being attuned to her—more than her mother and far more than she liked—made no comment until they had settled in at a small table with a drink each. Malada ordered water with a twist. The server explained the fruit they added as a "twist" gave a refreshing flavor to the otherwise bland reclaimed water.

"What bothered you about Zet?" Joun leaned over to whisper as the server moved away.

"I've been trying to isolate what made me uncomfortable. In the reading material we have, I've not seen any pictures of a creature built like the alien that walks erect. He reminds me of a tryanot, yet he is different. Might he be a hybrid?"

"I suspect no one knows. None of his crewmates use a designation for him as they do for each other. They joke around in here, so I've heard their teasing comments. They're up there." Joun's fingers turned her chin in the direction he wanted her to look. "That group up near the front, in the corner diagonally farthest from us. See them?" His hand dropped away.

"I do."

"The female closest to us is supposedly a Gossican-Human. The female directly across from Bunde is Xigant. She is the pilot and, I assume, pure Ellaerian."

"Her hair is a lovely color."

"Yes. The young male with the greenish cast to his hair, there. Do you want to take a guess as to his species?"

"Without being closer, no."

"He's probably a Ellaerian-Fantanian cross."

"How did this happen? How could there be so many crossbreeds? I've never heard of that before."

"They come from a pleasure world. One where certain unscrupulous parties go to great lengths to breed unusual creations. There are those who will pay well for a toy bred with their specifications in hand."

"That is wrong!" Malada hissed out.

"We find it so. Yet here they are. Alive and trying to build a life for themselves on that ship."

"What of the one I saw? You say no one knows his history?"

"Not to my knowledge. If anyone does, it will be his captain. Camat is a shrewd one. I suspect he may well be one of the youngest to command a ship that makes Estevan its home port."

"What are they doing to support themselves? I know those in the city use a financial system removed from barter."

"They take freight from one planet to another. Perhaps even passengers. Their ship will haul a substantial payload. Yet, they are shorthanded. Chronically so says Lute, but very picky who they take on as crew. Xigant is the newest of the lot."

"That is a grave responsibility for a youth."

With a laugh, Joun patted her back. "And being a healer at your age was not? Truly, girl, you don't know your worth."

Malada took a sip of the water. "There are springs in the vast that taste far better than this, even if we must filter the sand out."

"A good try at changing the subject of this conversation. You were interested in Zet, I believe."

"Ah. Someone has taken the stage. She must be a Human offshoot. Hush. I wish to miss nothing."

With a grunt, Joun sat back in his chair. Malada understood the discussion would continue once they left the restaurant.

Her eyes still on the group, Malada watched the shipmates. With a wave of his hand for the server, the young captain leaned his chair against the wall behind him. Silence fell on the room as the first notes filled the space.

Truly a gifted singer, the title of "songbird" draped the young female's shoulders easily. Malada almost eased the earplugs out slightly so the sound would fill her, but Joun gently nudged her hand down. He didn't speak. Her hand in his, they let the sound carry them away.

As the hour grew later, Malada's eyelids drooped. They ate. Enjoyed what Joun called wine, and all feelings of anxiety left. When he insisted they start for camp, she went along without protest.

All was tranquil until they reached the gate to the port. Standing tall in the fading blue light of the bigger moon was the ship she'd seen him on. Her skin pebbled as if an infection of sand lice had filled her clothing.

He was inside the dark and still ship. Zet, the alien. The one whose appearance was close to that of a tryanot on two legs, but more refined. What was he doing in there? Sleeping? Curiosity took hold of Malada. She wanted to know more about him and... Fear took over, and she moved to her father's other side, putting his bulk between her and the ship.

Once inside the safety of the junkyard walls, rather than listening to her father's views on her interactions with other species, Malada pled exhaustion and went to her nest. Sleep didn't come as quickly as hoped. She lay there beneath the covers, tucked away from sand and the chilling night air, thinking about what it might be like to not know your species.

Did he wonder if he was the only one of his kind? That must be an inevitable question, one that consistently ached for an answer.

The alien frightened her. What did she really fear? Before dropping off to sleep, the answer came to her. She sensed he could change her world. Giving up her position so another might heal had been hard enough to comply with. She didn't want fate dealing out more.

Her heart voice brought an idea she would need to examine when awake again. It was the last conscious thing she recalled. *We are all subject to the winds of change.*

Dreams came of a dance she knew of but had never taken part in. The complex moves of two people, mates, struggling to find a middle ground where they could exist in harmony.

Chapter 12

Griping about being shorthanded and calling the captain names under their breath for the lack would be normal on any other ship. Not one of the busy crew he encountered did. They rushed around, true. Food, hurriedly snatched, often got eaten as the entity hurried to a duty station. Things would ease once they were underway. Still, this was the most efficient and cheerful crew he'd ever had the pleasure of watching.

C'entala credited Camat with the health of his crew. The Ellaerian felt pride swell over his legacy. The youth could be like others he'd seen, seeds of those he knew of on his home world, cosseted and prone to arrogance. Camat worked as hard as his crew.

He also knew how it pained the youth to leave Eldara and take to the vastness again. A contract needed fulfilling and Camat meant to do his job. Leaving his mate being necessary, Camat did so without complaint. Nor did the Human make it difficult for Camat. Eldara left well before the hour they were to take off.

He'd offered the SUNs to Camat. They were the youth's portion, after all. He would have received it on his attaining adulthood by all Ellaerian traditions and C'entala found it necessary to remind himself that such traditions were not part of Camat's experience. Sometimes, reminding came more than once in a SUN daily cycle.

Camat displayed few of the objectionable traits of Ellaerian youth he'd met. That had to be Zatha's genes in the mix. There were times looking at Camat nearly stopped his heart. He so wished Zatha could see the legacy they had produced—together.

The government of Ellaeria swore mixing of species degraded the original, but C'entala wasn't so sure of that now. He felt Camat to be the better for his mother's ability to adapt to pressure.

If anyone wanted to see what happened to a pure Ellaerian when stressed, observing Xigant provided an excellent example. The pilot had gone into a dizzying spiral of destruction when she and her partner parted ways.

Itty, the little Houser med tech, was a fount of information about Camat. She relented and related facts. However, she swore he'd get nothing from her that the entire crew didn't already know. He'd learned how Camat and his small gang had stolen and negotiated their way into the funds to buy the ship at auction.

Several times, he'd watched the holos from both news services of that auction. Seeing his legacy take charge and bring the deal to fruition warmed his heart. He'd directed his family to the holos, sending copies to all their kin. They needed to leave the nonsense about mixing of species behind if they ever wanted to meet Camat. Otherwise, C'entala would keep the youth away from their judgment if they persisted.

The heads of other families had never deemed his status as a pilot and pilot trainer to be high enough to warrant a female. He'd never expected to have progeny, a legacy. He smiled as he took a seat and readied himself for escape from the planet's atmosphere.

Xigant, in the pilot's chair, would see the ship safely off-world and then on course for Pacifica. They had a load of seafood to pick up and deliver to Illsdl. Then the *Demon Lair* would hop back to Greenhouse 2 carrying a load of recyclables which would help pay for its repairs.

Once in the shipyard there, the ship would undergo extensive deep scans to determine any pressing needs. The lack of a log from the pirates complicated matters for Camat. He'd had to depend on inexact information from an AI that had, at some point, been scrubbed or had details altered.

With his implants tuned to the ship and Camat, he'd learned some tantalizing information. *Demon Lair's* AI had an almost paranoid fear of SUN. For an ex pirate ship, more than seemed reasonable. A "second" creator had planted information in the AI and, per the ship, other pirate vessels had also been affected.

Since that same individual had somehow made the AI more aware, C'entala thought its terror of the SUN fleet to be a good thing. It wouldn't ever attempt to battle it out with a SUN ship. The two premises taken together meant the chance of that AI, and others so modified, deciding to rebel were minimal. The SUN fleet would have to be eliminated for the ship to give consideration to revolt.

A ray of hope came as a decent meal, one he must chew. Food Keem took his time eating. He savored every bite of the conglomeration of something. Whatever it was, it filled his shrunken stomach, and he could almost feel the energy from it.

The captain had doubts about what to do with him. Otherwise, slop would be all they tossed his way. Why waste nutrients on a creature that would have a short lifespan? Everyone knew what Shung would do to him—if Shung got him. Keem hoped he had put enough doubt in Captain Buotch's greedy mind to keep him from the general's clutches.

He had to convince the captain of the riches to be found in the caverns which held the remnants of the old civilization that once ruled on Estevan. There had to be something there worth having. It made no sense for the Watchers to be living in that horrid desert without a good reason. Money always made an excellent incentive.

The entire matter needed research, a true scanning of everything about the Watchers. There were some things that required personal attention. A deep look into the sect and their reasons, stated and not, for remaining in the desert must happen.

If he were back on Estevan, a little side project would be regaining control of Eldara. Camat had no right to her—the female belonged to him. His songbird, regardless of the backward laws concerning slavery on the little dust ball of a planet, he would have her.

First came getting Buotch to turn his other cargo and put the ship's course on a heading for Estevan. He needed access to the ship's AI without the captain finding out he had it. With a sigh, he popped the last morsel into his mouth. Keem chewed slowly, savoring the taste of something with a smidgin of energy in it.

Getting ahead of himself wouldn't help. Nothing more would happen until the captain released him from the cell he waited in. If he were the Liderian, he would scour all available information on Estevan and its settlement for any sign of occupation previous to that of the Human colonizers.

If the male found nothing, he would either have Keem dragged before him to explain or—he sighed. None of the other possibilities would be helpful to him. Torture loomed large in his immediate future. Except Buotch had fed him something besides the usual slop.

That must be an indicator of better things to come? He hoped. Curling up on the cell floor, Keem pulled the blanket over him and tried sleeping again. He could do nothing. Everything sat in the Liderian's hands.

Praying had never got him anywhere. It seemed Saint Michael didn't wish to dirty his hands with an outcast. If the saint didn't want to bother with him, Keem certainly wasn't about to bother praying. Who knew if gods existed anyway? They were probably figments of the collective imagination.

Chapter 13

Eldara watched the *Demon Lair* rise into the atmosphere, her emotions conflicted beyond what she had expected. Pride in Camat, along with a longing to be with him, wove itself into a tapestry of regret. One that lay slightly overlapping her excitement at having been asked to perform at a private party in the city.

She had no intention of leaving Lady Pia and Tonio's restaurant. They had been too good to her when she needed help. But a private gathering for some of the most important of the planet's government would do her credit balance no harm, nor would it hurt her benefactors. Eldara suspected it might well bring some out to the port and the restaurant.

That was her hope.

The ship little more than a speck above her, she still stood watching until she could no longer see it. She lowered her hand and backed into the shade offered by the terminal. She should go back to the restaurant and practice in Pia's office for the upcoming party. Eldara didn't have the heart for it, though. She already missed Camat. Her mate. The male she adored.

Not enough to go with him. The nasty little voice in her head, the one which had been tormenting her since Camat announced the day of their departure, had to be put down once again.

"I must sing," she muttered. "He is with me on this."

Water bottle swinging from her left wrist, Eldara decided she would take a walk and try to clear her mind before going back. She had time, several days before the dinner and the gathering for the installation of the new governor.

With a giggle, she raised the container to take a sip. The port of Estevan was so far removed from the daily life of the city proper, it was a wonder it hadn't declared itself a city and elected its own administration.

She suspected that might get slapped down hard by those living in and around the port. They wanted no controls foisted on them. Even as they grumbled about the taxes, they paid them so long as Estevanana left them alone.

Tonio said it was a delicate balance of power. The port didn't restrict goods going to the bubble-covered city as long as Estevanana left those living in the port to do as they wished. More life forms called the city home, so if they wished to subdue the port, they might make a go of it.

However, the individuals of the Port Authority weren't delicate flowers living in a city with a controlled atmosphere. A dome that regulated the amount of light they received from this system's star, an aging covering that kept out the sand and grit that routinely blew over the port. No, those living in the port area were tough forms.

Tonio said if things got too bad, they could always take water, provisions, and escape into the vast wasteland as the first of the Watchers had generations ago. He said he suspected that might be the reason the first watcher, a woman per the old story, left. A bitter and vociferous disagreement with those who meant to set out the rules then.

Eldara kept to the shade of the buildings. Her feet kicked up little puffs of dust that immediately settled again. A shadow in the sky, slipping over the horizon, Billie, the larger moon, hung like a blue jewel above the furthest mountains. The little moon, Leda, wouldn't be seen for twenty Estevan turns. The season on them when farthest from the star, the heat wasn't as overpowering as when the planet's orbit took it closer.

She stopped in the shade of the big CNY junkyard to take another sip of water and to look around. She'd been this way in the dark... no, not dark, but in the blue light of the largest moon. The walls of the junkyard stretched high above her head.

It took up a vast area on the outskirts of the port. A transport with a Fantanian driver cruised down the dusty street and came to a stop just beyond her. The male left the vehicle and went to the big inset gates.

"Lute! Mondan here. I've a shipment of stuff from CoDee Nellis for you. Ya need to sign for it."

"Ah. Yes. I've been expecting that. Come in. And what might I do for you, Eldara? Or are you simply taking advantage of the shade cast by our walls?"

"Me?" she squeaked out.

Laughter filled the air. "We know who is within range of our walls. Since I know you aren't a thief, you didn't get zapped."

"Oh. I didn't mean to set off your sensors. But I am curious about what you have in there. Is it all right for me to visit and just look? Camat does business with you, doesn't he?"

"He does. And we encourage visitors."

A chuckle from the Fantanian, Mondan, had her feeling self-conscious. "The pretty ones," that form whispered.

Her face on fire from embarrassment, not the heat, she walked through the gates. "Oh, my! How in the seven hells do you know what's here?"

The Human male with the black hair and green eyes she knew to be the manager of the junkyard smiled as he walked her way. Lute greeted her with a grin. "Don't pay any attention to Mondan. All are welcome who have honest aims. There have been a few who didn't. As to knowing what I have here, I do. CoDee left me a comprehensive inventory when he put me in charge several years ago. I keep it up." Lute gave a mock shudder. "The gods know I don't ever want to cross Cat. That female is lethal."

"She is," Mondan threw in before turning to Lute. "Where do you want this?"

"Close to my quarters. In the shade, please. I need to go through that quickly. I suspect there's a part in there that needs to stay cool."

The Fantanian nodded agreement and walked back out to his transport. After getting in, he piloted it into the yard and down the wide center aisle.

"Cool day and warm night to you." The female's greeting caused both Eldara and Lute to turn.

"Same to you, Lady Malada. What do you and Joun have planned for this turn? Oh, have you two ladies met?"

"We have not. I heard her sing two turns ago." The female with the pale skin and hairless pate addressed Lute, then turned to Eldara. "That ship that left, was it the *Demon Lair*? I am Malada Tay Culat. They call us Watchers. We call ourselves the free families. It is good to see you face to face."

Made slightly speechless by the tall female with only eyebrows on a lovely face, Eldara hurriedly got her reaction under control. Here was a chance to talk with someone from the group that had frightened her the night she sang when they had changed direction and come toward her. "It is. Camat is my mate and he and the ship are off on a job."

"While you stay here."

"I have a commitment to Lady Pia..." Eldara wondered if the other female was criticizing her choice.

"I meant nothing in the way of censure. One must honor promises. It is to your credit that you do so."

"Thank you." Eldara buried her first impression of judgment from Malada. "It is very hard to see them leave while I'm still here. But I need to sing."

"Understood." The female smiled at her. "And you have a lovely voice. It would be a shame to have only the crew hear it."

"Ladies, it grows warmer. If you wish to visit, why don't you find some shade? I can have a bot bring you a cool drink if you let me know where you are."

Eldara turned to him. "Really, I must go. I have a job myself coming up in the city and must practice." She swung around to Malada. "I would love to talk with you more. Can you come early to the restaurant and have a meal with me?"

"I can and am honored that you ask me to join you. When Billie rises again, is that a good time?"

Eldara wondered if Watchers had communicators or if they eschewed modern devices. Getting to know Malada would be interesting. "Yes. Perfect. I will see you then. Lute, thank you for allowing me to see inside CNY. It's amazing."

"Come, let me walk you outside. I never thought to hear junk described as 'amazing.' That's a new one."

Her spirit lifted from the low point she had reached with Camat's departure. Eldara considered the things she would ask Malada. What a grand opportunity to learn more about the planet. She would be cautious with her questions, as she didn't want to frighten the other female off.

Chapter 14

A glance back at the system they were leaving, and Camat missed his mate already. Once again, he wondered how Silver and the Nizad's shaman managed. They did; so could he. Sitting a little taller, he turned to watch Xigant as she took the ship to the edge of the system.

All secure? He queried the crew through their implants.

Affirmative! Trund.

Ready! Oolden.

Go! Enkel. Impatient to see a new planet, he was always ready.

Yes, sir. Brown, for all he dressed like some holo character, couldn't shake those SUN fleet roots.

Yeah, let's do it. Bunde.

Med unit is ready. Itty. Their resident adult, serious as ever.

Aye, Captain. Programmed and ready. Xigant. The female had straightened up better than he imagined. He guessed he had Itty to thank for his new pilot.

Ready, Captain. The male who claimed to be his father. Camat shook his head. That one still had him perplexed.

Zet? Where was his major troubleshooter? Hey, Zet.

Sorry, Camat. I'm down in the engine room. Everything looks good. Ready when you are.

Camat shelved his need for Eldara. When the ship was in the yard, they would have nearly the half of one Estevan month to do what they liked. Whatever it was, they wouldn't be going far from the planet. He knew her. The female wouldn't want to miss a day singing.

However, at some point, it seemed he would need to make a trip to Ellaeria. He didn't want to go and planned to put that off as long as he could.

Xigant, you have the course programmed; set us in motion. Make the jump. A slight hesitation and the movement of the ship changed. That brief pause bothered him and remained the major reason for the trip to the yard they could barely afford.

Zet? Camat contacted him on the private channel. *All good in there?*

It is. I know it felt like the interval was of longer duration; it wasn't. Whatever is going on isn't any worse. We're bumping along about the same as always. But I'll be glad when this last job is finished, and the ship is in the yard.

Agreed. We've got close to ten jumps before she is safe in a bay on Greenhouse 2. Just continue to monitor things.

Will do. Brown says to tell you if anything, it was a scintilla less in duration than the last time. Whether that is good or bad is anyone's guess until she is in the repair bay.

Thank you both. Something about Zet was a nano off. He'd noticed that for the last few days before leaving, Zet seemed to be not exactly with him when they spoke.

The small hesitation mirrored Zet's feelings. Camat must feel the same, leaving Eldara on Estevan. In his case, regrets flowed over him. He had no knowledge of who the female might be... except that she had been with a Watcher. Joun, easily recognizable, had been her companion. Which meant she would vanish into the vast wasteland while he and the rest of the *Demon Lair's* crew sailed their way through the darkness toward another job.

Camat had some expectation of seeing Eldara once they completed the contract while Zet might never see the female again. He had an urge to... wrong. Honesty required he be truthful with himself, it transcended urge and hovered at need.

As the ship needed fuel to survive, he needed the female. It far exceeded anything he had experienced in life to this point. Her smooth skin... what would it feel like beneath his tongue? Dreams of wrapping his long tongue around each limb, using the sensory receptors to taste her instead of the air, intrigued Zet.

Gently, he would caress each curve of her body. All four limbs on either side of her, he could use his tongue and tail to explore the woman. Human, which made her a woman and not as strong as he, meant he must be careful exploring the treasure. If she would allow it.

Would she?

The chance that he might reach the limit of his life span because of the necessity of helping Brown nurse the ship through this last job added urgency to his wish to touch her. But the ship was a matter he dare not ignore. The fate of every crewmember and his own hung on getting the ship to the pickup site, to the delivery address, and then on to Greenhouse 2.

In his dreams, she welcomed him. On waking, he had doubts she would ever allow him close. He'd seen her reaction to him in the beginning. She hid beside Joun, concealing herself from his sight.

Was he too close to the animal they used to pull the cart for her liking? Did he frighten her? Did any way forward exist? If he could have time with the woman, perhaps he could convince her of his intelligence, his value.

The crew valued him. Itty saw him as a friend, a life form worth knowing. And he felt guilt flood him. Itty feared Greenhouse 2, and he didn't know why. In all the times they stopped at the planet to drop off shipments, she never asked for leave. Not once.

Worse, this time not only would she be forced to leave the ship but would need to either take passage on another ship to Estevan or stay on the surface until the *Demon Lair* was ready to go. And he had not spoken to her for days while lost in his own trouble.

When he could have gone to Lady Pia's, he hung back. Pride kept him on the ship. The way the woman reacted cut him left a wound that gave every sign of never healing. Even the vermin that Lady Pia disliked so much because they could destroy stores by chewing and defecating over them fought back.

Instead of doing what he could in the limited time he might have to change her mind, Zet hid and nursed his wound. ***Foolish child.*** There were things he could do to find out more about her. Lute would have some information.

With the ship in a repair bay for a good block of time, he could go back to Estevan and talk to Lute. Perhaps he could mount an expedition of his own into the dead ocean.

There were rumors of islands of green in the middle of the wasteland, places where a traveler might find water. Unlike other species, he could travel the desert far easier. He had a vast capacity for water retention and the ability to ration it. Heat didn't bother him as much as cold.

His night vision was excellent. Those who created him made sure of it. He could hide during the day and travel at night as he understood the Watchers did. A vast dead area easily seen from a ship circling the planet, how could one find a single woman in the expanse?

That question posed the single impediment to searching for her. The desert, rough as it might be, held no problems for him. Like the creature that pulled the cart, he was built for the terrain.

Beneath his boots, the ship gave one of those little shivers which terrified anyone who felt it. Here in the engine room, the movement was unmistakable.

"You felt that." Brown's dark eyes flashed to his, then back to the terminal he had been monitoring.

"I did. Greenhouse 2 can't come soon enough."

Swiveling in the chair, the Human engineer got up and jerked the door open into the engine compartment. "Swear to Saint Michael, this is giving me heart palpitations. I'm praying there isn't anything left to be found that the pirates squirreled away. Another load of those damned olta gems could put the lot of us in jail for years."

"I went over every inch of the skin and only found that one insane patch. What we need is a disclaimer of some kind from Sebe. The lawyer needs to write up something reminding Greenhouse 2 that this was a pirate ship, and anything concealed on it is from them."

With a shake of his head, Brown turned toward the compartment where the engines lay. "I'm not so sure that would help. Greenhouse 2 might refuse to work on her." He placed a hand on the door and felt the ship.

That hadn't occurred to Zet. He put his head in his hand, closed his first set of membranes over his eyes, and thought. The engineer was correct. That might blow up in their faces. The ship needed work and needed it now. They might well disintegrate while trying to find another shipyard if Greenhouse 2 rejected them.

Brown spun on what was his bad leg. Vastly improved now, the metal replacement for the leg he'd lost to Keem's plan to keep Brown working for him performed well. The ex SUN fleet engineer settled into the molded seat facing the terminal and sighed. "I'll take this watch. Go get some rest and relieve me in six hours. We can switch off until we get this baby to Greenhouse 2."

"Alright. First, I need to go see Itty."

"What's wrong with our med tech?"

"I said nothing about anything being wrong with her."

Brown leaned back and ran his hands through his dark hair. "That's right. It was Bunde. She's worried about Itty. The female never takes time off on Greenhouse 2. She won't confide in Bunde either."

Bunde and Brown? Now there was an interesting pairing. Although, Humans pulled Gossicans to them like magnets to metal. This was the first hint of anything between them he had seen. Not that he'd been watching. There were other things taking his attention, like finding hidden stashes of pirate junk. ***Or the woman***.

He left the second engineer's seat. "I'll check on Itty and be back in six hours. I can't wait until we get the ship into that repair bay."

"Me either," Brown said as Zet closed the door.

Chapter 15

"Didn't Xigant just make the first jump?"

Zet nodded as he strode through the door and into what Itty considered her sanctuary—her office.

He had a terrible habit of not honoring spatial boundaries, something she attributed to growing up solitary. Not that he ever confirmed her suspicion. Within millimeters of her, he lowered his head and those reptilian eyes stared at her.

"What are you going to do when we land on Greenhouse 2? I know you aren't going to take leave on the surface, and you can't stay inside while they work on the ship."

She thought about telling him she most certainly could but decided to not bother. "I was thinking of doing a retreat on Nizad."

"Alone?"

"Do I ask you these sorts of questions?"

A slight hiss from him told Itty of his frustration with her. "I only ask to find out if you might need company."

"Probably alone." She glanced down at her hands and when she would have picked at a loose piece of skin, a greenish-blue claw nudged her finger away.

"Itty, why don't you want to meet other Housers?"

"Zet, why don't you tell me how you grew up? What do you remember?"

The hiss she fully expected to hear lasted longer than the last one. "We are at an impasse then."

She nodded slowly and his second set of eye membranes slid slowly back and forth across those golden irises with the deep purple pupils. He reached down and picked her up, carried her to the desk, and placed Itty on it. Without another word, Zet put both arms around her. After a second's hesitation, she hugged him back.

"I just don't want to answer a bunch of questions. Where did you come from? Who are you related to?"

"You don't have answers and don't want to lie."

"Yes. How would it sound? I was born on Calius in a pleasure house and don't remember my parents," she sighed. "Can't you picture their faces?"

"And you're safe here, with us."

"I am."

"I'm going back to Estevan for the duration. You could come with me."

Zet's skin always looked scaly. Instead, it was smooth, supple, not rough at all. She'd looked a few things up and his skin resembled that of old snakes of Earth, cool and dry. Itty hugged him harder. "I really am looking forward to a retreat on Nizad. I might get to meet the shaman. At least Silver's second-in-command says he can arrange it."

With one hand, she wiped her eyes. "You're not supposed to make your friends cry."

"This is a rule? Where is it posted?"

"I'll get it for you. Now, you should be sleeping. If you're in here, then Brown is holding down the engineer's chair. He'll need you to relieve him." Using both hands, she gave him a little push. Itty didn't bother trying to move Zet if he wasn't ready. "Go on."

One long-fingered hand, claw retracted, tipped her chin up. "Is my friend better now?"

"Yes. As I've told you before, a burden shared is lighter."

Zet's shoulder wings and his spine-spikes, which had been flat, raised when he took a step back. "How many of our secrets do you hold, little Itty? Many, I suspect."

She grinned at him. "That would be giving out information you don't need. Go to your quarters, Zet. Get some rest. We all need each other functioning at peak power right now. We get this contract put behind us and our ship gets an overhaul. Your med tech insists you rest."

After a sharp salute, he turned and left her in the unit. She'd convinced Bunde to back off, Zet was another matter. Bunde understood she needed to be treated as an adult, regardless of her size.

Zet had been protective of her from the moment he'd accompanied Bunde home. Itty grinned. She and Zet were two strays the Gossican-Human found and brought back to the Demon's lair.

She would never forget walking into the basement of the abandoned warehouse and finding Camat, Trund, Enkel and Oolden there. Each one an outcast, they thought she had the same problem. Itty didn't. Prey is what Itty was. If it hadn't been for Shussha, she would probably have died by now of injuries suffered as a sex slave for someone on Calius.

At the time, she didn't know Camat was another of Shussha's rescues. The Kazzemian hadn't the capability of getting them off-world, but another city had sufficed. They would always be grateful to the female.

Hearing that Shussha had finally retired and had a comfortable and quiet place to spend the remainder of her days had eased the debt Itty felt she owed the other female. If she had to guess, Itty would say C'entala had probably done what he could to help the Kazzemian. Camat's father reminded her of his son, sober and solid.

Still, she didn't want to lose what she had here. They had all worked so hard to get the ship. She remembered crawling into spaces no one would ever have thought of guarding and opening entrances for the others to slide through. They never stole from those barely surviving, but the pleasure houses and the gaming halls... those they plundered as often as they could get away with it.

Did C'entala have any idea how fantastic a thief his son was? Itty giggled. Probably not. None of them stole for liquor or drugs—they stole for the things they could sell to amass credits. The credits that eventually bought the ship whose med unit she stood in.

When not planning a raid, Camat and the rest of them studied about ships and how to run them. Each of them took a subject and pursued it. But for her, it was never the ship she was interested in; it was the life forms who had given her a family. She'd slithered through some of the vilest places on Calius for them.

Another giggle erupted as she sat in her chair and let her gaze sweep across her unit. The med bed, the diagnostic machine, the shelves filled with holos and even old-fashioned books on how to keep her family healthy and happy crowded the space.

Zet, her protector, hadn't guessed how badly she needed a break. Itty did her best to keep her needs from affecting the others. She needed a respite because she had become too entangled with Xigant. Something none of them needed to learn.

The ship needed a pilot, and no matter how hard Trund tried, he would never measure up to the Ellaerian. He didn't have the education. She felt it wasn't a lack of brains or will. If Trund had access to the intensive training Xigant got, he would be every bit as good.

Oh, he had improved now that Xigant tutored him. But the female would always be just that little bit better. Trund had nothing to feel inferior over. In time he would be a better-than-average pilot.

Xigant was exceptional. And so broken. Used and tossed aside by a fool of a Gossican female. Which brought Itty to her dilemma—should she act on her attraction, or might that only cause Xigant more trouble? If the Ellaerian female's heart healed enough for her to go back to Ellaeria, would a relationship with Itty cause her to stay when she shouldn't?

Itty didn't need time away from the *Demon Lair;* she needed time away from Xigant.

Chapter 16

She and Joun left the yard early in the evening just as the smaller moon dipped below the bubble that protected the city from the Estevanian climate extremes. When Malada glanced back at the moon shining through the clear covering, it looked like a gem of some kind. Something she had seen in a holo.

Joun turned to grin at her. "Sometimes, in the right light, anything can appear beautiful. That is a sight I've seen a few times."

"It is pretty."

He made a clicking sound with his tongue on the roof of his mouth and the tryanot picked up the pace. "I want to be in the cavern before light."

"We're not going to the well first?"

"No. I spoke with Lute and there is something, if I can find it, that may prove lucrative." A slight shrug lifted his shoulders. "I suspect the pirates have another hiding place in there. I've not plumbed all the tunnels yet. With your help, I think I may finally get it all mapped."

"It is strange how none of the positioning tech works in there."

"Not so strange. I've observed many things we take for granted don't function in the old places. It is possible they had a superior blanking tech of some sort."

They reached the upper level of the old riverbed and began the downward trek to the floor of the dead ocean. Once, the river had deposited many a load of detritus at its delta, forming a broad plain that sloped gradually down. Travel up and down the ancient riverbed was far easier than the old ocean floor. The seabed had humps and valleys not easily negotiated if one didn't know where to go.

Having been that way dozens of times, Joun knew the route, as did the tryanot pulling the cart. For Malada, it was a learning experience. She paid attention while leaving as she had when journeying toward the port. Things could appear a great deal different depending on the direction of travel. "How long do you think this will take?"

He shrugged again. "Who can say? I've no real idea of the extent of the boring the old ones did inside the mountains. That makes it hard to guess at the interval of time this may require."

"You realize I left my jinge with Mother?"

A laugh flew out of the man. "Your mother has Tingle? Did you make her promise not to release her into the desert?"

"Certainly. I'm not a fool. But I didn't expect being gone for that long. You of all men should know how short Mother's patience can be."

This time, a chuckle filled the desert silence. "Oh, I do. But you must see how suited we are. When she can't stand the sight of me anymore, I go traveling. Since I need to travel for my mental health and she needs me gone for hers, it works."

"It does, I suppose. However, she has as little patience with me as with you. Thankfully, when I had no father to turn to, I had aunties who always gave me what I needed."

For a long time Joun walked silently beside her.

They were rounding the edge of what Malada had learned was once a colony of sea life. The creatures had deteriorated into jagged hunks of something not quite rock and dead for so many centuries they had baked and weathered into a mildly abrasive substance used by Watchers everywhere to make things smooth. When pulverized and applied as a paste with much rubbing and reapplying, the compound produced lovely results.

Those living in the city had no idea what the Watchers were privy to. The colonists who stayed on the plain and erected the bubble knew little of the actual history of the planet. A fact all Watchers worked to keep to themselves. The wonders of the ones who dug out the mountains when faced with the loss of the oceans, the heating of the planet and subsequent disaster were well-kept secrets.

In the beginning, those on the plain concentrated all their efforts on subduing the planet and looked to the stars for their needs. Trade and the largess of the original company who sent them there kept them alive throughout those early years. The mining they hoped to do turned out to be no more than a surface deposit on the plain and quickly harvested. Once they exhausted the deposit, the company cut the colony loose.

The first LaDonna, the woman who eschewed all the company stood for, went out into the wilderness and found something far richer—the remnants of a civilization significantly more advanced. She made a conscious decision to not share with those in the newly erected bubble, knowing they would tear the mountains apart for what they concealed.

Along the way, she discovered adequate water resources to keep a small group of people alive and healthy. Her descendants practiced strict birth control and portioned the land out. It never had to support more than it could.

Watchers honored the planet and those who had come before. Whatever they had done or whatever nature had done to extinguish them, each new LaDonna took great care to make sure they did not make the same errors.

"I am sorry. You were always so happy to see..."

Malada cut her father's apology off. "You return? I learned early if you two were quarreling, you left me alone."

"That does not speak well of our parenting of you."

"But I had the aunties and uncles. I suspect the One-Who-Sees-All told the first LaDonna to keep kin together until a group was large enough to split with no harm to either for support."

Joun clicked his tongue in a sharp sequence, and their tryanot came to a halt. "We must stop here and wait for the larger moon. There is a section ahead that is never good to traverse unless one can see the trail well."

They lifted the weathered covering from the back of the cart and sat on the edge of the bed. During the cooler months, Billie, the larger blue moon, rose in a slightly different quadrant from the small, pale moon. Leda, on the beginning of its waxing cycle again, didn't give enough illumination to travel by. Its faint light flowed over the landscape as water might have eons before.

At this time of year, Billie peeked at the land from the shoulder of one of the mountain ranges far from them. They must wait for Billie to fully rise before resuming their journey. When the orb breached the edge of the distant mountain range, the peaks appeared as low-lying shards, like the worn teeth of a tryanot.

He tapped her on the shoulder. "Come. Follow the cart and remember when we turn off this trail, there is a rock that is pyramidal at the entrance to the dangerous part."

This time the clicks he made with his tongue were fewer. She knew the sequences as well as how to use the stick to get the animal moving. Joun taught her when they began the journey, explaining that for his peace of mind she must know how to work with the reptile.

They traveled a short distance before she saw the rock he had mentioned. The trail undulated around a tumble of boulders and up a small incline. Malada saw nothing dangerous—until they dropped into a swale. To her right, there was nothing but space—no comforting rock to border the rough path.

The cart, with her father at the head leading the tryanot, navigated a narrow ledge barely wider than the two-wheeled conveyance. The floor of the old ocean had dropped away and she could not see the other side. Malada guessed the bottom to be far below. This had been a deep hole in the sea. She put out her left hand and gripped the side of the cart. An urge to look over the edge swam in her gut—she resisted. If she got dizzy and fell...

"Malada?" Joun's voice broke the spell. "How are you doing?"

"Fine."

"Not much farther. We will go up another incline and away from the edge."

"Is this the only route?"

"No. There is another, much worse. Without one of the transports the others use, this is the best way. There will be one more part of the trace that is similar. Once we are through it, we will climb toward the mountains."

"I can't wait."

Joun chuckled. "It's better that you experience it the first time like this. In the full light of the star, it is horrifying."

"That I can believe." She remained silent as they left that portion of the route and, a short time later, descended to another. Malada concentrated on the plodding gait of the tryanot and the side of the cart she gripped so hard her fingers cramped.

Chapter 17

Kneeling before the Liderian who captained the ship, Keem silently swore to get the other male on his knees at some point. It would take a great deal of work on his part, but would be worth it. The captain had no reason to keep Keem on his knees. None.

The Liderian thought himself a king and on this ship, he was. The captain decided who lived and who died—until the crew had enough and mutinied. Over the eons, who knew how many crews had risen against autocratic captains?

A fleeting thought surfaced in his mind to be dismissed. He saw no sign, heard no whispers of the crew being unhappy with the present captain. Down in the slave pens, the crew could exchange ideas if they were angry with the state of things.

They could write in the dirt on the floor, thereby keeping any signs of discontent from their implants and out of sight of the captain. Many decades ago, he had done the very same thing and earned a second mate berth, being too young to seek the captain's chair.

His silent mental exercises served one purpose—to keep him still and silent in the pose forced on him. Eventually, when Buotch thought he had suffered enough, the captain would come to the point.

Butcher would be a more appropriate name for the male. But consideration of what that name stood for was a dangerous place for his thoughts to go. That might lead to him wasting his only remaining resource—his life. No. He needed to let Captain Buotch have his little moments.

Eventually, the wheel of fate would turn if he stayed alive and relatively healthy. One never forced fate. A life form could only apply changes and see if that evoked a response. So, he would play Buotch's foolish little game and grovel a bit when necessary.

The Liderian glanced his way before moving the spreadsheet on his desk to the side. The male was about to issue an edict of some sort. Keem forced any sign of his amusement from his face. He would have kept the captain on his knees with his forehead on the floor and for far longer. No matter.

Buotch's inexperience dealing with captives now apparent, Keem knew he had the male's measure and would act accordingly.

He needed access to the ship's AI. Quietly, undetected by any of the senior officers. Tuning his implants to the ship would not be easy. Still, it was necessary for his goal.

"So, Keem. It seems your information regarding SUN fleet action on Estevan may well be true."

"Thank you for checking, Captain."

"It's nothing more than rumor. Nothing substantive can be located. As for these Watchers, they were easier to get information on. Still, none of it pointed to more than a group of desert dwellers averse to being under planetary government authority."

"Captain, If I may?"

"Yes."

"That junkyard, the CNY one, gets some rather interesting things occasionally. I've wondered where they get them."

"Have you seen anything?"

"No, sir. But people talk and on a world with as little to do for entertainment on it as Estevan, rumors get tossed around a lot. I suspect there may be some truth there."

"What happens to the 'odd things' found in it? Do you know?"

"I never had time to follow up on the information."

Buotch pulled the spreadsheet close and made a few notes. "If I have those restraints removed, and you placed in the deck ape quarters, am I going to get any crap out of you?"

"Not a bit, Captain."

"I expect you to work as the regular crew does."

"Certainly, Captain. And I have implants which can be tuned to the ship, if you allow it."

Allow it. Keem let his shoulders slump as he waited.

"I will. Humbor will remove the restraints and take you to your new quarters. You're sharing with three others. Do what you're told, and you'll stay out of the cells. We're due to drop off the slaves in seventy-two SUN hours. That done, we'll discuss the Estevan thing. Dismissed."

The orange Yadaxian, third mate on the ship, hauled Keem to his feet. "No fucking around, form, or you'll regret it," Humbor growled out.

"No, sir. Understood, sir. After you show me my quarters, might I check into the galley?"

Humbor freed him, then pointed down the hall. "Follow me. I don't see why not. I'll bet you're damn hungry after nothing but slave slop for weeks."

"Captain says it's acceptable for me to tune into the network. I guess I'll need the med tech for that."

"Guess so. Filute can handle that. Let's take you there first and get that done. Then I won't need to hold your hand to get you to where you need to go. The implants will take care of all that."

"If you would, sir."

"Yeah, yeah. If the Captain says your crew now, you needn't put on a show for me. I don't give a hairy damn where or what you were before. Just don't screw it all up. Got me?"

"Yes, sir. I understand."

And the wheel of fate has been altered. I wonder where we go from here?

Chapter 18

"Could I interest you in a trip to Ellaeria once the ship is in the yard?"

Camat had been expecting the question, or rather, the invitation. He shook his head at the male claiming to be his father. Camat didn't doubt he was—how many other forms were vying for the honor? Not a bunch. "Sorry. I'm planning on spending that time with Eldara. We don't get enough time together as it is."

The male seated in the chair across from him smiled. "I suspected that might be your response. Then could we make a short stop on Joloa?"

"That is a bit out of our way. We really need to get the *Demon Lair* seen by a competent shipyard. I'm not sure just what condition it's in and there is that nasty little hesitation. It worries me."

"All valid points. What does the AI say?"

"Not a lot about that. The pirates wiped its log. We haven't the faintest idea of hours on the engines or the frame."

C'entala's eyes glowed bright red for a moment. Another difference between them. Camat wondered once again how his father's family would react to his legacy being only part Ellaerian? It didn't seem to matter to the man who claimed him, but he didn't speak for his family. "That is a worry. I see your reasoning for not making any unnecessary stops."

To buy a little time, he could feel C'entala's need, Camat poured a tiny amount of whiskey into his glass and held up the bottle.

His father shook his head. "I see you're not much of a drinker. Neither am I. It muddles the thought too easily."

Now he had the perfect opening to take the conversation in a different direction. Camat knew what would come next, an invitation for him to take a few days out of his time with Eldara to make a trip to Joloa. He would not shorten their time together. Not for anyone.

"Xigant is a graphic lesson in how not to handle liquor." Camat held up his glass and took a sip.

"I suspect she was too alone for too long. When the Gossican came along, Xigant proved to be easy to relieve of all she had accumulated over her years of working." C'entala finished the last of the whiskey in his glass and put it on the table. "I did some checking. That female deliberately went after Xigant."

How much water can I actually saturate my cells with? There must be water out there. That female didn't look as if she suffered from dehydration. No creature can live without it. Watchers have sources...

C'entala opened his mouth, but Camat cut him off with a raised palm. Eyes closed, he used his implants. *Zet, you're broadcasting.*

Ah. Sorry, Camat. To everyone or just...

I caught that. You planning an expedition out into the desert? Oolden asked.

I've had enough desert for a while, Bunde added. *I'm going to find some place reasonable to rent on Greenhouse 2 and let my body rehydrate that way.*

Nah. You're going to prowl the bars and see how many bodies you can rack up. Just don't kill the jerks. Brown responded to Bunde.

Camat shook his head as his father chuckled in the seat across from him. Having tuned his implants to the ship, he heard all the comments. Time to bring this mess to a close. *That's it! The lot of you curtail it. Zet, you have the engine room in a half hour. Before you relieve Brown, I want to see you. Those on duty pay fucking attention. We're trying to ease the old girl along until we can get to Greenhouse 2. Next time, Zet, mind what the seven hells you're doing.*

Sir. Will do. Zet felt like a green kid who'd piloted his ship too fast into a bay on Greenhouse 2 and had to have the emergency fenders deploy. Embarrassed and not sure what to do about it. It seemed the entire *Demon Lair* now knew he had a desire for a Human female.

But he knew what had happened. He woke from another dream of the Watcher female and hadn't detached. He hadn't wanted to leave the wonder of it. Not monitoring himself as he usually did, he'd wallowed in the feeling of someone wanting him.

Coming out of the gym, he found Itty waiting. She smiled and reached up to pull his head down. "When you get off watch, come see me."

With a nod, he acknowledged her request, then hurried to get to Camat before he was late relieving Brown. They were working twelve-hour watches because no one else could monitor the engine room quite as well.

The disturbing little pause that took place every time they made a jump had everyone on edge. But in six hours, they would be at the job. One twenty-four hour shift and then they could jump for Greenhouse 2.

They carried the parts for the system upgrade to the shields for a small mining world. Dropping off the parts was the simple part. Sticking around to make sure they got it done and no pirates swooped in to give the admin on planet 854 circling the dwarf red sun any trouble was the problem area.

Zet knew Camat had spent a lot of time getting information out of his father. If they didn't have C'entala with them, they would have bypassed this contract. As it was the most lucrative one to date, they had to take it.

He had to forget about the female on Estevan and concentrate on getting this job done and them on the way to Greenhouse 2. Prepared to get his ass chewed out by Camat, he hurried to what Camat called his office with an apology poised on his tongue.

"Sorry..." Zet started as he entered when his captain gave permission.

"What you broadcast is your problem. The rest of the crew isn't going to let you forget it in a hurry. That's not what I called you in about. You plan to go to Estevan while the ship is in the yard? Did I hear that right?"

"I do."

"So do I. Did you investigate how you plan to handle that? Is there a ship going that way from Greenhouse 2?"

Zet felt his entire body relax. He so didn't want to say more about the Watcher. "I did. There's a shipment of used parts going to Estevan from Greenhouse 2, and it should leave about twelve hours after we get into drydock. If we don't get jammed up on time, I planned to take it. They ferry used stuff back and forth between Greenhouse 2 and Estevan all the time."

"Since you set that up, can you book passage for me? I want to spend time with Eldara."

"I can. How about you share the berth with me? I got a berth because I thought we might be putting in a lot of hours and I planned to catch up on sleep and"—he felt his heart rate speed up slightly because he didn't want to explain but thought he had to—"do a full hydration. Pack on as much water as possible. Since they do the run all the time, the *Luda* usually has full tanks."

Camat nodded. "They do a little water smuggling on the side."

"Yes, I suppose they do. I hadn't thought about it, but... yeah. We've done our share of that."

"In limited amounts, we have." Camat laughed. "A few liters of water go a long way in some circles on Estevan."

You on the way? Brown's voice asked in the implants.

"Brown wants me," Zet told his captain.

"On the private channel?" Camat pushed the chair away from the desk and stood. "Ask him if anything is wrong."

Zet did. At the same time, he used his private channel to the AI. "Something wrong?"

His spine ridge rose slightly as he listened, then flattened. With the ship on one channel and Brown on the other, both saying nothing untoward had occurred, he relaxed and turned to Camat. "Not at this time. I think Brown just needs a break."

Camat waved him away. "Go. We don't want to burn our chief engineer out."

Sprawled in the seat with his metal leg stretched out in front of him, Brown found the ability to grin at Zet when he entered. "Since there were only two Watchers in Port Estevan, and I know you've already met the male, that leaves the female. So, got a case of a honey you want to do?"

"You Humans have some oblique ways of saying things. A female got my attention; I'll admit to that. Whatever else is going on in my brain is not shareable."

"Don't flutter your little shoulder wings at me and put those back spines down. I don't give a SUN credit about that as long as you get your ass in here and relieve me when it's your watch."

Taking the second engineer's chair, Zet kept his mouth shut. Brown seemed irritable enough without making it worse.

The ship's first engineer scrubbed a hand over his face. "Swear by Saint Michael, I'm going to sleep the next twelve hours straight."

Then he glanced at Zet with a sigh. "Nothing shows up on any gauges—I can't point a finger at a damn thing. Something simply feels off. I'm going to feel a whole bunch happier when the ship is in the Greenhouse 2 yard."

"Agreed. Now get your cyborg behind out of here. Get Caran to make you some of those Selvian roll sandwiches she's been experimenting with. Somehow the juxtaposition of the sweet roll and that savory olla nut paste with a slab of mushroom works. It's filling and you'll sleep better if your eat."

Brown used his upper arm strength to get to his feet, pushing on the chair's arms. "I wish I was a cyborg. Then this damn leg wouldn't bother me so much. It's better, but not exactly great."

Before the door closed behind Brown, Zet caught the sound of Bunde's voice in the hall berating the Human for something. He had a sudden epiphany. The female cared about Brown but didn't want to let the engineer see she felt something for him.

Emotions were strange things. Up until the moment he spotted the Watcher female, he'd had no problem with feelings. Having few, he went about his business logically. What he felt churning away in him now could not be denied. It could be subverted, shunted aside for stretches of time, but not eliminated. He didn't know what to make of what the sight of one Human female had done to him. It didn't make sense.

Chapter 19

Having passed the word on about the latest in the finds Joun had brought in, Lute waited to see what the owners of CNY Universal Salvage Yard wanted him to do with them. So far, Joun's finds sat in an isolated corner of the yard, one he had no trouble keeping other life forms out of.

There were things under cover he wouldn't mind having in his module, but had been cautioned against that by Lady Cat. He no longer feared her speaking into his mind. Still, he kept most of what went on at the quarterly meetings to himself. Allowing anyone to know the depth of Lady Cat's abilities could cause them nothing but trouble. Particularly on Estevan.

When Cat and CoDee rescued him years past, he'd resolved to never betray them. Things had changed over the years. With Lady Cat a member of the Life Foundation, anyone foolish enough to try hurting her would find themselves buried or jailed. It didn't hurt that CoDee belonged to the Mercenary's Union. Mates and family members of those in the Union were every bit as protected as those in the Life Foundation. Still, he could see no reason to give out information.

The communication from a ship called the *Rolatr*, under the signature of a Captain Buotch, bothered him. The male wanted to know if the yard had any "artifacts" related to an ancient civilization that once flourished on Estevan.

He immediately forwarded the message with a plea for instructions, asking what he should tell the captain. Although Dave Yerks was located in Port Estevan and a short distance from him, his response came in last. No doubt he was busy working on something in the fabrication shop and hadn't checked his messages.

CoDee and Cat responded first. One word began the message—"nothing." They advised he was to reroute any such inquiries to them. And not to worry, they would respond to Buotch. Cat added it might be a good idea to see what he could arrange in the way of extra security as she had a bad feeling about that male. CoDee added a short "agreed" as a postscript.

So Lute found himself in the market for forms he could trust to patrol and secure the yard, night and day. He wasn't sure where to begin.

When Dave finally replied, he agreed with Cat and CoDee and added he would be there at midday and bring lunch. Dave suggested they use CoDee's old living quarters dug into the side of the hill in the far back of the yard as a meeting place.

So Lute waited there, staring out at the rows of items spread out in the warmth of a midwinter's day. He made sure when Dave arrived at the gate to have the sensors, all of them, check carefully. The time to be cautious was before anything happened, not afterward. He wondered why Dave wanted to meet in the old shelter.

When he arrived, Dave praised him for being cautious. Then he explained that if any listening devices were being used, they were probably directed toward Lute's living module, an old Tuff-Built yacht he'd turned into his home.

They discussed the probability of Captain Buotch fishing for information. Why—that was the first question. Dave felt the captain had met someone who influenced him. When the meeting ended, Lute looked forward to meeting a female Dave called Yarla.

She had been at the pleasure house and it didn't work out. The female who ran it, only known as The Diva, came to Dave and asked him to give her some kind of job to get Yarla out of the house.

From Ummarrii, no one knew quite how she'd landed on Estevan. Smart and capable, Dave wanted Lute to work with her in finding and maintaining security not only for the yard, but for his fabrication shop and smaller gym business as well.

Known as keen observers, to the point of seeming telepathic, an Ummarrii could easily handle the job. Dave explained she would winnow out the undesirables from the candidates that neither he nor Lute had time to interview and train. If Lute agreed to work with her, Dave would send her to Sebe to sign a contract and a non-disclosure clause about the finds Joun brought in.

When Dave left, Lute heaved a sigh of relief. He hadn't the slightest idea how to proceed when it came to guards. Tech security was another matter. An order for things he needed to increase that level of security had already gone out. To keep the Estevanana admin's nose out of their business, the order went to suppliers on Greenhouse 2.

Being shoved along the corridor toward the captain's ready room by a Gossican female who licked her lips when she eyed him unnerved Keem at the beginning. She had informed him of her interest with a grin that allowed her to drop that second set of teeth. The ones she made sure he saw.

Then Buotch waved a tablet in his face. Whiskers quivering, eyes narrowed, the Liderian demanded an explanation of the message he'd received in response to his inquiry.

Keem politely asked to see the messages. At his back, the Gossican made a slurping sound. She had plans for him that likely involved a great fucking which would end in his being a meal—hers.

He had to read the messages twice. "Sir, might we talk alone? Please. I think this matter is best discussed between the two of us."

"E'nnty, wait outside."

The door hissed shut behind him, and Keem nearly jumped across the top of the desk. "By all the household gods of Selvia, whatever possessed you to send them a message? Of course, they are going to tell you they have nothing and know nothing. I saw the Watcher with my own eyes bringing in a cart that entered the salvage yard."

"But I needed verification..."

"Are you that low on funds that a trip to Estevan is going to break you? If so, take me to Shung. He's got brains enough to know not to alert the prey."

"But Shung..."

"Wants to kill me and resurrect me until he's tired of doing it and then use a Gravity Diffuser on me to make sure I can't come back again. But he'll listen every time and once the seed is planted and his anger dulls, then we'll go to Estevan and take what we want."

Keem gave the tablet a shove, and it slid off into Buotch's lap. "Being the middleman, buying and selling slaves has kept you from learning a few things. Never flew with pirates much, have you?"

The captain shook his head.

"I can tell. You never alert the prey. Never. You want them docile and going about their business as they normally do. Then you swoop in and round up slaves, steal their treasure, load up their harvest." He slammed his fist down on the desktop. "Idiot! By the seven hells, call that sex-starved Gossican in and have her take me back to the cells. I'd rather be a slave or killed by Shung than deal with a fool."

Arms folded over his chest, Keem turned and took a step toward the door.

"Wait!"

The sound of the chair moving told Keem the captain had left it. Then a hand touched his shoulder. "Surely there's a way to remedy the situation?"

Keem lowered his head and acted as if he was thinking, all the while grinning. This had worked out to his advantage. Soon, he would be in control of the ship and its captain, with Buotch nothing more than a figurehead. *A blessing on all those many Selvian household gods*!

"Perhaps. I'll need to think about it. I'd like to go back to my quarters. And tell that female to behave. I don't mind a little sex, but no chunks of flesh are to go missing. Maybe if I get my mind off things, when I return to the matter, something may come to me."

"That's reasonable. She was watching you, I noticed."

You noticed something? I wonder if you're trainable. "This has been terribly upsetting."

He rubbed his forehead. "You and"—he waved a hand at the door—"E'nnty frightened me. That drives all productive thought away."

Let the snake shit chew on that for a while. Buotch didn't need to know how formidable he could be. Never let the prey know they are in danger.

Chapter 20

Listen up, all.

Zet swallowed the last bite of the roll filled with something Caran called breakfast meat and tossed the last of his tea down. He hoped, as they all did, that Camat's alert meant they could leave their orbit around planet 854. That world didn't have a name—yet. What to call it was an ongoing, heated debate in the governing body.

Zet smirked as he hurried out of the galley and off to the engine room where Brown waited to be relieved. His vote was for *Trash Bin*. Since they couldn't come to a decision, the entire planet had devolved into a state of chaos. The Demons were lucky to have had their contract paid. Camat had made sure they were taken care of by not releasing the upgrade until the credits were verified as on deposit.

The entire time he'd been in negotiations, some genius middle manager thought he could try bargaining for a reduction in the price and Camat had been picking names for the place and tossing them out via his implants.

Trash Bin. Dump. Bargain Basement. Dung Heap. Those were only a few of the ones the crew laughed over while listening to Camat. Calm, rock solid, Camat refused to budge one inch on the money. The only concession he would make was to give them three extra days of the *Demon Lair* in orbit around the planet in case any pirates were stupid enough to try raiding it. Privately, none of the crew thought there were pirates desperate enough.

He took the winding emergency stairs and slid down the rail all three stories to the hall leading to the engine room.

We're done with this one.

A cheer went up from the crew at Camat's words.

Does any section need time to prepare or are we good to kiss this loser bye and make for Greenhouse 2?

Zet slid into the second engineer's seat in time to watch Brown fist pump the air. *Engineering is as ready as we're gonna be. We vote leave now.*

He agreed with Brown and added his confirmation. All sections concurred. They had all had time to catch up on sleep while orbiting.

Okay then. Let's give it a countdown. Thirty minutes and we're gone.

Another cheer met that statement.

Brown turned to grin at Zet. "Fingers crossed we make it to the yard before whatever the hell is wrong falls apart. Damned if I know what the fucking matter is. Swear to any god who's willing to listen, I've checked this pup up one side and down the other. I can't find it. If it decides to give way, I hope there's time to make it to the escape pods."

A slight moan from the little-used speakers had Zet closing both eyelids in exasperation.

Brown sighed. "Shut the fuck up! Damn AI. That's what you get for tuning in to every miserable thing that takes place on this ship. I'm only joking with Zet."

"That's not funny," came through the speakers again.

"Who the fuck asked you? Pay attention to getting our butts out of orbit and to the edge of this system to make the first jump. How the hell many is it going to take to get us to Greenhouse 2?"

Both males looked at each other and nodded. *Give the damn thing something to do,* Brown wrote on the monitor with a finger.

Neither male needed the thirty minutes. They had been ready to leave for two days and Zet thought the rest of them were probably just as prepared. One SUN hour later, they had made the first jump, and the ship was still in one piece.

After a huge stretch, Brown levered himself upright. "We're back to twelve on and twelve off until we get to Greenhouse 2."

"So it would seem. How many jumps do you calculate between here and Greenhouse 2" Zet asked again.

"Too many. Sorry, shouldn't have said that." He waited for a few minutes. Zet understood Brown wanted to see if the AI had any comments to make. "Maybe four if Xigant and Camat have calculated it for the shortest distance possible."

"What do you plan to do when we get there? Are you traveling?"

"No." The chief engineer shook his dark head. "I plan to stick around in case the yard has questions. And there's someone on Greenhouse 2 I need to see. I understand there's a med tech there who works with those like me. If anyone can help me integrate this leg better, I'm all over that."

"As I would be."

"Fucking Keem!" Brown slapped his leg. "The bastard could have put me in his med bed with the leg and it would have been as good as new. The thing is, he didn't want me able to run off." Brown turned to Zet. "You know, he took the old one I made away from me every night to make sure I couldn't leave. I couldn't make even a crutch. He had me watched and any time I tried, he sent someone to take it away."

"Keem. Yes, someone who needs to be at the bottom of the Pit of Shealin."

"He does." Brown rose. "What are you going to do? Oh! Wait. I already heard. You're going to chase some Watcher female on Estevan."

He felt his spikes rise.

Brown laughed. "Down, green boy. Stop fluttering those tiny wings at me. I wasn't the male who didn't shut down and broadcast to the entire crew." He laughed.

Realizing he had done exactly that, Zet sighed and nodded. "I did. So I can't blame you for saying something. However, since you and Bunde are both staying on Greenhouse 2, is that in separate rooms? Or..." Zet let his voice trail off.

It had taken him a very long time to get over his anger at being teased. Then Oolden had taken him aside and urged him to tease back. Learning what he could use to tease and when he had gone too far had been a long time coming. But he had learned.

The chief engineer's punch landed on his shoulder. Not as hard as it could have, but there was a reasonable amount of force. "Don't push it, you jumped-up lizard," Brown growled, then a laugh shook him. "Alright, let's call it a tie and leave it there. I'm heading for the kitchen."

Zet turned and called out to the other male as he made for the door. "Caran has some things she calls breakfast bites she's been experimenting with. They aren't bad. Kind of toothsome."

"Thanks, I'll check them out." The door closed behind Brown, leaving Zet in charge of Engineering.

It would be his first twelve-hour shift of the journey. *Four jumps with how much time between each one?* He didn't bother asking Xigant or Camat. He would mind his station.

Time to execute second jump, ten seconds. Hold on. Camat's voice in his head began the count.

Zet's eyes riveted on the station, he waited. His hearing tuned in on the low hum coming from the engines. Every nerve in his body waited.

Jumping.

The ship seemed to hesitate that same minute amount. It didn't seem any worse or any longer than usual.

Zet? Camat.

Nothing different. It's the same as always.

Alright. Nothing different on the screen? No systems changes?

Nothing but that slight hesitation. Brown and I have looked at everything and everywhere. Nothing. By Saint Michael, not a hint of anything other than that little stumble.

Camat sighed. *Got it. We aren't going to push it. Xigant and I talked it over. This is going to take us slightly more than forty-eight hours to get to the yard. Oolden is giving them our projected ETA via email. Sorry. I wish we had someone who could relieve you and Brown, but it's long shifts again.*

That's fine, Camat. We already knew it must be like that. It's hard finding a decent engineer's mate. Understood.

Thank you both.

He didn't bother responding. If they didn't have Brown, it would be him on duty with no relief. Another of Bunde's strays, having the ex SUN engineer on board made his life easier. Not to mention he'd learned a lot from him.

The best part of the entire thing was being far from Calius. If anyone ever hoped to find him on the planet, they were bound to fail.

He got comfortable in the chair. Four shifts. He could handle that.

Chapter 21

She knew it existed, but had seen nothing like it before. The caverns themselves were enough to have Malada feeling awe for those who had gone before. Watcher dwellings were nothing like this. Nothing. Tents colored as the wastelands were like the tiny beetles on the backs of tryanots, mere specks.

"This is amazing! I'm happy SUN didn't simply blow the mountain apart."

"That would have been a disaster." Joun continued walking deeper into the rock. The entrance hall, as he called it, led to a place where a series of tunnels fanned out before them. He strode to the furthest one on her right and turned at its mouth. "Don't stand there gawking. Come along and turn on that light."

Malada scurried after him, touching the control to turn on the lamp mounted on a skullcap. "Wait! I'm coming."

His laughter echoed off the walls surrounding them.

"What is so amusing?"

"Do you feel somewhat smaller than you did before entering here?"

Closer now and feeling a bit safer, she could touch him if necessary, Malada thought about his question. "Yes. I had no idea..."

"Your brother refused to enter with me after we cleared out the entrance."

Malada could certainly understand why Stapen would refuse. "I know he wasn't the only one to help you gain access to the site. Didn't any of the others enter with you?"

"Not a one. Nor will they."

"I don't understand. Aren't they the least bit curious?"

He stopped and turned. Joun held out his hand. "You are the only one interested. Now, take my hand and I will lead you in. Look up. Oh, you may turn off your light now."

"How..."

"Hush, child. Trust me."

Her hand in his, the light off, Malada followed him into a vast space. The extent unknown to her, its size manifest itself in the echoes of their steps.

"Be still a moment. I must release your hand," Joun said.

Then three loud claps echoed and the space illuminated, taking her breath with it. Above her—up, up and again up—her gaze traveled to tiers and tiers of balconies. "By the LaDonna! This is huge!"

She hurried to the center of the space and turned slowly. "We could all, every Watcher on Estevan, fit in here."

"Yes. And there are five tunnels, remember?"

Her circuit finished; Malada turned to Joun. "How much have you explored?"

"Far too little. It is only me, as no one else is brave enough to venture here."

"There are two of us now. I will help you."

"I hoped you might since your brother..."

"You understand, even the tents oppress him at times. I can understand how knowing a mountain encased him might drive Stapen to do something rash."

"True. I shouldn't be so harsh with him."

"Where to now? The pirates, where did they keep their ships? What is on the higher levels? Do you know?"

Joun joined her in the center of the space and took her hand again. "One question at a time. First, I've kept my explorations to the lower levels where most of the tech is to be found. The pirates had a place on the far side of the complex. It's sealed. Whatever SUN used to accomplish that..." He shrugged. "We've nothing capable of opening it. I suspect we might discover something if I continue searching. Still, this place is huge. For your next question, I explored the upper levels at first. But as all the things I'm interested in are down here, I haven't gone back. Up there are where most of what I suspect functioned as living quarters are."

"Which holds nothing of actual interest for you. Understood. Could I go look? Is one easily lost in here?"

"I've mapped what I have explored. As I said, I went up there but didn't find anything of value. Go investigate and get it out of your way. Then you can concentrate on helping me. I find those SUN spreadsheet things quite helpful. Lute showed me how to work them."

He pulled something out from beneath his robe and held it out. "Here is one I took the precaution of getting from Lute for you. I've already put the maps into it. You can attach it to your wrist and consult it when necessary."

"Spreadsheet? What sort of name is that?"

"Probably an old Earth designation. Here. Let me engage it."

Joun showed her how to find help on the thing that he curved around her wrist almost like a bracelet.

With the instructions ringing in her head as she repeated the ones most applicable, like where to find the help section, Malada began the upward climb using the spiral stone stairs. Joun said he thought that there were other ways to move between the floors, but he didn't know how to make them work. He'd discovered how to make the lights work by accident. Three hard claps turned them on, and four turned them off.

The ornate carving on the lintel above one entryway on the third floor drew her attention. The flowing figures reminded her of robes rippling in a fresh breeze. Intrigued, she entered and clapped.

The lights were not the bright white of that of the cavern. These had a softer, warm tone. Chests lined the walls, one of which still stood open. She assumed Joun had looked inside and not closed it. Perhaps a pirate had lifted the lid and found nothing of value.

Still...

Curious, she walked to the chest, which stood outside its niche. A soft sheen met her glance. Malada kneeled and reached in. Fabric, material softer than anything she had ever handled, met her searching fingers. She pulled what had looked to be a blue-gray length from the chest and it pooled in a heap before her, then changed color as she pulled it close.

"Oh! This is amazing. How much is there?" She tugged one end around her shoulders and returned to the chest. Everything inside was a shade of gray—until removed. Puddles of material that changed hue as she moved them lay in a circle on the floor in front of the chest. Ten lengths lay there, with several more still inside.

"Joun, these are worth every bit as much as the tech," she murmured.

"You think so?" His voice came from behind her. "What makes you say that?"

She lifted the one around her shoulders in both hands and brought it over her head. "Look at how it changes color. Mother would forgive all if you brought her one of these."

He shrugged. "Would she? Really?"

"I think we will try it and see. You will be surprised." She doubled the material over and threw the length over her shoulders, wrapping it around her upper arms. "Is there more in the other chests?" Malada lifted her chin to the wall in front of her.

"I suppose. I only looked in the one. Right now, I've come to get you because I need help removing something. I need you to hold it up while I take out the last connector. Falling to the floor might harm it."

"In a moment. Let me put these back first and close the lid. They shouldn't just lie here and wrinkle. If you hand them to me one at a time, I'll layer them back in."

Grumbling something under his breath, Joun moved from the door toward her. Malada chuckled. As soon as she closed the lid, Joun spun on his heel and left without a word. She turned and clapped to shut off the light before hurrying after him.

Chapter 22

"When do we leave?" Camat asked Zet as they all watched Xigant ease the *Demon Lair* into their assigned bay.

The 365 degree gantry scaffold would surround the ship as soon as she cut the power. He and Brown stood on the bridge watching. Zet turned to the chief engineer. "I suppose this isn't anything new for you."

"True. Still, it never gets old. This scaffold is a little more basic than what SUN has." He waved a hand toward the screen. "That doesn't make it less interesting."

"Captain, may I cut power?" Xigant asked.

"Do so. Good job, Xigant. I understand it will take them close to twenty-eight minutes to get us integrated into the shipyard. That gives everyone time to get packed and ready to leave. I want contact details for the lot of you. And they need to be with the AI as well. If those change, you are to email new information to me and the ship immediately. Have a good time, everyone."

Zet turned to look at Camat. "I'm going to be wandering around Estevan out in the wasteland. Keeping in contact won't be easy."

"Turn fucking tracker mode on in your implants. Tune the thing to me and Trund. Don't give me any damn arguments about it. That isn't negotiable—life forms die out there."

Mouth open to say something, he bit the protest back when Camat glared at him. "By Saint Michael, one argument out of you and you'll have company on that trek."

"You asked when we leave. Sixty SUN minutes from now. We need to get our tails in gear." Certain he'd ended the discussion for the moment, Zet turned away, leaving Camat mumbling behind him.

The crew hurried off the bridge, each one wasting no time getting to their quarters and packed. Zet took care to engage Xigant's attention.

"Excellent job, pilot." He blocked her view of Itty, who had been first off the bridge. The little Houser scuttled away with Bunde and Caran right behind her.

His reasoning being if Itty wanted to talk to Xigant, she would have stuck around. Pilot or not, the female wasn't going to chase down his friend. As Brown said, "Not happening."

The Ellaerian stopped trying to see past him, straightened her spine, and sighed. "Nowhere other than the surface of Greenhouse 2. Since both Brown and Bunde are sticking around in case of problems, I will. We can coordinate, if necessary, on any questions the manager may have."

And you won't be chasing Itty. Good plan. Zet kept his thoughts contained.

Glancing around her, Xigant took one step closer to him. "Causing Itty any harm and disapprobation aren't part of my plans. Ever. She helped me when no one else knew how."

For the first time, Zet felt a lessening of his disapproval of the Ellaerian female. "Glad to hear it. She's special, is our Itty."

"I agree with no caveats. I've never seen a more dedicated med tech, not ever. Itty cares about us all."

"Indeed." Seeking to ease the tension between them, Zet took a step back to give her space. "Be careful if you decide to take a tour of the swamp. There are things in there that can eat you alive. A good pilot is nothing to waste."

For an instant, her eyes flashed red fire, then she grinned at him. "A compliment? I'll take it and ask no questions. Well, perhaps one."

He nodded. "I may choose to keep silent. Ask away."

"Where are you going while the ship is in the yard?"

Zet walked to the door and motioned her through it, remembering the gesture from the holo on how to act at court on Messeria. "Back to Estevan, as I told Camat. I've heard of interesting things that are supposed to be out in the wasteland. I want to look around a little."

She acknowledged his bit of courtliness with a slight inclination of her head as she preceded him out. "Take care, First Assistant Engineer. I'm not sure we would have made it without you and Brown in the engine room."

For the first time since she had come aboard, Zet smiled at the female. "Your concern heartens me. I will."

They said no more but went off to take care of their luggage. He hadn't believed that the holo with all the instructions on how to behave with a high status Messerian would ever be useful, but it had helped with Xigant.

The freighter took a few passengers. He and Camat would be on board for two extra jumps, as it had a stop to make at a mining asteroid. Nothing else was bound for Estevan for several cycles, a factor Zet had already explained to Camat before booking his passage.

But, as promised, they set down on Estevan seventy–two hours later and a smiling and bouncing Eldara met Camat at the port authority gate. After greeting her, Zet turned toward the CNY Salvage Yard.

Lute had his provisions and had agreed to let him store anything there he wished. Having soaked up all the moisture he could prior to leaving the ship, Zet thought it best to be on the move. There were many unknowns when it came to his desert expedition.

After a long conversation with Lute, Tonio, and Dave Yerks, he felt luck was in his corner. The ship had gone into the yard during what was the apogee of Estevan's circuit around its star, the greatest distance possible from its heat source and the best time to explore.

His small pack gathered up, he went to Lady Pia's to check in with Tonio and let the other male know he would leave after a full meal. He wanted as much fuel on board as he could manage.

Zet grinned at himself. That language was so much a part of him now. Xigant had acknowledged him, and Brown's acceptance cemented his position on the ship—First Assistant Engineer. He had a berth and a title. Not bad for a creature whose race was unknown. No one would ever guess he was an engineered species, a one-off creation.

As soon as night came, he would be on the way to testing his limits, something he had wanted to do for a very long time. Once he knew about how he reacted to the wasteland, it would be the high reaches of Haakonlan next. How would he function in the cold of Fjellskog?

Other races had documented their physical properties. Itty had manuals for each of the crew. In some cases, like that of Camat, more than one. That left it up to him to give her what she needed. He must discover what he could tolerate and what might be too much for him. All of which he must be careful of. Itty understood him better than most and had pointed out if he pushed himself past what his body could handle, there would be no one to rescue him.

Zet entered the cool restaurant and immediately regulated his body heat. He didn't need to sleep or get sluggish. He needed to be alert and cognizant of his surroundings. If he let his body heat get too low, he wouldn't eat.

Greeted warmly by Lady Pia, she took his order. Zet already knew what he wanted and asked if it was possible for Tonio to take a little time off to talk with him. With a smile, she told him it might be and went off to give Tonio his order.

He spent an enjoyable space of time chatting with Tonio when the male delivered his meal in person. Tonio confided he had always entertained a desire to explore the vast desert, but the thought frightened Lady Pia so much he had never tried.

Evening came and, as the brightest of the system's stars appeared in the darker parts of the sky, Zet followed Lute's instructions to take the path to the dry riverbed, which led down to the floor of the ancient ocean. Full dark came while he followed the path to the first place where it split.

Lute had said this was the farthest he had ever gone. Standing on what had once been the delta of the dead river, he allowed his sight to adjust to the absence of artificial light. A slight breeze he'd first noticed became bolder as the night deepened. The cold seemed to flow over the rocks and into the hollows that had once been full of water. How had the planet lost its ocean, its water? He wondered if anyone knew the answer.

Estevan seemed to be a puzzle that no one wished to explore. Those who lived beneath the dome were content with their lot. The spacers weren't interested in a planet with so little in the way of resources. They favored the desert world for the same reason the *Demon Lair* had originally made it its home port. There wasn't a cheaper alternative anywhere near the most settled regions of the universe.

Then he thought about the Watchers. Generations of them had lived in this desert. What kept them here? How did they live? All good questions deserving of an answer. He might not discover what he wanted to know on this trip, but he had time.

Faced with a choice, he picked the left fork of the path. He could always return and take the other if this one led nowhere. A noise to the right had him zeroing in on the sound. He tuned his night vision higher and watched a small creature scurry off to take cover beneath a stone filled with holes.

A tryanot! "Would you communicate with me? Can you?"

The little creature burrowed deeper. A tenuous sensation of anxiety caused him to back away before an acrid odor filled the air. The little creature feared him. Zet walked slightly past where the animal hid, and the fear scent became minimal.

Interesting. Do I release scent?

There were so many things to learn about himself. For now, he would keep the tryanot's reaction in mind. How did that relate to him? Was there any correlation? Already, the journey he had planned was presenting him with ideas. His exploration of Estevan would be about himself as much as this vastly unexplored planet.

Chapter 23

He needed to control the ship or the captain. One or the other. Keem used the holo program in the ship's exercise unit. Sweat rolled down his body as he traversed a steep path in a wasteland reminiscent of Estevan.

Having obliquely mentioned gaining possession of his slave again, Keem got it brushed aside by Buotch. A snicker from the captain's second in command, Humbor, led Keem to a disturbing realization. They planned to find what he suspected lay on Estevan and then turn him over to Shung, enriching themselves twice.

Over my dead form. By all the seven hells and every miserable snake in the pit, no. There had to be a way to take over. He could kill Buotch and Humbor, but what would the rest of the crew do then? What he truly needed was the ship's AI on his side.

There was a distinct possibility that E'nnty would back him. The Gossican female with a taste for him in more ways than one, the head of the stevedores had the respect of those serving under her. Respect, or sometimes fear. Which didn't matter to him. What did was her ability to control a percentage of the *Rolat's* crew. How she did that was of no consequence. Would she support him if he tried to take the ship over?

If he didn't take a chance when offered, he might find himself back in Shung's torture chamber. The thought caused more sweat to cover his body. He would approach the female. What harm could it do? If she got angry and lost control, she might kill him. If they got him to the med bed in time, the med tech would regenerate his body.

Having determined that approaching the Gossican must happen, how and when remained to be determined. He must plan carefully—E'nnty had a volatile nature. He could not rush her, nor could he wait much longer. Estevan would be the next port of call as soon as they delivered the slaves. He didn't have long to put a plan in motion.

The Gossican female sniffed him before running her tongue up his neck to his ear. "What's in it for me?"

She took another sniff and every hair on his body rose in response. On alert, he still couldn't help the erection that she brought on.

Not having had many interactions with female members of that race, he hadn't realized that fear could be an aphrodisiac. She repelled him, while making him tremble with a need to have her.

"A ship. I only want my slave and a ride to a small system somewhere out on the frontier. One as far from Elthsetaine and General Shung as I can get. What you do with the ship after I get what I want is up to you."

"You don't want to stay with me and do some illegal trading?" E'nnty asked before she bit his ear.

Keem felt a trickle of blood just before she began licking the wound she had caused. His whole body trembled with a need to be inside her. The female was heaven and all seven hells personified.

"No. A quiet life will suit me with my slave to see to my needs."

When her hand reached for him and tugged hard, he almost exploded.

"Not yet. I have plans for you right now. Have you any idea how we might get away with taking over the ship?"

When she turned her head and nipped his shoulder, he shook as if in a drug-induced frenzy. Perhaps he was. As soon as she finished with him and he could move again, Keem intended to look up more about Gossicans. Did they exude a poison that turned their prey into gibbering sex maniacs? Victims willing to allow all their life force to go to the predator in exchange for gratification?

"Well, I... I have... Please give me a minute to explain."

Hot breath scented with blood drifted across his face. "Get on with it. I grow impatient."

"What if the captain somehow inadvertently got caught up in the chaos when the slaves were offloaded? If a warning about the SUN fleet or a couple of Union mercenaries somehow got broadcast, there wouldn't be time to look for him, would there?"

"How very ingenious. A beacon dropped off close enough to the edge of the system with just enough power left to issue a warning would replicate a ship being blown into debris by the fleet."

She opened the wound on his shoulder before licking it closed. "You didn't give me much time. I've less than forty-eight SUN hours to tinker with the beacon and get the captain in the proper frame of mind. You had better make this good. When we finish here, I'm off to see Buotch."

Shifting over him, she thrust down, taking all of him at once. "Move. Do that swirl thing. I enjoy that."

E'nnty stopped talking and her mouth went to his. The sting of her teeth on his lip got lost in the fury of mating with her. He swore to all the gods he knew that he would never again let a Gossican anywhere near him. Female or male.

Chapter 24

"Have you any idea what this does?" Malada stood and straightened her back.

"None." Joun used the dizkezz he controlled with a virtual glove to make what would be the last cut to some item that stood in a row with others in the cavern filled with dust-covered objects.

"This thing..." She waved a hand around the enormous space. "Any of these things in here could kill us or bring the entire thing down around our ears."

"I've been removing things from here for several years and nothing bad has happened yet. Get ready. We're almost through. I need you to catch it. Perhaps they are set to implode or explode if roughly handled."

She sat again and turned her back to the wall, both hands under the thing he meant to take away. "If we don't know what any of this is, why are we taking it out and selling it to CNY? I assume they must be where you got the cutter."

"Almost there. As soon as the dizkezz makes the last cut, I need to move away so I don't inadvertently cut through anything I shouldn't. Until I get it away and shut off, you will need to hold this thing for a little while."

"I've got it."

"Now!"

Joun stepped away, and for a moment the entire weight of the equipment rested in her hands. Then he was there, his strength making it far easier for her.

"Lean forward and turn a little. We will lower it gently to the ground."

When it sat there, inert, Malada turned to her father. "Why are we doing this? If it is never used, has no purpose we can determine, what is the reason we are defacing all this?"

"A valid question." He reached out and brushed a bit of the fine rock dust off her head. "We may discover something. The owners of CNY are making a trip back here and will spend time with the things we have gathered. If anyone can discover anything about this ancient civilization, it will be them."

"What makes you say that? How can the owner of a place that specializes in used items have any idea what to do with this? It seems foolish to pull the place apart for no good reason."

"Child, child. How can you be so dismissive? You know nothing of the two I speak of and already you are judging them. Bring the gravity luge over and we'll load this. As for Cat and CoDee Nellis and Dave Yerks, all three are highly intelligent and own more than a used parts yard. Dave owns the best machine works between here and Greenhouse 2. CoDee is an engineering genius. Cat... well, she is another matter altogether. You must meet them; it will broaden your outlook on others. I fear your outlook is too narrow for one so young."

Under her breath, she grumbled about his judgement of her. Joun said nothing, but his expression told her he had heard. With a sigh, she helped him lift the thing and settle it gently on the sled.

Deciding to give back some of what he had heaped on her, Malada pointed to the sled. "You could use this instead of the tryanot and the cart. Surely that would be easier."

"I could. But then the beast would have no purpose. He needs one. You have no idea how much easier it would be. I could ride it over the trails and never touch a toe to the wasteland. Profit and ease are not what I'm looking for. My foot falls on the paths with pleasure. My eye scans the wasteland and I remember how many of us have done so before me. But this..." He waved a hand at the cavern and the things inside it. "What did the ones who came before look like? What were their hopes and desires? Did any of them escape? Are there any records? How will we know if we don't explore what they left? Have you another method?"

Silenced by the passion she hadn't realized he held for the civilization that came before them, Malada could only nod.

After having loaded the device into the cart, they retired to the cavern where they had set up camp. A deep well there provided water. The metal cap which had once kept it hidden lay to the side where Joun had moved it. He had explained that he could cover the shaft again and no one would ever know it was there.

She wanted to ask how he had found it all and didn't, feeling somewhat chastised by his comments earlier. *Was she too judgmental?* Malada asked herself as they sat on cushions, eating. He could be correct in his assessment.

Her thoughts turned to the alien standing on his ship. What about that one had disturbed her so much? She had felt like prey, but why? That life form had done nothing to threaten her in any manner. He had simply been so different from anything she had ever seen before. There lay a kernel of what her father had seen. She saw an alien so physically unlike her that her immediate reaction was fear.

Time to pierce the inflammation and let the bad part out. "The alien on the ship; you remember my reaction?"

"I do. Come." He left the cushion and held out a hand to assist her. "Let us go out and check on the tryanot. Evening approaches and he needs to hunt. We can watch the star set."

On her feet, Joun gave her a hug. "Planet-shattering conversations are always better when held in sight of something far greater than ourselves."

She chuckled at his attempt to make her spirit a little lighter. Malada waited as Joun made several trips with the bucket. He filled a container with water for the tryanot that would be dispensed to the lower level shelter where the beast waited. Joun turned the valve, which allowed the hollowed-out rock outside to fill, then they left the cavern to check the animal's supply. Before drinking, the animal butted its rough head against the man. Her father scratched its big head and when the creature finished the water, released the beast to hunt.

"Look how soft the land looks. One could almost call it welcoming. Which it is if you understand it."

"Ah. Like the creature I allowed myself to fear could be a friend if I had taken the time to know it."

Joun looked at her and nodded. "And Zet is a male, not an 'it'. A living organism with thoughts and, I suspect, dreams of his own. I mentioned Cat to you. The female you have never met is alien as well. From a feline strain. Think of Tingle, your jinge, only the size of a small human."

"Does she have claws?"

"That I can't tell you because I've never made her angry. I suspect she does. Another thing, she can't talk as we do. She makes herself understood through thought transfer. For some years, until she joined the Life Foundation and CoDee became a member of the Mercenary's Union, they couldn't bring her back to Estevan as anything but CoDee's pet."

"She is a real telepath? I thought they couldn't exist because the barrage would burn them out."

"I can't speculate. But I can tell you her alien aspect has frightened others in the past. She and CoDee are a couple. And I know of another odd pairing. A Messerian and a human female. Attraction, a melding of souls, can often take strange forms."

Malada thought about what she knew of Messerians. "But Messerians live perhaps four times the life span of Humans. How can he..."

"I'm positive all of it bothers them both occasionally, how could it not? Still, it seems they have embraced what they can for as long as the universe allows."

"You and Mother. Is it the same?"

"Our differences bother others more than they bother us. I'm sorry that you felt cheated by my absences. I find I must speak with your brother and see if he feels as you."

"Sorry. I shouldn't have mentioned anything."

He put an arm around her and kissed the top of her head where a stubble of hair grew again. "I'm glad that you did. I wouldn't want anything festering between us. Better to drain the infection."

She laughed. "Well, that is what I thought to do now. I don't want to be judgmental. A closed mind learns nothing. The next time we are in the port, would you introduce me to the alien? Zet, I mean."

"Happily. I suspect you will like the crew of the *Demon Lair*. They are all young people who have worked hard to better themselves. And several are halfbreeds. You should get to know them."

"I agree. The breeze is rising. It will be cold tonight. I hope the tryanot finds dinner."

"He will. If not, I'll find something for him. A thing you may not like."

Malada leaned into her father and sighed. "I know other creatures eat meat."

"And Watchers don't." He laughed. "I'll tell you a secret. Those sausages of Tonio's are not meat. Purely vegetable."

She gave him a nudge in the ribs. "Now you tell me. I worried quite a bit about what he used to make them."

They both laughed as night closed in on the wasteland. There would be much to do the next cycle. Malada and Joun went inside to rest.

Chapter 25

Meeting the large creature nearly nose to nose on the narrow trail above the void came as a shock. From what he knew of tryanots, the larger ones pulled the carts and wagons used by the Watchers. The creature uttered a squeak and began backing away.

"No. Halt!" Zet cried out when its hind leg dislodged a few rocks which tumbled down into the dark. The creature froze. It was a long time before the faint sound of the rock hitting far below wafted upward and broke the silence.

The large animal made a low groan.

Unsure if it would understand him, Zet spoke. "Wait, I'll turn around and you can follow me to where we may go our separate ways."

A feeling he thought might be acceptance briefly touched his mind. ***That, I must investigate.*** The feeling touched him again. As he walked back the way he had come, Zet thought about the implications. Was communication with the large beast possible? How, or better still, why?

Off the rough trail and on a level spot big enough for them, probably a cart and a wagon or two as well, he waited. Surprisingly quick, the tryanot hurried to him and put its large head against his chest. A feeling of gratitude touched him.

"You belong to someone, don't you?"

A faint picture of the Watcher who frequented CNY salvage floated through his thoughts and vanished. That faint touch excited him. Had his creators planned this? Then he recalled the slight anxiety he had felt on encountering the smaller tryanot.

I felt its fear. It wasn't simply the scent of its reaction to seeing me. I felt it.

The larger animal pushed its head against his chest. He forgot the sensation as a picture of another creature, a mammalian denizen of the wasteland, scurrying away from the large tryanot played out in his mind. He saw the tryanot capture and eat it.

"You were hunting."

Another huffed-out grunt filled the surrounding space. Communication between them was possible. But why? What races in the universe had anything close to his physical composition? He wished Itty wasn't so far away so he could turn his implants back on and ask. If anyone on the ship knew, it would be her. On Nizad in a retreat, he couldn't reach her and must figure this out by himself.

"Finished hunting?"

The creature rumbled, and a picture of another creature flashed through his thoughts. "No, then. You need another. Show me how you hunt."

The tryanot lowered its head and moved away a short distance. It turned its head slowly from one side to the other and then partially back again. Quietly, but extremely quickly, it took off with Zet following.

Did it hunt using scent or sight? As he followed the creature, he decided it might use a combination of both. Its prey, barely a mouthful for something that large, was dug from the hole it ducked into by powerful claws. Much like his.

After gulping the animal down, the tryanot turned to go back the way it came, the same direction Zet had taken when they met. It turned to glance back at him. It seemed to want him to follow. Zet did.

He didn't expect to find what appeared to be a wall constructed from stone at the base of a cliff. Nor did he expect to see the male Watcher and his female companion waiting there.

"Zet! What are you doing out here?" A note of something, perhaps irritation, tinged the male Watcher's voice.

Something else, grudging acceptance perhaps, came with the other's next words. "It will be hot soon. The tryanot needs water and we need to get out of the light before it gets too high. You have not met my daughter. Malada, this is one of the crew from the *Demon Lair*, Zet. Please, follow me inside while I get water for the beast. I hope it has filled its stomach and will spend the rest of the day digesting its meal."

"Greetings, Malada."

She gave him a curt nod but said nothing. He felt conflicting emotions run through her as she backed away toward a crack in the cliff face. Zet couldn't read her father, but he certainly could read the female. Fear, then curiosity, followed by something no other female had ever given him before—a look of physical interest.

His body responded immediately. Zet's organ began descending. He countered that reaction with a command to his brain to stop. Not appropriate behavior for any male on first meeting a female.

In his thoughts, the tryanot disagreed. It would have seized the female and begun mating without a second thought. He was supposed to be above that. A thinking creature with the ability to control his body and basic desires. The urge he felt was every bit as strong as the need to survive had been the day he escaped his creators.

He hoped Joun would again put his body between him and that of the female. Hopes dashed, he wrestled his need to grab the female as she walked away from him, her body moving in a manner that threatened to turn him into a frenzied beast.

Behind him, the tryanot found a spot that would remain in the shade and dismissed them all. It knew water would soon flood the small rock pool near its head. What other creatures got up to was nothing to bother itself over. Watchers and its new friend were all slightly strange. One ate, one mated with willing females, one drank, and one worked when asked. What more was there to life?

Much more, my friend.

Chapter 26

Would Joun allow Zet to see everything? How could he keep him from entering the site? In fact, they must allow him entry before the daystar got much higher. Could Zet's body cope with the higher temperatures?

Inside the small cavern, Joun came to a stop and turned. "I can't leave you out in the heat. However, we need assurances from you regarding this place."

Zet also came to a halt. She watched him take a step back. A second set of transparent eyelids blinked, and little wings of skin fluttered at his shoulders before flattening out. She wanted to touch them. What would they feel like? Was his skin rough?

"Assurances? I won't ask more because I sense you aren't about to explain until we settle this," Zet said.

Malada took another step to the side. The males needed to decide things. This discovery belonged to her father by rights. She should move up the corridor and see to watering the tryanot, but had to watch.

"Correct. You are to tell no one of what you see here," Joun said.

"I cannot do that. You are admitting me because of what the conditions will be outside. If there is a need, an emergency, how can I keep others out?"

"Define 'emergency,'" Joun said, his hands in fists at this side.

"Life and health at risk, with nowhere else to go," Zet replied.

Zet made his reply to her father's question with a slight hiss of his words she hadn't noticed before. Did that give away anything of what he might think or perhaps feel?

"I don't consider dealing in artifacts to be sufficient to qualify as an emergency."

With a blink of those clear second eyelids, Zet leaned back against the rock wall behind him. The small shoulder wings fluttered again. "Why is it something you can do but not acceptable for others?"

Joun seemed to grow an inch or so as he drew himself up. "I'm not trading them for money, but for things to allow my work here to proceed, and sometimes for things that make life out here better for other Watchers. Not that it is your business, since I'm the one who found this in the beginning."

"Do I recall something about a pirate base on Estevan and SUN entombing them? Is that correct?"

The slight hiss increased. Zet seemed to realize it and made a sound in his throat that she guessed their tryanot would understand. All fear she once had of the alien vanished. Now she wanted to learn more about him. Particularly when she took another step to the side and watched a row of spines lift in the air on the back of his neck. How far down did they go?

"Yes. Your recollection of that is as it happened. However, I knew about this place long before the pirates took possession. They nearly got the place destroyed. I do not know how old the civilization that dug into the heart of the mountains was when their world began its slide into the desert it is now. I hope one day to find out. To do so, I must have silence about its whereabouts and how to enter. I cannot protect it if all find out about the place."

The wings and spines settled. Malada guessed what her father said made sense to Zet.

"I understand your concern. You have my promise if we can agree that in an emergency, life and health being at risk, I may make use of this knowledge."

Joun's fists relaxed. Malada silently applauded her ability to derive information from the small clues she got from watching the alien. It seemed the males had settled on an acceptable agreement.

"Let me explain," Zet said.

Her father tensed again.

"As the creature you call a tryanot can, I can also stay out there. Come summer when it is hotter, I would need to find shelter during the worst of the heat, but I was built for this kind of terrain."

Built? Malada silently mulled Zet's word choice over. Why did he use that word? Had she been speaking, the one she picked would have been "born." Could he have used hatched? Tryanots laid eggs.

Using his tail, Zet pushed away from the wall, a movement Malada noted.

"I have no need of rescue. However, you may trust me to keep to this bargain with you," Zet said.

What she suspected passed for a smile with the alien highlighted their differences rather than minimized them. She wondered if he realized how fierce an image he portrayed. By the slightly wary expression on her father's face, Malada understood Joun recognized the warrior in the alien before them. The tryanots they had bred and used for traversing the Waste in no manner resembled the form who stood just inside the entrance to the wonders inside the mountain.

She remained at the side of the narrow cavern when Joun took a step forward and Zet came level with her position. He didn't move a muscle when Joun placed a hand on his shoulder.

Her father smiled but withheld the pat he would normally have given another. He had noticed the little wings and the spines on Zet. "We have settled the matter. So, come along and have a bit of food with us after we take care of the tryanot."

She wished she could have touched Zet so she would have an idea as to the texture of his skin. Joun's robe swirled when he turned and grazed Zet's leg. Since the fabric didn't catch, Malada thought his hide might not be as rough as a tryanot's.

Striding together, the two males moved past her. Malada followed, observing the alien from the back as he walked away. Thick and muscled, Zet carried his tail off the ground. It didn't drag as did those of the tryanots. Did he need it for balance? She had so many questions.

A sudden urge to laugh took her. She suppressed it by biting her lip. The two walking ahead of her would wonder at her reaction, and Malada didn't want to explain. Joun would understand; the alien would not.

Her fear gone, she wanted to investigate Zet. Feel his tail, his hands, and fingers. How were they different? How were they similar? Were the small wings capable of anything useful? Could he use them to cool himself when overheated? Were those spikes now lying flat on his spine sharp? She could see where they might be of use in a hand-to-hand combat situation.

If any Watcher males became interested in a wrestling match, she would try to discourage them. Well... unless she knew Zet could keep them flattened in a sporting match. Watchers liked to wrestle.

Different bands often came together in this season for that reason. Both women and men competed. The matches had another purpose as well. They allowed young unattached Watchers, or those who had no partner for whatever reason, a chance to meet and maybe pair up.

With that tail, it would be hard to put the alien down. When he used it to push off from the wall, Malada realized how useful it would be to a wrestler pinned on the mat. It occurred to her that others would be as interested in Zet as she was... now.

Chapter 27

The scent of water tickled his nostrils. It was close. He didn't need to refill his reserves... not yet. Before he left, it would be necessary. He'd planned a longer trek, but the scent of the female behind him required rethinking his goal.

Her fear of him had ebbed. ***What had replaced it?*** Zet wondered, grateful the woman didn't have implants or wasn't able to tap into his thoughts as the larger tryanot had. They stopped at an alcove and Joun bent over what appeared to be a valve. The Watcher counted to ten, then shut it off.

Straightening, he waved a hand at the mechanism. "I feel there must be a better way to do this, but I haven't deciphered their symbols. So I installed this system to give me a way to care for the animal without hauling buckets of water out into the heat. I fill this container and from here, fill the basin outside."

"I encountered a smaller version of the tryanot out there before meeting yours. Were the larger ones genetically modified to be larger? If so, did your people do that?"

"We did." Joun sighed. "It may not have been particularly fair to do so, but we needed the larger animals to pull carts. The distances are too great between some of our enclaves for a single night's travel on foot. With no places to stop between them, we needed the creatures."

"Do you name them, or are they nothing other than creatures to use?" Zet watched Joun carefully. It pleased him to take in the slightly embarrassed expression which flitted across the Watcher's face.

"Most of us do name them. We try to keep the numbers of the larger ones under control. It wouldn't help the wastelands to have herds of them gobbling up the resources." He smiled at Malada. "She named the last one I had, and I haven't named this one yet. He is new to me. I had to retire old Slug as the trip had become too much for him and I haven't settled on a proper name for this one yet."

"What does 'retirement' look like for one of them?"

Joun's answer would give him a better understanding of the Watchers. Zet waited silently.

Joun grinned. "We don't allow but one female to breed in perhaps two or three turnings of Estevan. Too many would lead to overpopulation. Since they are our creation, it is up to us to care for the creatures. Retired ones, like Slug, care for the female's clutch once it hatches and they help train them. I hated losing Slug. As his name implies, he was slow but dependable. I haven't named the new one yet because..."

His voice trailed off. Then he glanced at Zet. "You saw him hunting?"

"I did."

"Was he fast? A good stalker?"

"He did well."

"Good. He is a fine beast."

The Watcher turned and made his way up the incline toward a platform. He stood to one side and waved Zet forward. "This is only a small portion of what is here and there are two other sites."

A hiss escaped Zet as he stepped onto the rock landing and looked in the cavern spread out before him. Several floors ranged around the central open area; balconies dotted the walls, all faintly lit in a manner he couldn't quite see.

Several steps down and he followed the scent of water to the center of the room. A small pool, too dark to see to the bottom, bubbled up, then flowed away to rise again a few millimeters tall before draining away. "How is this here? Do you know how deep it is?"

He turned to see Joun striding toward him, an odd expression on his face. "How did you do that?"

"What? What have I done?"

"Brought the water to the surface. It has never done this before. I must lower that bucket and bring up what we need."

Malada came around to his other side. "It was empty earlier. See?"

She touched his arm, and he turned to look where she indicated the camp they had set up. "For the last few days, it had been dry as the wasteland outside."

"I don't know. It came up on its own. I did nothing." Zet took a step back from the small pool. "Let me walk away and tell me what happens."

He strode back to the landing and turned. "What is it doing now?" he asked the two forms standing next to the water.

"It's gone!" Malada called out and turned to him, eyes wide.

"Please come here. We need to see if it will happen again." Joun waved him forward.

Zet didn't want to see if the water rose again. An urge to turn and run out into the desert took him and he teetered on the edge of doing just that when Malada added her voice, asking him to come to her. Finding his feet reluctantly moving him forward, Zet suddenly appreciated Camat's situation with Eldara. How did the male get on the *Demon Lair* and leave her on the planet?

Almost a meter away from what he gathered had been an empty water feature, he watched the fluid rise into the bowl. Joun uttered something about being damned in the Waste with no shelter. Zet took that to be a Watcher's curse with one part of his brain while watching in appalled fascination as the column of water in the center lifted a few millimeters.

"By all the vermin in the southern wastes, what is happening here? Do you have ancestors from Estevan? Did you come out here to find this? What is going on here?"

Joun's rapid-fire questions had Zet taking a step back.

"Not that I know of. I do not know what is going on," he replied.

"But you must know something of your ancestry..."

"No! Cease your questions and believe me when I tell you I know nothing of my history."

"How can that be? Surely, there must be some memories, some information," Joun pressed him.

"Stop. I will tell you why I don't know. Others manufactured, genetically engineered me as you created the tryanots. Certain life forms brought me to life for purposes I've no knowledge of. That information is to go nowhere. Just as I am to keep this secret. Now stop pestering me."

"Then we will ask them."

"We cannot." The last word came out in a hiss, one even Joun couldn't miss. Zet tried to tamp down his anger and anxiety.

"Why would they keep that from you? I don't understand," Joun asked.

"Leave him alone, Father. You're only upsetting him."

"Because!" Zet felt his tail beating the ground. "They are gone, dead. And I killed them rather than let them torture me further."

He spun and turned to run from his tormenter. Malada would be upset if he hurt her father.

"Zet! Wait!" Malada called as he ran to the landing. Nearly blind with rage and hurt, he caught his shoulder on the rock of the entryway. A quarter of the way into the corridor, he felt her hand on his back. He forced down the spikes so as not to injure her.

She gripped his arm, and he slowed.

"Wait... please. Where... will... you go?" She panted the question out.

"Out there. Somewhere. With the tryanot, perhaps."

When she pulled on him, he felt compelled to turn toward her.

"I... know." With a hand on her chest, she tried to catch her breath.

His arm automatically went to her and urged her close to lean against him. Which she did. Her body seemed to mold to his. Zet rested his head on hers, giving her time to recover.

"I have a place. Stay here with me. Joun is sorry, but let him worry a little. He should know better. Will you come with me?"

Her hand on his chest made comforting small circles. As he held her, Malada eased his anger and anguish. Out in his enclosure, the sleepy tryanot sent him a thought picture. Zet closed both eyelids and shook his head. "Yes. Wherever you lead."

Aware of what he had agreed to, he wondered if Malada understood and decided probably not.

Chapter 28

Her gaze went from her father to Zet and back again. How could Joun continue to press the alien after seeing what his efforts produced? When that thick tail pounded the floor of the cavern, eons worth of dust floated into the air. Even more disconcerting was the anguish mixed with the anger when Zet blurted out that he had killed his oppressors.

It took her an instant to overcome the frozen state the encounter had engendered in her. A glimpse of her father's face revealed his realization of what he had caused. She dashed after Zet, barely catching him in the corridor.

Even as she reached for him, she noted how the raised spikes flattened against his spine. When he drew her close, Malada did something she had never done with a male before—acquiesced, allowed her body to lean against his. A smooth covering met her touch. She had expected rough skin like that of the tryanot, but instead found him slick, cool, with supple skin that rippled beneath her touch.

The feel of him drew her in. All her life, everything seemed to be a varying degree of warm. He was a change she found intriguing. When it grew cold come evening, would his temperature change?

Malada made the offer to take him away from her father, thinking of the room with the material she had discovered. Zet's skin was much like the texture of the cloth. There had been a stone bench, and she could cushion it with some of the material. Perhaps if she looked in all the chests, there might be thicker lengths. Ones that would lend themselves to comfortable bedding.

Bedding? What foolishness was she getting into? Then again, was it foolish to comfort another creature? One her father had injured by hounding him for information. No. Her family had caused the harm and certainly she should try to make it right.

Her mother had impressed the need to even things up when offenses occurred. Wounds of any sort would fester if not handled properly and Zet's wounds certainly needed salve. The healing touch of kindness and consideration. Of affection.

She nearly stumbled on the stairs to the upper floor when the word "affection" crossed her mind. Did he have some way of controlling her? A glance from the corner of her eye showed her a life form suffering from the horror of his thoughts, not thinking about her.

Her mother taught her there were no true telepaths. The Human mind couldn't handle the barrage of thoughts that would produce and would find itself overwhelmed. Insanity being the result for any telepath.

Zet wasn't a Human.

What was it about him? He was a male. Wasn't he? Could he be asexual? She had too many questions, none of which would be answered now. It would be cruel to subject him to more of what her father had begun.

Malada led him into the room. His eyes flashed around the space and settled on the chest she had first opened. Closed now, with the material safely tucked away, it gave no hint of the contents.

"What is that?" He pointed to the chest sitting in the middle of the room.

It was at that moment she realized how imprudent her father's tirade had been. One slightly curved claw had extended before Zet retracted it. With one swipe of his hand, Zet could have killed him then and there. She filed that information away to present to Joun later when they were alone. He needed to know of Zet's abilities. What little she could find out without prying, as her father had.

"It's a chest filled with material. Wait a moment and I'll pad the bench with some of it. That stone will get uncomfortable after a while."

He glanced in the direction of her chin nod. "It will be fine."

Then he gave her a slow perusal. "Unless it will cause you discomfort?"

Shame clawed its way through her. She had been prepared for almost anything but consideration from this life form. Both she and Joun had equated Zet with the tryanots they used, beasts with no genuine feelings. Did they know anything about the mental life of the beasts? Were they truly unfeeling animals? Unable to answer her speculations with clarity, she felt as if she had mishandled a child. "No. I will be fine. Let us sit for a moment."

"The chests." He waved a hand toward the shelves and their contents. "What do you think they are made of?"

"Wood. There were trees on this planet at some point in its history." She turned to the chest and lifted the top. Taking the top length of cloth, doubled it over, draped it over her shoulder and walked to where he sat. "Feel this. It reminds me of you..."

She regretted the words the instant they left her mouth. Far too personal, she should have picked something else to say.

When he reached out, not a claw could be seen. At least he could control his body. His fingers stroked the cloth and slid off to touch the skin of her forearm. The gentle touch woke a sensation she hadn't experienced before. The clear eyelids blinked over golden eyes with the deepest of purple pupils, elongated and lanceolate. Narrow and pointed at each end and wide in the middle.

Unable to move, Malada stared at him. Male to the tip of his tail, Zet's eyes held her motionless. His hands moved upward and clasped her waist. Without a word, he picked her up and sat her in his lap.

When she opened her mouth, a finger touched her lips. "No words, please."

She felt something on her back and realized his tail had come up to brace her. A gentle pressure urged her to lie against his cool skin. Malada did. The length of cloth came around her, wrapping their bodies together. Terror should have driven her to her feet. Instead, she relaxed against the alien and didn't resist when he stroked her beneath the slick slide of the amazing cloth hiding their movements.

Aware of every touch and glide of fingers, when a delicate scrape of what she knew to be a claw slid across her skin, Malada shivered. A need to touch filled her. She traced muscles beneath the cool skin and they rippled in response.

This is insane! He is an alien. A being who has killed. No matter what she told herself, her body would not be denied. The stroking took on another dimension when those fingers touched the skin of her breasts, and she audibly sucked in a breath.

"You dislike this?"

The hiss in his words drew her in further. Somehow, those soft words lulled her. "No. It feels... good."

Supported by his tail, Zet used both hands on her body until she quaked in his hold. When he reached the inside of her leg with one hand, Malada grabbed it and pushed him in the direction she desired.

Beneath the cover of the brightly colored cloth, she gasped when he demonstrated how fast he learned. Bowed over that thick tail, she broke into a thousand tiny pieces at the hands of an alien she had met twice. *No, once. I have lost my mind.*

Chapter 29

"I am yours. Only yours." He couldn't keep the words captive; they insisted on being said to the woman lying in his lap, his tail supporting her head. He had lost every brain cell he ever possessed. Gone now, they had migrated to the pulsing organ nestled against her lean flanks.

"M... mine?" Eyes the color of the sky of Estevan at first light of the daystar turned to him. "I don't understand."

Lifting her off his lap, Zet cuddled her against his chest. Her light robe settled on his skin, intensifying the pulsing. "I hardly understand myself. I've not this encountered before. Something inside me feels we are a pair now. What that means is beyond my experience."

One small hand stroked across his chest, causing his skin to ripple in response. Her soft breath on his neck had every nerve ending pumping his reaction to his brain, which shuttled it to his organ, which threatened to leave its protective sheath and invade her. Something he could not do without her agreement.

"Malada, I wish to take this one step further. Without your permission, I..."

"Does that throbbing thing I'm feeling beneath me have anything to do with your desire?"

He hissed out a breath. "Yes. Most certainly. I understand you know little about me..."

He growled when she wiggled, a movement which intensified his urge. "You know I killed someone, but little else. I can tell you what I remember, if you need to hear it."

"You owe what to the ship? Loyalty? What is your position with the *Demon Lair*?" Those seeking fingers reached one shoulder and a light touch on a wing caused it to flutter.

"Loyalty, certainly. They rescued me, kept me safe and away from those who meant me great harm. They are my family. I killed the form who tortured me to find out what my body could endure. Some entity meant to create warriors. For what planet or conflict, I've no idea."

"Then you feel a duty to the ship?" she asked before bending her head to lick from his chest up to his jaw.

"I do." The words came out on a hissed semi-moan. "What you are doing makes it hard to think."

"I'm only returning the favor. What you did earlier didn't give me much time to object."

"Oh! Sorry. I didn't mean to compromise your will."

Malada lifted her head and licked at his jaw again. His nostrils open wide, Zet sucked in her scent. He wanted to remember it until he left the plane of the living. She smelled faintly of dust and heat combined with something else he had no word for. But it made him rigid beneath her.

"Do you know what race you came from?"

"No, my race is unknown. I suspect I may be a combination of different genes manipulated into this shape."

"Has your med tech tried to find out?"

"I've not asked her to. It seemed somewhat pointless. I am what I am and must make the best of it. What could she do?"

She leaned away from him, and the robe came off to land on the floor. Opening his eyes, which he had closed to better direct all sensory perception to monitor their interaction, he noted the white skin and the disordered length of material wrapped around her hips. "What is that?" Zet released her long enough to point at the cloth.

"A covering to keep sand and dirt out of delicate places." Placing her feet against one of his now trembling legs, she lifted her body and pulled the wrapping away. "You've undone it, anyway. How do you keep delicate tissue from harm? Let me see."

A minute later, she stood to the side, one hand on his leg closest to her. "That's terribly pointy. It may be too much for me."

When those fingers stroked his sheath, Zet grabbed her hand. "That is the covering which keeps me from harm. Here, give a hard stroke and you will see something else emerge."

The hard tip softened and enlarged, allowing what he kept hidden to burst into view.

"Ah, now that is more like it. Lie back on the bench."

Nearly blind with need, he did as she asked. Malada mounted his body on the hard stone shelf. Suddenly, he was in a place he'd never dreamed existed. Mind numb, his body took over. Hands on her waist, he thrust as she descended. When her hands went to her breasts, he growled at the sight.

Her grunts turned to a scream and his body bowed as he pulled her down tight to him. A rotating motion finally brought him release. Locked together, he couldn't move for a space of time. Slowly, he slid back down on the bench and the female's body lay limp atop him.

Tail wrapped around her legs, his arms around her body, Zet worked to leave the beast behind and let his mind engage again.

A soft laugh came from the female. "You know, I thought if I ever took a male, it would be someone unlike Joun. I wanted a man to be beside me, not off wandering the Waste as he does. I suppose you will leave me here while you go off on that ship."

"You could join the crew. Come along."

"Could I?" A wistful note colored her question. He understood she didn't ask it of him, but of herself.

"Perhaps. I will think about it." She pushed up and lowered her legs to the floor. "Do you think you can bring water up in the pool again? I'd like to wash a little. And we need to find out where Joun is or what he is doing."

His sheath back in position again and all tucked away where it belonged, Zet rose and held Malada's robe. "This is a momentous day. I'd never thought to find anyone as Camat has."

"Camat is your captain. The mate of the female who sings in the restaurant."

"He is." Zet clapped a hand over his mouth when a strange sound left him. *I am happy.* It came again, and this time he allowed the rumble to go unchecked. Itty always told him there was nothing wrong with being happy.

"What will Joun make of this?" Zet asked. He watched as she expertly wrapped the long piece of material around her hips and then between her legs. "It will stay that way?"

Malada reached for the robe he held and grinned at him. "As long as you keep those fingers to yourself, it will."

She bunched the robe on her arms and slipped her head in. With it on, she gave a wiggle which shifted the cloth into position. "He has no say in the matter. Come, I want to get a container of water and then we can come back here."

"Washing would be good. Why is your hair so short?" He followed her out of the room.

With a shake of her head, Malada strode toward the stairs. "Now you ask questions. Because I shaved it. A shaved head was a sign of my position. Thankfully, I no longer hold that place in the kin. I will explain all later. Now, I'm thirsty and wish to clean up. No more dawdling."

Zet interpreted that to mean she required his silence, and he should follow along. Having a female required certain adjustments, ones he would make willingly.

Chapter 30

It had all gone well, so like a snake's glide across the bottom of the pit. Nothing disturbed, no one the wiser until the fangs sank in. Keem had difficulty keeping his face a mask of confusion. The questions flew around the ready room.

Where was Captain Buotch?—asked and left unanswered several times.

Keem had asked to be the one to bring the requested drinks to the ready room. His mission completed, he sank down on his haunches in a corner. If anyone questioned his presence, he planned to say he awaited additional requests should there be any.

As usual, Buotch had picked a female from the cargo of slaves and left the bargaining to Humbor, his second-in-command. The first officer on board the *Rolatr* did as he always had. Got on with selling the cargo, accepting the funds, and then took the ship out to the edge of the system.

Buotch should have left his cabin by now, fully sated and ready to deal with the business of dividing the take. After several hours of pacing the corridor in front of the captain's cabin, Humbor conferred with the third mate, Uuld; E'nnty, who had charge of the stevedores; and the med tech, Filute.

Uuld, a Felskoglander, was all for taking the door down by any means available. Overruled by the others, he muttered expletives while Humbor negotiated with the ship. At long last, the AI, after agreeing something could be wrong as it couldn't reach the Liderian, breached the privacy controls and opened the door.

Empty except for the slave, evidently drugged, the officers retreated to the ready room to discuss what they should do next. Uuld, as most of his kind, pounded the table and insisted they go back to the planet and take hostages until they got the captain back.

Humbor immediately voted against that strategy. They were only one ship, and a short-staffed one at that. A thing they had all agreed to as it kept shares larger, although it made more work for them all. They could easily find themselves in jail on that world with their ship confiscated.

Filute volunteered that the captain had been feeling overworked and vastly underappreciated for the last two runs.

E'nnty agreed. Several independent traders, as they referred to themselves, had disappeared over what SUN called a year. She suggested Buotch might have taken early retirement. That planet didn't have a huge colony of life forms, and he could probably do fine.

As a slave. Keem had a silent laugh over that. If manipulation and sleight of hand were courses to be studied, E'nnty would take top honors anywhere.

Silence took over the room. After a few seconds, Uuld mumbled it would be entirely possible that Buotch decided to jump ship. After all, he had more than enough stashed somewhere to set himself up as a rich landowner on a world like the one they had just left.

It didn't take long for the others to agree. E'nnty, last of all. Then the matter of who got to be captain came up for a vote. As he and E'nnty expected, everyone simply moved up a position except for her. She moved higher up the chain of command to third officer.

Which Uuld might have disputed. That portion of his duties required far too much time with logs and other paperwork that he despised. E'nnty had been helping him out for quite some time and he turned it all over to her, along with the promotion, readily.

"I have another thing to bring up." All heads turned in her direction, which the Gossican female ignored as she turned to Keem. "Bring a bunch of snacks. Go on."

He didn't bother to answer, but surged to his feet and hurried out the door. Keem knew what was coming next. When he returned, they had broken into the captain's liquor cabinet and drinks waited in hands all around the table. A single one sat on the other side of Uuld in front of a vacant chair.

She pulled it off! He wanted to run over and kiss her and didn't. Very soon, things would take off.

He put the tray on the table and Humbor waved a hand toward the empty chair. "Sit. Tell us all you know about that desert planet. Esta something. I think we need a bigger infusion of credits. What's going on with that world?"

That the query came from Humbor told him E'nnty had worked her magic on the Kazzeman. How she accomplished it, he couldn't begin to understand. With his dark blue skin color and body lines of a slightly paler hue, the slender life form was more attractive than the captain. What bothered Keem was the tendency toward a mild form of telepathy in Humbor's race. He surely must have picked up on E'nnty's duplicity.

Then again, perhaps not. The Gossican female held the dubious position of being the most sexually-orientated Gossican he had ever heard about, and he had heard tales. A quick glance around at the officers with what he hoped was a confused expression would help to keep him from suspicion in the captain's disappearance.

Everyone knew E'nnty had bedded him. As the only Human on the ship, that would be a given for a Gossican. Everyone in the great expanse of the universe knew no Gossican could resist a Human.

Keem took a seat. He waited until after he gave everyone all the information he had on Estevan before taking a sip from the glass.

Eldara, I'm coming for you.

If things went as he hoped, Camat might end his life on that dirty old world. It would be such a pleasure to take care of that young fool.

Chapter 31

Zet didn't fear Joun, but worried about Malada's reaction to what her father might think. Having found something, someone he craved more than anything, he hoped they would have no impediment to discovering the depth of the relationship.

No, I know I'm hers. It is what she thinks of me that is my concern.

He smothered a groan, unwilling to allow any doubt into reality by voicing it. Having no parental experiences to relate to, the closest he could come was the interaction with the crew of the *Demon Lair*. Camat, as captain, got a certain amount of deference. Minimal to be sure. If he were to categorize what he felt for the male, respect came to mind first.

Highly intelligent, Camat had sifted through the clues brought to him and planned the best thefts. Ones guaranteed to bring in enough credits to finance a decent amount of food and toys while putting away funds toward the ship. Had it not been for Camat, they would still be nothing more than an aging gang on Calius trying to stay ahead of the government and narrowly avoiding jail.

Not one of them feared Camat. None of the crew of the *Demon Lair* felt any level of inferiority or superiority toward another. They knew each other's strengths and weaknesses and used those for the advantage of the whole. Would Malada understand? Would Joun?

He waited close to the miserable pool that had caused Zet to blurt out things he meant to keep secret. If Joun wished his secret kept, he would do the same for Zet. Would he use what he knew against Zet with Malada? So many variables existed they spun in his brain.

One thing drew his eye. A contrivance made of metal that lit up the area where her closest male relative waited. The Watcher stood, hands at his sides, Joun had mastered any emotion. Zet could detect nothing from his expression or his stance. The long robe enhanced her father's ability to keep his thoughts to himself.

The light gave Zet a place from which to begin conversation. "Is that a Kiar crystal?"

Joun waved a hand toward it and shook his head. "I suspect we have other matters to discuss of greater import than this light source. However, to put it aside for now, no. That is not a K crystal."

He folded his legs in a graceful manner that allowed Zet to understand Joun was still fit and probably strong for his age. Living in the Waste took mental agility and physical strength.

"Father." Malada sank to the floor in an equally graceful movement.

Zet knew his movements were not as fluid. Living on a ship in the vast reaches of space required a distinct set of muscles and he acknowledged he had been far more supple when they lived on Calius. That had required a different attitude as well.

No amount of mental exercises would keep this encounter from happening. He had mated with Joun's daughter. What that would mean for them all, he had no prior understanding of. Recognizing his deficiency, Zet refused to blunder further into unknown territory by speaking. He waited.

"Malada. What have you two done? Is this an exploration of different species or..."

Ah. With that much out of the way, Zet realized Joun wanted to know what his daughter meant to do about the incident. Zet agreed. Malada's perception of how he fit into her life would dictate his reactions.

"Exploration and perhaps something more." One hand picked at the cloth of her robe.

She was nervous. Malada wasn't sure of her position either. Not a good beginning. Zet allowed a soft growl to escape. "To me, we are more than two curious life forms embarking on what our chief engineer would refer to as a planetside fling. I am committed to Malada."

Joun took a deep breath and released it slowly, gaining time to formulate a reply. Zet held steady, exemplifying as calm an outward appearance as possible. He wanted to hear what the male's response would be to an outright declaration.

"Malada has never been off Estevan. This is the first time she has gone into the mainstream of Estevanian life. I fear being on a ship would be difficult, as she is a creature of the Waste and all the vast space that encompasses."

Zet made sure his wings and spines stayed flat. If Joun were paying attention, he might notice the extension of his claws. "I will never ask more of Malada than she can handle. Camat's mate stays on Estevan when the ship is out on a job."

"The songbird. Yes. But I suspect she is used to many more things and life forms than Malada."

"You two will cease discussing me as one might a small child. We will decide what to do from here. If I chose to go with him into space, I will."

He heard the words and doubted she had any plans to set a toe on the *Demon Lair*. Shoulders tight, sitting erect, compromise wasn't in the female's posture. Zet thought Eldara and Camat would have company in their arrangement. The one he knew to be shared by the shaman of Nizad and Commander Silver of the *Poignard*. Nor would he push for her company and risk driving her away. A nudge toward the port and perhaps a friendship with Eldara would be as far as he intended to go.

She reached for his hand and Zet retracted his claws even as he forced his body to be at ease. It would further nothing if she got the wrong idea; that he wanted compliance from her. Malada turned her head in his direction. "How long did you plan to stay in the waste?"

"I think I have four more days."

"Good." She squeezed his fingers. "There are things I wish to show you. If we travel tomorrow night, there will be enough time to get there. Father, may we borrow the beast?"

"Unnecessary. I will carry you. I only need direction." Malada turned to him with a questioning look. "I'm much like the tryanot. Although I traveled here in the dark for the most part, I can deal with the Waste during the light hours. There are some advantages to a mate built to withstand a desert environment."

Malada grinned. "It seems that I have bagged a prize."

As have I. He didn't speak the words his heart knew to be true. There would be time enough when they were alone. And he wished to be alone with her more than anything.

Zet waited on his mate. What made her happy would make their lives better. He couldn't give up his family on the ship, however. That would be the only thing he insisted on. All else could be negotiated. With nothing left to say, the discussion came to an end.

Zet ate one of the high energy bars Caran had given him with instructions to only eat two per day. Malada and her father had something he suspected might serve the same purpose as the energy bars.

That taken care of, Malada asked Joun for the use of the second crystal lamp.

"You have me and I can see quite well in the dark. What would you like to do?"

"Go back to the room with all the cloth. We can take my bedding."

She wished to be alone with him. That fit his needs nicely. "Gather your things into a bundle."

Malada did so and turned to tell Joun to rest easy. "Shall I hold your hand? Or how will you lead?"

"No worries." Taking a step toward her, Zet put one arm under her knees and the other behind her back, lifting her and tucking her to his chest.

"Oh! That is a long distance. I'm surely too heavy."

Laughter rumbled through his chest. "Be still and keep your head down so I can see."

When they were far enough away that Joun couldn't hear, he whispered to her, "There are some good reasons to mate with me. You are like a drift of dust in my arms. I can handle a great deal more than your weight. Much more."

The strange little sound which left her throat, not quite a laugh, lifted his spirits even higher than having her in his embrace. Malada sounded happy. The prospect of being alone with him again didn't frighten her.

Chapter 32

Borrowing their tryanot's spare harness, Zet created a seat for her across his chest. He refused the use of Joun's largest robe, saying the heat wouldn't bother him, not in the winter. Malada rode on his chest like an infant would, her water container strapped in front rather than behind so as not to rub against his skin.

A bit of grit, sand, or fine rock dust beneath a strap could cause an injury taking days to heal. Joun gave him directions to the first of the waterholes where her kinhold would be found and a place where they could wait out the heat of midday if Zet found her extra weight taxing.

Zet listened quietly and nodded agreement. The entire time, Malada got the impression Zet meant to be polite and not anger Joun. In the pale light of the setting smaller moon, they left the caverns, their tryanot raising a sound she hadn't heard from one before. Zet told her it acknowledged their leaving.

For all the length of the treacherous path on the edge of the great rift, she wondered how he knew, reaching the conclusion that Zet being of like form might have better communication with the tryanots. That thought led to another before she drifted off to sleep; what would her mother make of Zet?

She resolved to ask him how much water he had stored in his cells. Enough for a quick return trip if her mother proved too intractable? Since he hadn't come this way before, how could he gauge it until he had made the trip? She must ask before they descended into the bowl where the rift waterhole stood, the first of the three her kin cared for.

The steady rhythm of his stride across the Waste lulled her into sleep filled with images of the night before. An inventive and considerate lover, he pleased her more than she let on. Malada woke herself several times to keep from doing anything that might make him lose concentration or set him off balance, the dreams having become far too real. Landing on hot sand or a rock jumble could easily injure them both.

She jolted awake when the sound of a keening wind dissolved a dream full of sensations caused by his fingers and slightly rough tongue. "How long has it been since the wind came up?"

"Not long. It's coming from the direction of your family's location. What do you advise?"

"We need shelter. A rock formation would be best, one that will block most of the dust and sand I see coming our way."

"There is something to our right. We will run into the storm, but the space is big enough for all."

"That dust is thicker than you realize." Zet had already changed direction and sped off to something she couldn't see. His vision must be much better than hers.

"She will guide us in."

"What? Who?"

"The small female tryanot who has already taken shelter there."

Above the singing of the wind, at a slightly lower pitch, Malada heard the moaning call of a wild tryanot. Pulling the long robe up, she eased the material over her head and pulled both knees closer as she adjusted the cloth to protect her skin.

The first wave of flying debris spattered against them. Malada couldn't hold the first cry in as what felt like thousands of tiny slaps hit. Zet's arms tightened their hold, and his tail curled around her head. Louder now, the cries of the tryanot grew closer together.

Zet fell to his knees. "Roll forward into the shelter," he called out against the keening of the rising wind.

Battered no longer, she opened her eyes to see the roof of stone above her head. Malada understood neither of them could sit in the small space. Grateful it was wide enough for them and the beast, she lifted her body to her elbows in time to watch as Zet wiggled in. He got no further than the entrance and turned on his side, his back to the storm. His body nearly plugged the narrow opening.

A small sound, much like a growl, drew her attention to the area by her feet. There, a green tryanot with narrow black stripes from her throat down into her chest stood on her four legs. Nestled between her stout legs were two smaller beasts. Malada thought they must be her offspring.

An answering sound from Zet startled her. She glanced swiftly from him to the mother with her babies.

"They are thirsty. These three were trying for that waterhole where we are going. Hunting wasn't good last night and they stayed out too long."

"How do you know this?"

"I don't know how it works, it just does. I mean to help them as she helped us. You should move as far to the back of the shelter as you can. This is likely to be a little messy. There is nothing I can do about that. Just give her room to come near my head, please."

On her back, Malada scooted as far away as she could and turned on her side to give the female as much free space as possible. In the semidarkness, she watched the beasts. The tryanot must be wondering what she'd called in.

Zet's body seemed to convulse. His stomach muscles rolled as he opened his mouth to allow liquid to fall to the rocky floor of the crack in the rock. The female made a strange chirp and nudged the smaller of her two offspring toward the puddle. It lapped up the liquid greedily.

With her snout, she moved him aside and nudged the larger one forward. When the one finished, all that remained was a damp patch. Then Zet did the same thing one more time, and another puddle of liquid hit the floor. Hurrying forward, the female pushed her face into the puddle, and it vanished in a few loud slurps. A series of several chirps followed before she scuttled forward and put her nose to Zet's.

She swiveled and, with the smaller beasts between her forelegs, herded her family to a corner of the shelter.

"How much more water are you carrying and how did you do that?"

Zet sighed. "Quite a bit more. But I suspect a refill will be necessary when we reach your people. I have several pouches concealed within my body. My tail holds more than you might think."

She leaned over and twitched some loose dirt over the damp spot in front of him and wiggled closer. "I'm sure she appreciated your kindness. Do they come to the waterhole when we are sleeping during the day?"

"I think that is correct. Nothing is entirely clear. I can't understand everything. I suspect your tryanots alert the wild ones when it is safe to drink and hunt. You understand that your larger beasts hunt for vermin, but you should know that the larger ones call on the wild ones when an infestation gets too great for them to handle. Like her, they are small enough to get into places like this to hunt."

"No, I didn't know that. Although I suppose it makes perfect sense when you think about it." She turned her back on him and wiggled close. When his free arm fell across her, Malada felt comforted. "I don't suspect this one will last long, still it may be too late for us to travel when..."

What she classified as his amused response rumbled through his body. "I can see far better in the dark than you. When this blows out, we will continue. While we wait, I suggest we rest. I expended much of my energy getting here."

Malada pulled his arm tight around her and mumbled agreement. She already felt tired, and he had done all the work.

Chapter 33

The shrieking wind abated. He became aware of the change when the mother tryanot nudged his legs. Zet drew up his feet, allowing her and the two babies to leave the shelter. Before vanishing into the twilight, she sent a thought. A rough outline of the area she called her territory, where he and the other female would always be welcome.

With a low rumble, he acknowledged the information.

Malada stirred in his embrace. He suspected it would be best to move on. Zet had hoped to reach what Joun called their kinhold during daylight so he might scout the area out. Being with the Demons for as long as he had, Zet learned the value of prior knowledge. A thing denied him in this case.

Lazing in the small shelter might be entertaining, but would do nothing to provide either food or water, a situation not to be ignored in the wasteland. They must be going. "Malada. It is time to move on."

She seemed to come awake instantly. Her eyes opened, and she turned on her back. "The storm is over. How long?"

"I don't know. As you did, I slept. The female tryanot woke me and left a short time ago."

"Then we should be moving on. I don't believe we are far from the kinhold."

"Agreed. This shelter is part of the female's territory, and it extends to the outer edge of your waterhole."

"How do you know these things? If you will roll out of the opening, so will I. Then we will see where we are."

"As before, I can't give you an answer." He rolled away from the shelter and got to his feet. Malada followed and bent to dust off her robe.

"Why?" she asked.

"Because I don't understand any of it myself." After shaking to get most of the windblown sand and dirt off his hide, Zet glanced out at the area. Scoured of anything light enough to be caught up by the wind, bare rocks met his gaze in every direction.

"Do you know about implants? Have you heard of them?" he asked her.

"A little. After I empty my boots, follow me. I know where we are. The kinhold lies off to our right." She sat on a rock, lifted the material from her legs, and removed her foot coverings to eliminate anything that might hurt.

Zet grinned. He didn't need boots for anything but clinging to the hull of the *Demon Lair*. As easily injured as her feet were, he recalled how she struggled to escape when one of his claws scraped the bottom of her left foot. The scrape hadn't hurt, or so she said. She claimed he had caused a nerve reaction that she had to get away from. A spot on her side had done the same thing when touched. He had made a game of it, one they both enjoyed.

She stood and smiled at him. "What are these implants? They give you something very like telepathy with others and your ship. Do I have that right?"

"They do and are capable of much more, depending on how many credits you have at your disposal when you buy them." He reached for her hand. "Will your eyes work as well as they should in this low light? I wouldn't want you to fall."

"You do understand that we have adjusted to our circumstance? Any Watcher can function in the light of our star, but we prefer to move about at night. Our bodies have adjusted to that over all these eons. I may not see as well as you do, or as far, but I can navigate."

Which Malada proved as they walked. The land gradually sloped downward until they reached the edge of another rift in the planet's landscape. This one didn't seem to be as deep as the one that the trail to the caverns skirted.

He thought he caught a faint glow from the bottom and turned to her. "Are those lights down there? If so, how is it we never see them when on approach to the port?"

"The standard approach lane for ships is far from this sector. A matter we happily endorse. See those two large boulders? That is where the trail starts to the bottom of our kinhold."

"It doesn't appear wide enough for a tryanot and a cart."

"That is the apparent one. We have another we keep secret. Come along, let's get this done."

Her tone and the words left him wondering how difficult this meeting with her other parent would be. As she said, they should get it over with. With nothing to say, he followed her lead.

On reaching the rocks guarding the approach to the waterhole down in the depths of the fissure, Zet noted it would barely accommodate a tryanot and cart. And the animal would have a difficult time unless a full-grown male.

An enticing scent wafted up from the cleft, the smell of growing things and water. Then another aroma came to him. The wild female tryanot had reached the edge of the fissure—along with her two little ones. She wasn't on the trail, but slightly more to the left. He wondered if she knew of the secret route.

An impression came to him which left Zet trying to understand what was happening. How and why? Had his creator somehow come across tryanot genes? That could have happened, he acknowledged, even as he and Malada started down the twisting trail. He knew so little, that most of the time he pushed all the questions to the back of his mind and left them there.

He turned his attention to the trail and the deep fissure they worked their way to the bottom of. The soft feel of moisture in the air became more apparent as they descended the rock walls in increments via a trail that folded back on itself.

How had the first Watchers found these places? Someday he would ask Malada for a lesson in their history. Later.

The trail leveled somewhat, and she turned to him with a sigh. "Can you wait here for me? In the shadows? I need to alert everyone that I have a guest. There are two small children here, and both mothers could get upset if they think there is a threat to them."

"I will wait. I see no reason to upset anyone. It would be to our advantage if all are at least somewhat receptive."

Her hand stroked his jaw. "I find more things about you that I like the longer we are together. I don't quite understand what is taking place between us. Being attracted to you is so out of character for me."

"This is beyond anything I ever thought might happen." Taking her hand, he licked her palm. "I feel as if I were adrift and being slowly pulled toward a negative system."

"As do I. But, somehow, this feels right. Now, don't stray from here. I'll be back for you soon."

Zet leaned against the rock wall at his back and watched Malada stride off. Their being together truly felt beyond insane, but watching her move away from him without following proved to be a difficult thing. He wanted to follow, but must trust her to see them through the next few hours.

Nine tryanots made him aware of their presence. Two males and four females were the resident herd kept by the Watchers responsible for this kinhold. The little wild female and her offspring had made it down to the water and were busy replenishing their reserves.

A conversation took place between the wild ones and their domesticated kin. He and Malada were included favorably, Zet noted.

Around him, beneath the overhang which sheltered the tents—spaced out for privacy, he assumed—the crystal lanterns he counted had three sides blocked off, resulting in all illumination being focused on the tents. He understood now how they kept from being seen from space. As soon as the lesser moon rose, it would be impossible to pinpoint the location he now stood in.

Still, the next time they were orbiting Estevan, he would investigate further. Knowing what to look for made a difference. That thought brought him back to the situation he now found himself in. Malada was no more suited to life on a ship than he would be to life on a cold planet.

I must introduce her to the crew. That was where he would be their guide. It couldn't come soon enough for him. He wanted that out of the way as well. Then they would need to decide how to go forward. Zet understood compromise would be his watchword with this relationship. He couldn't give her up. Nor could he desert the *Demon Lair.* His life had suddenly become so complicated, he felt disoriented. Malada might see him as calm and composed, but he felt like an out-of-control ship, end-over-ending toward a very hard landing.

Chapter 34

"What? An alien who resembles a tryanot? I do not understand. How can one be intelligent enough to…"

"He is not a tryanot. Zet is an alien. I don't quite understand what happened between us, but it has. I have somehow chosen him, or something like that."

"You should never have given up your position and gone to the port with Joun. He should have watched—"

"If you even utter the words demeaning me, reducing me to a child, I will take Zet and we will leave. You will see me no more!" Malada glared at her mother; arms folded across her chest.

"Ah." Emara turned away to stride to the far side of the tent. With a powerful slap, she set the strings of beads that delineated her sleeping area from the living area to swinging.

"Don't blame Joun for my actions. He questioned the circumstances also. Quite a lot, in fact. I nearly cut him off as well." She hurried over to stand behind her mother. "Somehow, we couldn't avoid what happened. This is far beyond anything I might have considered. There are other forces at work none of us understand, including Zet and me."

With a sigh of resignation, Emara turned. "Then this… this alien isn't forcing himself on you?"

Malada chuckled. "As if Joun would let that happen and still be among the living. Please, Mother. You, more than anyone, should know he would allow no one to bother a child of his. That hot temper of his would surely explode."

With a nod, her mother reached up to take her face in both hands. "Child, does he walk on four…"

"Mother!" she huffed out. "Enough. You will meet him and that will answer your questions. Stop making this harder than it needs to be. Zet is a kind, intelligent life form. Come with me to greet him."

The soft swish of her mother's clothing behind her encouraged Malada. Without turning to check, she led the way out of the tent and back in the direction she had left Zet. Leaving the faint glow lighting the area where the tents huddled beneath the bulge of stone, a hint of panic threatened.

It fled the moment he stepped out of the shadows and into the light of the rising lesser moon. Malada hoped her mother saw what she did. A bold, confident life form who no more resembled a tryanot than she did.

Having come to know him better, the barest flutter of those wings on his shoulders gave away his nervousness, which put a smile on her face. Pushing all other considerations to the side, she continued forward and reached up to touch his jaw. His wings settled, as did her hint of anxiety. If this didn't go well, they had options. Perhaps she could learn to live in close quarters on the ship with him.

Turning in the half circle of his strong arm, Malada smiled at her mother. "Emara Culat, this is Zet. Mother, this is the life form I have picked to be with."

The female before him held herself rigidly, exerting a great deal of self-control, and he suspected his physical form bothered her. The answer blossomed in his thoughts immediately. He resembled a tryanot on two legs. Somewhat. Not that much, if he gave it thought. It had to be his overall appearance.

This Human female had some preconceived ideas about what, or perhaps who, she had in mind for her daughter. Which left him wondering, because Malada had mentioned the position she gave up required celibacy. No matter, he would conduct himself in a dignified manner as befitted one of the crew of the *Demon Lair*.

Truthfully, all thanks must go to Itty and those holos on Messerian court manners.

Not a pirate, he was part of a legitimate free trading ship. One with ties to some very well-known Mercenary's Union members, not to mention a high-ranking member of the Life Foundation.

Zet would assume this female's status was ranked high in her community. He released Malada and made a bow which would be the due of a retainer to one of the high kings of a Messerian enclave, holding it for the required amount of time. His eyes tracked Emara Culat, thanks to his better field of vision. He noted the slight relaxation of her still posture—which amused him. Zet sucked in the noise he almost made. How she would take a massive bellow directed her way was a question he didn't need the answer to.

Instead, he stood to his full height, several centimeters over them both, and waited for her to speak, all while being careful to keep his spines flat. The female's jaw worked twice.

"A... I greet you, Zet. As my daughter's..." Emara stuttered to a halt. "Her choice, her ma... ah... mate. Come to my dwelling. I'm sure you need water."

One quarter of his supply remained. Not enough to get them back to the caverns or to the port. He could not afford to be unduly prideful. He needed to refill, and the sweet scent of open water drew him.

"If you please. I would be grateful." He watched her posture relax one more notch. Zet considered refilling while she watched and decided that was best done later. The mother of the female would find the process too like that of a tryanot's.

The time in the enclosure with Emara remained tense. Not to the level he originally sensed at first sight—lesser, but not comfortable yet. He thanked whatever gods held sway on Estevan on discovering Malada had her own dwelling. Zet happily retired with Malada shortly before the lesser moon slid below the walls of the valley.

Thankfully, she seemed to be the same female as the one he'd spent the night with in the cavern. Her mother's attitude had not changed Malada's view of him.

The faint light of the daystar oozed down the rock walls into the lower reaches of the cleft in the earth. Leaving a well-loved female comfortable in their nest, Zet looked out into the narrow valley. There were terraces up both sides of the rock walls with stairs cut in to allow access. Things grew there. Zet didn't know what the plants were called and thought he would ask Malada later.

At the lower end of the stream, the small herd of tryanots had gathered for their daily drink. He joined them. Varying images bombarded him as he approached. Then the cacophony vanished as the oldest female stepped forward to touch her nose to his.

He still didn't understand how they could communicate in this manner without the usual implants, but left the mystery for the moment, choosing to accept the information the matriarch of the herd felt he needed to know. The Watchers might think they controlled the tryanots, but if they could experience what he did, they would find the beasts they had engineered had assumed the position of guardians of their originators. A fascinating concept. One that diverged wildly from what he had experienced.

The difference in the Watchers' treatment of their creatures and that of his experiences at the hands of an unknown team of scientists provided the reason. The Watchers valued their animals. Tryanots got the first drink when they reached a destination, the first meal. The beasts were valued and prized for the service they rendered.

He had been bred for war on a world much like this one. A prototype, they had used Zet to refine their creation. How many others had they produced and destroyed as they improved the concept? The question had always bothered him. When he escaped, though, there were no others in the cells.

Zet was the last of his line.

He lowered his head to the pool of running water and drank. His creators had given him two sets of lungs. The second set would hold air or water, whichever he needed most in a situation. He could saturate his cells with either. Water being least plentiful on this desert world, Zet filled his body, making ready for the trip back to the cavern.

Chapter 35

The ship orbited Estevan with the crew glued to the screen. Water would be difficult to get; they could all see it and comments regarding the lack of water floated around the control room. Surreptitious looks darted his way and slid past again.

Keem held his irritation in. Now they understood why he had insisted on filling his small allotted space in the hold with containers of water. He'd told them and they didn't listen. All but his Gossican partner. E'nnty had done as he had. Together, they stood to make a fine profit from the sale of water. And not just any water, certainly not water provided by the ship's reclamation system.

No, this was water they loaded on Lideria after making the obligatory stop to change the registration of the *Rolatr*, the captain of record, and carry the hard news of his loss to Buotch's family. E'nnty had insisted it was foolish to set pylon on Lideria, but Humbor insisted, and the crew supported it as the only correct thing to do.

She and Keem had dithered and fretted the entire time they spent on Lideria, a full six SUN days, fearful that their mutiny would somehow come out. It would be more than horrid if Buotch's family learned they had sold him into slavery. Being torn to pieces appealed to neither of them.

Then he ran afoul of his Gossican lover's temper. She refused to allow him to reclaim Eldara. If he brought the female on board, E'nnty said she would sell the songbird off at the first opportunity. After E'nnty had a short session with the young singer.

Keem knew exactly what that would entail. If there was any blood left in Eldara after that, she would be less than useless. He still felt angry about E'nnty's refusal to allow him his rights. Having a Gossican for a partner had its nasty complications.

Still... the sex... that, he had no complaints about.

Captain, there is much grumbling by the stevedores. They don't like what they are seeing of the planet on the holos. The ship's AI hadn't confined its comments to the captain only, broadcasting them to all those with implants, officers all—except for him.

Shut down the holos! Immediately! Humbor commanded.

Done, Captain, the ship responded.

Put me on broadcast mode. I wish the crew to hear this, and I want responses from all of them documented and noted. Tell them if they dislike what they see so much, they will all find themselves confined to the ship and there will be no on-shore leave for anyone not an officer.

As you command, Captain Humbor, the ship's AI replied.

A few moments later, the AI broadcast again. *All their names are being noted and each department head will provide documentation as soon as I have it.*

Keem wondered why the ship's AI had made everyone aware of what was going on below command mode. He intended to ask E'nnty her opinion of it all once they were alone. Close to the planet now, there was no hail from the port authority.

"Why isn't somebody questioning what we're doing here?" asked Humbor.

Keem took that as his cue to make a bit of headway with the captain. Humbor continued ignoring him, using E'nnty as a go-between. A fact which irritated him far more than it should. "They are always short-staffed. It's up to us to call in and ask for a berth. You won't get one otherwise."

"Backward place for sure," Humbor muttered. He turned to Etienne, their Canarian officer. "Contact that backward bunch of sand fleas and get us a berth on that dustball. Do it in a hurry. I'm tired of burning fuel for no reason."

An hour later, they had settled on Estevan to find the port surprisingly had more ships docked than expected. Heads of the detachments had come forward and pleaded that they receive some shore leave. Otherwise, they doubted they could control the crew.

Humbor grudgingly gave them twenty-four hours. Any crewman foolish enough to wind up in an Estevanian jail would die there. No exceptions. Any funds due them would be confiscated and returned to the common pot.

The captain then turned his beady, black gaze on Keem. "How do we find this treasure? You better have a real good handle on this. Otherwise, you can join any stupid drunk crewman in jail. No, wait. You're worth of lot of money to a certain party. One way or the other, I will get money out of you."

That didn't scare Keem if it was supposed to. If worse came to worse, after killing him and resurrecting him a few times, General Shung would listen to reason and take on the project himself. If the general got enough out of it, he might, perhaps, stop killing Keem and put him back to work.

"We need to go talk to a youth, one who manages the big junkyard. Lute has been trading with the Watcher, Joun, for a long time now. Joun is who we need to find. He knows where the ancients hid everything."

Chapter 36

Lute watched the holo of the three people standing at the gate to the yard. He recognized a Gossican female, a Liderian, barely, then came the other one. Of Human origin, he stayed in the background. Somehow, that one looked somewhat familiar. Lute was sure he'd seen him around—somewhere.

If they had met, why was the bald male hiding behind the other two? Unsure, he didn't open the gate or speak to the three. Instead, he copied the holo and sent it off in an email to Dave and Cat and CoDee.

A niggling sense of unease slithered up his backbone. It felt a lot the same as the first time Eletto Troon contacted his father all those years ago. That had nearly ended in disaster for him. Only Cat's intervention had saved him from a beating that would have killed him. One his father would have administered for his failure to eliminate both CoDee and Cat.

Cat told him to trust his instincts—he planned to. Until he got something back from the three partners in CNY Universal, the parent company of the CNY Salvage Yard, none of the three would set foot inside. He'd increase security while waiting for instructions. Since almost nothing ever happened on Estevan, he'd let a few things slip.

The first response to his plea for instructions came from Dave. Not a surprise as he was still on planet while Lute had no idea where CoDee or Cat might be.

"I'll get hold of Jerak. We'll use his transport to get you out. Do you think they might be armed?"

"I don't know. That Gossican scares the seven hells out of me. Still, the thing that really bothers me is what reason does the form behind the Gossican have for hiding? He must be up to something, but what?"

"How's your security?"

Lute laughed. "Way better than when those three showed up."

"Good. Jerak and I will be over as soon as I can reach him. I'll bring along an apprentice in case we need a bit of muscle. As soon as you see the transport in front of the gate, jet on out. Then we'll go over to Lady Pia's and ask if anyone knows who that form is. It's almost the evening rush and the place will be packed soon. Sooner or later, everyone in the port makes it over to Pia and Tonio's. Someone is bound to know something. I've sent a message to Neelah asking who brought that ship in earlier. We'll know something soon. Then we'll have more info to give to Cat and CoDee."

"I just don't understand what this junkyard might have that would cause someone to think about raiding it."

"Why do you think they want to raid it?"

"It's just the feeling I get from the three of them. If I had to put a label on it, menace would be the word."

"That's enough for me. I trust your instincts. Be there in a flash. We'll park so you can hop right into the back without having to see them."

In his quarters, Lute gathered a few things in a pile, then scooped them into a jacket and sealed it. He wished he had a small container, but didn't. Never in his life so far had he thought he might have to make an emergency exit from the yard. Once they had this situation under control, he would make a plan. One that included another way out of the place other than through the gate.

The jacket clasped to his chest, he waited for Dave and the crew to rescue him. The entire time, the young manager of the salvage yard tried to imagine what those three wanted. They hadn't come prepared to trade or buy, their body language gave that away.

Pacing around the yard, his gaze came to the covered section where the things from Joun sat waiting on Cat and CoDee to assess them. A chill flew up his spine and the thought nearly exploded in his brain.

The relics were the only thing he had that lay out of the normal range of salvage yards around the universe. The leavings of a long-dead civilization. He had read about the Yodoran Funeral Boats. Little was known about them, but their funerary boats were legendary. A total of ten were publicly acknowledged to have been located. There were rumors of other nations having one or more to study. Each had delivered a quantum leap in technology to whoever found and studied one. Although the study and cataloging often took generations.

He'd read that the oldest one ever found was estimated to be just over a billion years old, the newest around half a billion. The first one known to be found in Human history was about six thousand years ago by a nation called

Udesh. Within a hundred years of finding one, the Udesh had become an empire that flourished for over a thousand years.

There had been wars fought over possession of a funeral boat. He should have taken better care of the things Joun brought him. Having thought of them as nothing more than remains of a dead culture, he'd been too lax.

"Time to go." Dave's voice came through the communicator.

He had no time now. What he needed were armed guards and didn't dare, as that would draw more attention to the things beneath the covering he needed to treat as nothing more than weird relics.

"Coming!" He groaned as he ran down the central aisle toward the small door in the large double wide gate.

Joun.

How could he warn the Watcher to stay away for a while? Inside the transport, it was the first thing out of his mouth to Dave. "We've got to warn Joun to stay away. I think I know what they want."

Cat woke CoDee reluctantly. They had been through some tough situations recently and he had fared somewhat worse than she. He needed rest, and it seemed they were not to get as much as she hoped. At least the trip back to Estevan would be easier with the modifications to the ship's AI. The *Bond* could function for longer times without interaction.

A delicate balance between AI and Humans needed to be kept. No one wanted a resurgence of the AI wars. Then again, what use was AI if it couldn't do what it was created for? She didn't need an implant now to control the AI, her telepathic ability being enough, Cat had made sure that CoDee slept while she maintained constant contact with the ship.

The coder on Pacifica had done a marvelous job of reconfiguring the ship's AI. Glad she had insisted on taking the layover on the water world, her slight mew of pleasure filled the hall as she left the control center.

They had needed to have a few things looked at and asked around. A relative of the coder recommended him. The youth worked out of his home with his mate. The Arkalian male didn't advertise and had no formal business, helping only family as a rule.

Why? That was a question Cat had hesitated to ask and stopped CoDee from voicing. She felt the Master of the Universe prompting her to leave it alone. The young male with the wave rider mate would have denied it all and done nothing for them had they pushed the matter. There was a mystery there that could remain unsolved. Not everything in the universe needed to be probed.

But the communication from Lute, followed by a joint one from Dave and Lute, meant any idea of a leisurely journey had come to an end. No one threatened Lute or Dave. That would not be allowed to go on. Whoever the Liderian and the Gossican were, they had no right to start trouble.

The matter of the third life form would be investigated and answers obtained. She would do what she felt necessary, which included a bit of snooping in their minds. Cat acknowledged to herself, as she gazed down at her mate, that Lute was their adopted offspring.

Kneeling on the gelbed, she shook CoDee gently. As she sensed his emergence from sleep, her thoughts went to him. *Wake, dear one. We are needed on Estevan.*

Chapter 37

He could happily carry Malada forever strapped to his chest. But with his time limited, he must consider the last possible moment he could set off for the port. Camat would expect to see him in seventy-two hours. Then they would be off again to collect the *Demon Lair* from Greenhouse 2.

That he looked forward to. With the ship in top sailing shape, the anxiety-causing stutter in the engines should be gone. Still, he would miss Malada. In so short a time, he'd grown to need her presence. No longer alone, his lack of an identifiable race didn't bother her.

A heady thing—acceptance from a Human female, it buoyed his heart in a way he'd never experienced before. Along with that, he gained a better understanding of their pilot's reaction to losing her lover.

Xigant had gone far beyond what Zet thought he would allow himself in a similar situation, but he understood her better. Not only that, Xigant's feelings for Itty and her ability to put them away or not made more sense.

He certainly couldn't put what he felt for Malada aside. As Camat did to make Eldara happy, he could leave Malada here on Estevan with the other Watchers. With the site of four kinholds firmly established in his mind, and the ability to contact any of the beasts as needed to obtain her location, he could crew on the ship.

The credits he earned would go to buy her things to make her life easier. So far, she had no plans to move into Estevanana or the port. With her sharper hearing and better night vision, there was too much noise and light in the port for her. He understood, as Joun, she could manage for a short time, but not on a permanent basis.

Nor was there any possibility of her living closer to the port. The kinholds needed the water in each location to survive. The Watchers maintained a delicate balance with the Waste, one that must be maintained if any of them were to survive.

Over all the generations since the first colonist, the LaDonna, walked away from the settlement, Watchers had been adjusting themselves to the living conditions of the desert landscape. It would be no easy thing for her to adjust to the port or the ship.

Zet didn't dare ask her to live on the ship with him. Too confined, too much noise, too many life forms in close quarters might make her turn away from him altogether. So, he would leave her at the caverns with Joun when the time came for him to leave.

They had declared themselves, both to Joun and to the rest of her kin. All knew Malada had chosen him. The wonder of it still caused him to shake his head.

And a Human female at that.

An expectation of perhaps mating with a creature like a tryanot had nebulously existed in his mind. He considered it simply as a means of catering to certain needs which had recently been manifesting themselves, nothing more. An actual relationship with an intelligent, lovely female had never been part of his innermost desires.

What female would want a single male, race unknown, with no supporting kin to look to if circumstances warranted it? Malada said his lack didn't bother her, the male he was being more than enough.

She stated she would be happy to travel with and help Joun. Her father needed an assistant. Her suggestion, that he get them a place in the port area so they could be together when he did land made sense. Zet had promised to ask around and see what might be had.

At worst, he would see if a plot of land couldn't be purchased and he would do as Lute had in the interim, get a life module from the salvage yard to use until they could put up a place. If large enough, Joun could stay with them when he came in out of the caverns.

So many possibilities sizzled along in his brain, yet they all had one constant—he and Malada together, blending their lives.

The wild tryanot from the shelter put a picture in his mind, which caused him to halt his steady forward progress. It alerted him to the need for caution. A small storm brewed in the northeast. It might or might not grow to the same proportions as the last one.

"Is something wrong?" Malada mumbled as he stopped to turn and search the horizon behind them and off his right shoulder. Below the ring of mountains far in the distance, he could see a dirt-colored haze.

"No. Still, we shall make for the caverns a bit faster. A rising wind is at the base of the far mountains. It might expand, or perhaps not. I think caution is best out here."

"Don't go too fast. You don't want to fall."

He caressed her shoulder. "Never. I won't drop you."

"I don't want either of us hurt." She yawned. "You haven't had much rest."

"I don't need as much as others. Go back to sleep. I'll wake you when we near the caverns."

"Alright." Malada nestled closer to him.

After a quick stroke down her shoulder to her rounded body lying against his skin, he put both arms at his sides to maintain balance as he picked up the speed. *Silly female. As if he would be stupid enough to do something that might injure her.*

Keem thought he'd surely be on his way to General Shung when they were denied access to the salvage yard. Instead, E'nnty and Humbor smiled and nodded. On the way back to the ship, they became animated when discussing what the youth who had suddenly left might be hiding.

They made plans to get inside the place and see what they could find, all while acting as if he didn't exist. Which angered him, and Keem had to grind his teeth to stay silent. Later, in the room which he now shared with E'nnty, she made it up to him with fantastic sex. At the end of it, she sucked him so much that he had to check to be sure there were no blisters.

He wasn't exactly complaining. Still, he couldn't sleep. The Gossican lay on her stomach and hardly moved while he tossed. What he needed was action, not sex, but some kind of action that would give him an inkling of what the junkyard had inside that he needed to know about.

Keem had no intention of allowing them—Humbor and E'nnty—to cut him out of the action. They planned to do just that. Not part of the crew, they still regarded him as a slight cut above a slave. Another thing he must not think about...yet.

Control was what he needed. Of E'nnty, Humbor, and the cursed ship. Being cut out had been their aim from the start, if he had given the matter proper thought. Which he hadn't. Blinded by the physical side of things with his Gossican lover, he hadn't kept track of matters as he should. A failure he would pay for if not careful. The form of credits in which he must pay being decided by Humbor and E'nnty. Something he could not allow to happen.

The female wouldn't move for some time. Keem took himself into the cleaning unit and contacted the AI. He needed more information on the damnable junkyard and the AI would supply what he needed or else.

What he got first put a smile on Keem's face. Not sure how it would affect him, it would be amusing when those two tried using a flyer on Estevan. When he traveled from the city to the port the last time, he hadn't realized that no one used flyers and Keem had put it down to some kind of backward laws regarding disturbing the planet.

The information jumped out at him from the history of the port prior to the founding of the salvage yard. Sand and dirt constantly flew around the planet causing flyers to crash far more than anywhere else. They weren't cost effective to use and the loss of life caused the colony massive problems. Not a soul could be spared in the race to make a habitable place for Humans.

Snippets of data on the man who started the junkyard provided little information. Still, he shut down the holo and went back to bed with a smile on his face. Tomorrow, when some bright form came up with the idea that they should patrol the desert with a flyer while searching for Joun, he would warn them. A sign of his superior knowledge of the planet and a token of good faith. It didn't matter to him if the flyer crashed, if he wasn't on board.

Chapter 38

Malada insisted he sleep for a few hours and took herself off to help Joun. Zet knew she had made the correct decision and still hated her loss for any amount of time. With a muted groan, he splayed his body flat on the lush softness of the material belly down. What in the seven hells would he do without her for long stretches at a time?

Instructing his mind to stop all thought and concentrate on rest, something he did often and worked without fail, didn't work this time. It took him several tries to get his thoughts under control and let sleep take him.

Only to wake fully later when his hand sought Malada and didn't find her warm body. Instant awareness brought with it the sinking feeling that he must leave, and soon. Rising, he realized bodily needs would take him to the one cleaning unit Joun had discovered and set up.

Inside it, Malada's scent teased him, bringing up thoughts of her writhing on his body only a few hours before. A thing which could not happen in their limited time, but he ached for as he couldn't be sure when he might be with her again.

"How do Camat and Eldara manage?" His voice filled the small space.

Joun hadn't discovered how to make the thing work properly, a container of water and sections of soft cloth were make-do stopgaps. Zet had the feeling he could deduce more for the Watcher if he had devoted any time to the effort. Unwilling to give up any time with Malada, he'd not bothered to even mention the possibility.

Although, he suspected after what happened with the fountain in the main area, Joun knew it to be a possibility, but the Human hadn't bothered trying to pry him out of the room he and Malada occupied. He felt grateful to the male he now shared kinship with through his mating with Malada.

As he picked up the cloth to clean his hands, he first sniffed the tips of each finger, enjoying the thought of where each had been and how they had given them both pleasure. Malada had clung to him, trembling as he raised her to heights of passion.

Zet hesitated to remove the scent of her from his body. It got worse when he reached the tip of his tail. Coated with her delightful juices, he stopped and stroked it as he recalled all the new uses he'd devised for what some had called a useless throwback to prehistory.

His organ on the edge of descending, he put a stop to reliving what would cause him to delay leaving. He dared not stay any longer. It was time to find Malada, fill his water-holding mechanism to capacity and leave.

A soft moan of acquiescence left him as he hurried out of the small space. Others waited. The rest of the crew would want to get to the ship and get it back into space. Jobs, contracts might have come in while he spent time with Malada. For now, their time was over; he belonged to the *Demon Lair*. But he would be back.

Making the leave-taking as short as possible, he found her with Joun. They both accompanied him back to the main cavern, where he pulled as much water into his body as possible. A quick hug with Joun and an embrace with Malada, and he left the cavern.

Outside, the tryanot who had already nestled into a large patch of shade provided by a ledge of rock, rumbled a greeting and a farewell which Zet returned. Then he was off down the trail that he now knew well, having memorized it both coming and going.

Several hours into the journey, nearly at the halfway point, a wild tryanot made contact. A greeting and acknowledgement of knowing the beast that served Joun. Surprise caused him to stumble, and Zet came to a halt. He hadn't realized that the wild ones and the larger, genetically engineered beasts had a vast network of contacts. He berated himself for not thinking it through. Why shouldn't they? The ones at the kinhold knew the local wild tryanots.

This wild one put a picture in his mind of a huge storm brewing on the far side of the basin that comprised the ancient ocean bed. The creature pictured itself digging in with a wall at its back. It faced the port, obviously seeking protection from the storm which must be coming from the east.

Too far into the journey to backtrack and too distant from the port, the warning was enough to have him searching for shelter. A noise much like the one that the wild female had used to guide him before sounded off to his left.

A bit more guttural, Zet homed in on the sound and followed it to a ridge of rock that undulated off to drop away at another rift.

Closer, the sound led him to a hole in the rock, with the opening at waist height. He peered inside and found a male tryanot who appeared to be at least a third larger than the female they had hidden with before. Sensing the welcome, he crawled in and settled to the far side of the small shelter. The wind quickly rose in volume and soon had Zet wishing for a pair of Itty's fancy noise reducers.

It took him a few seconds to understand not all he heard was from the storm. *A flyer*? What insanity. Everyone knew flyers didn't work on Estevan. The crash came after the engine shrieked out its last. Beneath them, the ground shuddered. Zet knew it had to be close.

The tryanot on the other side of him trembled as it scooted a little closer to him. He understood its fear of the unknown. The violent storms that could sweep across the dead ocean were something the creature had experienced enough to be knowledgeable about how to survive one. Having the foundation of its world move as it had, the cause unknown, terrified the creature.

Creating a picture in his mind of the flyer with an upright form occupying the pilot's seat, Zet let it sit there, hoping the tryanot would understand he wasn't frightened. Then he curled up and decided he may as well sleep while waiting for the storm to die down.

The other creature woke him, pushing its head against his shoulder. Nudging him from the shelter, Zet felt the sense of urgency the tryanot projected. Vermin, a horde of them, were coming their way. Tryanots, wild and engineered, fed on them, but a flood of vermin might overwhelm a lone tryanot. The life form in the flyer would soon be dead, if not already.

He needed to get there first. Jumping from the hole to the ground, the tryanot raced off to the southwest. Zet immediately understood that was a safe direction. A gust of wind brought a strange odor to him. He turned in that direction and ran toward the scent, which got stronger.

On the far side of the ridge, he came on the twisted wreck of the flyer. The dead thing inside resembled what he thought must be a Liderian. A neck hanging of some kind dangled from the body.

With no med bed immediately available and the vermin coming closer, he jerked the piece from around the Liderian's neck and took off again just as the first of the pack came in view. There wouldn't be a bit of hide or a bone left in a few hours.

Metallic chain in hand, he sprinted away from the pack. A couple of them followed him, one nipping at his heel. Zet increased his pace and hurried away, knowing the creatures would lose interest in him and return to the sure feast in the wreckage.

Over another ridge, he slowed his pace and absorbed some of the water he'd stored. The heat from the star overhead had increased now that the cloud of sand and dust no longer obscured it. The rays baked the surrounding land and drained him of moisture. Spying a slight overhang with a sliver of shade, Zet stopped and regurgitated enough water to slide a film over his head. He would need a cleaning unit desperately back at the port.

The Port Authority must be his first stop. He would beg a spare sleeping berth from Neelah, the customs official nominally in charge. She could take the piece he'd brought back and notify the Liderian's life forms of his death. He didn't want to be faced with angry Liderians when they realized this would be all they would have of the pilot. He didn't feel a need to explain why he couldn't have brought the creature back. Neelah could do that and hopefully keep his name out of it.

Everyone on Estevan knew taking a flyer into the Waste to be a foolish gamble. One of the first things any ship new to the planet got handed with their ticket for a berth was the sheet telling them of the dangers of the planet. Not only was it stupid to try using a flyer on Estevan, but implants could and did experience glitches the further one got from the city or the port. No one understood why, it just was how things were on this world.

He had to stop one more time to allow the water he'd taken in to rehydrate his cells. An immense feeling of satisfaction at having survived rolled over him when Zet jogged up the ancient riverbed to the plain. Inside the port administration building, he went first to Neelah's office.

"Zet? What brings you here?"

Dangling the neckpiece out with one hand, he took another step closer. "You know I was exploring in the waste?" At her nod, he continued. "Some foolish form crashed a flyer where I was sheltering from that storm that just blew through. A bunch of vermin nearly got me when I stopped to get this and bring it back. There won't be anything left of him when they get through."

She stood and walked over to take the chain from his fingers. "Eew! You smell."

"I know. Can I beg a bed and cleaning unit from you for the night? I'm exhausted and don't think I have the energy to go looking for a room."

"I suppose you want me to notify the ship that he captained of his crash and death?"

"Please. I don't want to explain why I couldn't carry a dead Liderian who weighs more than I do out of the desert while trying to stay alive myself."

Neelah's brow furrowed, and her lips formed a straight line. Angry, she nodded. In all the times he'd seen her dealing with many life forms and their ships, he never seen her become irritated and this was pure rage. "I'll tell them. You don't need to worry. There is no way you could have brought him back to get him in a med bed or fought off a herd of vermin. I warned the fool about taking a flyer into the Waste and got ignored for my trouble."

Shaking her fist, she turned her head and glared at the chain and pendant. "They better have someone who can captain that tub. I'm almost ready to order them off the planet. Real close."

Then she lowered her hand. "Yes, you can have one of the quarantine rooms for the night. But don't come out if you hear any shouting. I'll take care of this notification. Space-juiced idiot just wouldn't listen. Second door on the right is yours. You go get settled. I've got a ship to deal with."

Zet left the office, grateful that she'd already had words with that ship. He would get the name from her later so he and Camat could steer clear of the lot of them. There was something very wrong with a ship and its crew who didn't listen to the locals. As the nominal head of the port, Neelah could order them to leave. He wondered if she would and if so, when.

Chapter 39

The Human female demanded entrance to the ship, the captain's absence being the main reason she had to see the other officers. A confused group of officers, with a gleeful Keem lurking in the background, escorted the irate official to the ready room of the *Rolatr*.

He so hoped his enthusiasm wasn't showing. Neelah Orn's arrival absolutely must be good news for him. It had to be. Humbor hadn't returned, and they were discussing what to do when she arrived.

After the big storm blew through and they heard nothing from the captain, Keem quietly exulted. Keeping his mouth shut had only helped him. No one could say that he encouraged Humbor to take the flyer out. The opposite, in fact. He'd whispered to E'nnty that no one used flyers on Estevan.

The Gossican female mentioned it to the group sitting in the very same ready room. Ships entered Estevan space and landed on the planet. Why couldn't flyers be used? Humbor put the situation down to the inability of the planet to produce a decent vehicle. They were behind tech-wise. Liderian tech being superior to Human products, their flyers would surely handle anything the planet could throw at them.

Then the storm hit. Keem had seen the expressions of discomfort on the faces of the remaining officers. Propelled by the howling wind, dirt, dust, and tiny pebbles flew unhindered across the plain, slamming into the skin of the ship. The ferocity surprised the others. Keem had already experienced an Estevan storm and understood why there was a thick bubble around the city.

The customs official who ran the port authority strode up to the table. *Rolatr's* officers turned her way when they reached the safety of the far side of the table. Humbor would have stood in the middle, right behind the captain's chair.

Keem sidled into the room and eased around so he had a good view of the Orn female and the officers. Focused fully on Orn, they all ignored him.

With what sounded like a grunt, the official pulled her hand from her pocket and slammed something on the tabletop. A series of indrawn breaths and heartfelt groans came from the others.

Keem recognized the chain and pendant that Humbor had worn on leaving the ship. Both hands flew to his mouth to contain the very inappropriate laugh he felt surge upward. E'nnty would take charge now. Neither the second officer nor any other heads of departments would dare to dispute her authority. As vicious as she was both strong and beautiful, they would all need a med bed if they gave her any argument. If he kept her happy, he would now have something to say about what the ship did and where.

"You arrogant little twits! You thought you had it all figured out. We're nothing but backward citizens of a third class planet with little or no economy and don't know our asses from shit recyclers. I warned you about taking a flyer out—did you listen? Oh, by all the seven hells, no! Now your captain's dead. Which one of you smart life forms is taking over for him?" Orn glowered at the officers.

As he had thought, E'nnty took three steps to the side and positioned herself behind the captain's chair. "Me."

Bruttan, the Liderian and Humbor's second-in-command, mumbled something. E'nnty punched him on the shoulder and after swaying slightly, the male became silent.

Didn't take you long, my beauty. This time, Keem allowed a slight smile to touch his features. There was something to be said for being a kept male, if the keeper was Gossican.

"We will need his body back to return him to his home." E'nnty inclined her head slightly.

The official laughed, startling all of them, including Keem. "What body? There are herds of vermin out there, and they are always ready to reap the benefit of stupidity. They smell blood and it draws them from everywhere."

Not ready to be put down by an official of an insignificant desert planet, E'nnty scowled at Orn, dropping her second set of teeth to impress on the official who she was dealing with. "His bones then."

"There won't even be bones to find. They will drag them off once all the meat is gone." Orn pushed the necklace toward E'nnty. "Is there a locator beacon on the blasted flyer?"

"There is."

"It might still work. As a courtesy, I will give you and two strong males three days to gather what you can from the wreckage. Then you are to leave

Estevan and never, and I mean *never* return. You…" Orn glanced around at the others. "All of you and this ship are banned from Estevan."

With that, she turned and stalked from the room. No one spoke until they believed she was out of range to hear them.

Uuld wanted to take off and use the ship's weapons to reduce the planet to a gas ball. No one readily agreed. Violence was the Felskoglander's first reaction to anything.

"Shut the seven hells up!" E'nnty reached around Bruttan to give Uuld a push. "Don't be an idiot. You really want the Life Foundation whining about us being pirates? We've managed to keep the slave trading we've done quiet. An investigation is not what we want here. We can't take a chance on using another flyer. That's obvious. We'll have to walk in. That means carrying lots of water and lighting so we can travel at night."

"What about the treasure?" Etienne, the Human Canarian communication officer, asked.

E'nnty slipped the necklace over her head. "We'll give this to the family. We have three days to scout this out. If there's something, we will take advantage of it. Otherwise, we leave this overheated dust bowl and who the hell cares? A load of slaves picked up and delivered is sure to fill our accounts and we know how to do that, don't we?"

No one argued.

Had Zet found a good place to shelter from the storm? Malada stood near the area where the tryanot had curled up in a tight ball to wait it out. The sky again clear and the winds reduced to a light breeze, she worried over him. How could this work without some way of communicating?

Later, she would ask Joun about getting a communicator. Although, so many things of a technical nature didn't work in the Waste. Her father suspected the old ones had left something running, or perhaps the very nature of the land interrupted with all but low-tech applications.

That lay beyond her sphere of knowledge. There were spirits, or something that seemed like a minor god or spirit, that controlled the planet.

Those in the city were too insulated from Estevan to feel what the Watchers knew existed, even if they didn't comprehend the nature of it.

A slightly scaly snout bumped her arm and Malada glanced at Joun's tryanot curiously. It had never done that before. It rubbed against her. Malada reached out to stroke the broad head with eyes much like Zet's, only with different colors for the iris and pupil.

Several click-like sounds came from the creature. Was it trying to reassure her about Zet? Perhaps. Malada thought about how the wild female tryanot had led them to the shelter and safety.

Why hadn't her father named this tryanot after retiring Slug, his old beast? The one Joun had used from the time he was a young man. A thought came to her as she stroked the rough beast. "I think Father still misses Slug."

Another nudge from the tryanot had her feeling it was in response to her statement. How much did they understand? Perhaps a great deal more than Watchers wanted to admit. That thought took her in one direction she had never ventured before. Watchers had bred tryanots for beasts of burden from the smaller, wild strain. Had anyone really taken the time to learn what the animals were truly capable of?

Estevan had an edict against slaves—were the Watchers inadvertently in violation of that law? The beast made another series of clicks and butted against her palm as if it meant to tell her something.

I must ask Zet about the creatures. When she saw him again... but who knew when that would be? Malada sighed and continued stroking the beast. Finally, she smiled at the tryanot. "Shall we call you Speedy? You're quick when it's needed."

A rumbling sound came from the tryanot. "Well then, Speedy it is. I'll tell Joun you have a name now. He is to use it."

Chapter 40

Leaving the quarters he'd enjoyed for the night, Zet gave in to duty and activated his implants, although it might be too early to try contacting Camat. He now had a better understanding of his captain's needs. Were Eldara and her mate awake, they could be engaged in something they wouldn't want interrupted.

That line of thought led him to consider his other crewmates. Having determined he would apologize to Xigant at the earliest opportunity, he stood at a window in the hall that would take him to Neelah's office and watched daylight ease over the land.

He'd grown content with Estevan. Once one learned to cope with the dust, fine dirt, and debris that often flew over the planet, it wasn't a horrid place to live. Those cocooned in the city had less to worry about. Inside the dome of Estevanana, he could see the apartment buildings soaring into the protected space.

But he'd heard talk of building another dome as the one protecting the city was getting old. If the city administration built another protected city not too far from this one, they would move everyone to the new one and replace the older dome. The city population had grown, and they needed more dwellings.

Camat hoped, as the *Demon Lair* listed Estevan as its home port, they might get a chance at any contracts for haulage that were needed. Their attorney, Ivan Sebe, was monitoring the situation. Camat swore the man would move for them when the opportunity arose.

Daylight with a slight blue tinge lit up the port. Brown being the predominant color of everything, buildings and the areas between the buildings, splashes of color moving past the salvage yard toward the dry riverbed that provided access to the Waste caught his gaze.

Zet felt someone moving in his direction and identified Neelah by her distinctive odor.

"Ah, they are leaving," she said while stepping up beside him. "I gave the crew of that Liderian ship three days to get what they could from the wreckage. They told me there is a locator beacon on the flyer, I hope it works.

When they have what they need to take to the man's home world, they are to pack up and leave. They make me nervous."

"The question I might ask is, what do they seek here?"

With a sigh, the Human female raised a hand to the window. "If only we didn't answer to Estevanana. As long as they collect credits from ships that land, the Authority..." A deeper sigh rolled up out of her. "I can do nothing to monitor who lands. I'm to collect the fees, make sure nothing violating regulations gets planetside, and that's it."

He took a glance at the female in her dark blue uniform. "You're the only one out here. That must be a difficult job."

"More so than you can imagine." A ray of light pierced the glass before the shielding blocked it out. Her dark skin glowed for a moment. Taller than Itty by several millimeters, the female's Houser ancestry was apparent. Her smile eased the serious expression on her face. "At least I get free housing out of the job. And all the food I can grow."

"Much like being on a ship. You get fed, have a decent place to sleep, all the holos you want, and work your tail off while on board."

Her dark eyes shone and a laugh bubbled up out of her. "Yes. But I don't need to worry about colliding with space debris and getting vacuumed out into space."

Zet nodded. "True. However, if you think about it, getting caught out in a storm—for instance, like the one that took the flyer down—creates much the same effect."

"Huh. I never thought of it that way before." She turned and watched the three life forms disappear as they walked into the depths of the old riverbed. "You're correct, of course."

"Like the form who crashed out there. What was he trying to find, I wonder?"

"Something I asked myself for a long time last night. I have a few theories and wish I had a few other forms out here. If I did, I'd send someone out to shadow them. As it is, I keep asking myself if I should have simply told them to leave."

"How do you think you can make your command stick?"

Brow wrinkled, lips thinned, she glared up at him. "Cut them off from all services. That's the only weapon I have. Once I lock this place down, they can't force their way in and reconnect."

Leaning down, she picked up a bag he hadn't noticed.

"You need more. The port needs more."

"We do. The port should separate from the city and form our own government. Then maybe I could get some help." She turned toward the transport tube she'd used to get to the floor he was on. "Dream on. Are you going off to find something to eat? Tonio and Pia probably have food ready by now and I'm hungry. You coming?"

Zet followed the female. "I am. I didn't know they served food this early."

"It's not official, but they cater to my needs. I'd rather eat Tonio's cooking than mine. Since you're part of Camat's bunch, I don't see them turning you away."

Intrigued, he followed Neelah to the tube and down to ground level. The air had heated with the arrival of the star's light and he thought about the three headed out into the Waste. It would be hot. Far more than they realized. He hoped they had enough water with them. Otherwise, three more from that ship might die out there.

The female circled around to the alley behind the restaurant where she knocked on the back door. When a sleepy-looking, bleary-eyed Tonio answered, she held the bag out.

The male took it with a grin. He glanced at Zet before opening the container. "Ah. Good, good. I'm nearly out. Come in, Pia is almost done with the scramble and bread."

He stood to the side and Neelah went in. Tonio grinned at him and gave Zet a gentle push inside before shutting the door.

In the kitchen, around the big table Tonio used to hold his equipment, sat Camat with an arm around Eldara. The two were laughing at something, but turned to greet Neelah and Zet.

"You finally activated your implants. I thought you might contact me," Camat said.

"Ha, and get yelled at?" Zet said as he pulled a chair out and slid his tail to the far side. "But we do need to talk. I learned a few things out there in the desert."

Kitchen tool in hand, Pia turned to smile at Zet and Neelah. "You are both welcome. I would have sent Camat for you, Zet, when I found out you were staying with Neelah. What were you doing out there?" Without waiting for a response, she turned back to the stove.

For a moment, he wondered if he should keep his news to himself. Then decided these people were his family and had a right to know. "Not what I planned at first. I... ah... found a mate."

The kitchen erupted into chaos with everyone shouting questions. Tonio picked up a big spoon and hit the side of a pan several times. "Belay the noise. Let him talk or we'll never learn what happened."

"Me first," Camat cut in. "Okay, how in the seven hells did that happen? Tell all. No, not all, don't give us too much information. No deep-diving into private stuff."

Zet inclined his head. "I met up with a large tryanot out there, Joun's beast. I followed it as I wanted to see if I could find the place where Joun got the things he trades. The plan was to explore, and I thought he could point me in a direction. He has made a discovery of an old civilization. But he swore me to secrecy as to the location. I can't tell you that. He had his daughter with him and... and... well, we talked and... other things..."

Camat let out a low whistle. "Joun's daughter is your mate? Aren't you a dark one? I didn't even think you two had met."

Plates with food on them appeared on the table. Pia took a seat, picked up a utensil and waved it at him. "What did her father say?"

Eyes on his plate, Zet picked up his own tool and pushed at the food. "Joun said quite a lot at first. We are both full grown, and I simply wanted Malada to be happy, so having Joun accept matters helped. Malada and I saw each other when she first came here to hear Eldara sing."

"Saw each other? And that's all it took?" Camat asked.

His gaze still on the food, Zet thought about how to deflect the questions. "Yes, but there is more going on. You know someone landed a ship here recently that hasn't been here before. They didn't listen to Neelah and took a flyer out into the Waste. The captain flew it and he crashed and killed himself is what happened. A pack of vermin descended on the site, and I had to run for it. Neelah told them they could send out a search party to see what they could find. When the vermin finish, there won't even be bones.

But what bothers us, Neelah and me, is what were they up to? Something isn't right."

"Yes. And what the hell can anyone do about it?" Tonio waved his tool in the air and a bit of food slid off onto the table. "This is getting far too much for Neelah to cope with. We need to keep up pressure on the city admin to cut us loose. I'll be taking this to Dave. He needs to alert CoDee and Cat to the problems we are facing now. That article in Galaxy Wide News and GalDocs about the pirates and how SUN routed them hasn't helped. Every idiot in the universe thinks they left treasure somewhere on planet and they want to have a look."

"Oh, it that what started this?" Neelah picked up her empty plate and took it over to the sanitizer.

"It is." Tonio followed her after shoveling in his last bite. "You need people under you so you can monitor who gets to land. Business may be great, but how many of those fools are going to go out into the Waste and end their lives? Then who will deal with the fallout? The city will surely push it all on us. You know they will. I'm finished giving them money for doing nothing to help the port."

Those gathered in the kitchen were silent for a few minutes.

"Who have you spoken with besides Dave?" Camat asked.

Tonio laughed. "Believe me when I tell you, Dave, CoDee, and Cat can make things happen. We have been in talks with the city for the last SUN year. CNY Universal can wield some power. And CoDee is tired of having Cat act like his pet animal when they come here. With them being part of the Union and the Life Foundation, I think we now have a good shot at taking control away from the city." He leaned over to kiss Pia. "I'll be back. I'm off to give Dave the latest news. It's time we got serious about becoming our own entity."

"Wait!" Neelah hurried toward the door. "I'm with you on this one."

Those left in the kitchen exchanged glances.

Pia rose from the chair and reached for the empty plates. "So it begins. I knew something would go wrong when that article went universal. Camat, what do you think?"

"That it's time Neelah got some help. And I'll side with the port. The city does nothing for me." He turned to Eldara. "We need to find a place out here.

Maybe build something if necessary. I don't trust the city to deal fairly with those who come out here to work."

"Our old place is sitting vacant," Pia said as she stacked plates in the sanitizer. "It's on the street that dead ends at the hill behind the salvage yard. Someone tried to run a business out of it but didn't work diligently enough. You want to buy it, Tonio and I will sell it cheap."

Zet watched Camat and Eldara exchange a glance that spoke without their saying a word. He looked forward to Malada and him being so close they could do the same.

"Can we get the code to get in?" Camat asked Pia while smiling at Eldara.

"Certainly. Give me your communicator or your spreadsheet and I'll give it to you. Go look around. It may be in rough shape. The tenant didn't do much."

"We will." Camat grinned at Zet. "Want to come along? You may be on the hunt for a place too."

"So it seems. Although Malada isn't comfortable in the proximity of so may life forms."

Camat gave Eldara a quick hug. "You'll work it out. We did."

Pia gave him the code. After a hug and a brief thank you to Pia, Camat reached for the back door and opened it to find Tonio with Dave Yerks right behind him.

"We've something to discuss. Don't go anywhere for a moment," Tonio said. Camat, Eldara, and Zet moved to the side.

A clatter caused them to start as Pia tossed their eating tools into the loaded sanitizer. "What is wrong?" she asked as she put an arm around Tonio. "Where is Neelah?"

"Back at the Authority, planning to do some research," Dave answered before taking a holo cube from his pocket. Placing it on the table, he activated it. "Anyone know who the form behind the Gossican female is?"

A sound barely short of a scream came from Eldara as she turned her head into Camat's chest. "Keem! He's lighter and more muscular, but that is Keem. I'll never forget that miserable creature."

"Who took that?" Camat asked as he pulled her close.

"Lute. He's been hiding out in town with Sebe while I asked questions. I didn't come to you two because I didn't want to interrupt anything." He ran one hand over his gray hair. "I suppose I should have."

"There was no way for you to know. How did Lute get that picture?"

"Those three wanted into the salvage yard and were making a stink because he wouldn't let them in. I already contacted Cat and CoDee. Then Tonio and Neelah saw me this morning and—something isn't right here."

Zet thought of all the things they should do and getting Eldara to safety came first. Then he could discover what the crew of the *Rolatr* with help from Keem, had planned. He rested a hand on Camat's shoulder. "Use my fare and take Eldara to Greenhouse 2. The ship should be almost ready."

"What are you planning? You can't tackle this on your own."

A picture flashed into his mind. Right outside the back door of the restaurant, hidden by several boxes, an older wild tryanot male munched away at the vermin he'd just caught. Like a series of holo shots, several more pictures came his way. He knew where the Gossican female and her two companions were. Keem wasn't with them.

Zet grinned at Camat. "I'm not alone. This is just the kind of warfare they created me for."

"Will the Watchers help you?"

Supposing they probably would if for no more reason than to keep their secrets, he replied, "Yes. Take Eldara to Neelah, get her to hide you two out in her guest quarters until you can get a ride off planet. Stay out of sight. Keem is still in the port. I'll handle the rest of this."

Chapter 41

Malada felt a shift in the Waste. Something felt wrong. She might have given up her position to another, but there were things she couldn't eschew. The tenor of the land would always be something she instinctively felt. The health of the land they lived with and that of the Watchers would affect her.

Insight of another kind made her smile. Her mate's health and safety would contribute to her wellbeing. She felt he was well and not in harm's way. As nothing else could, not their physical attraction and meshing nor the ability to come together mentally, her internal awareness of Zet convinced her of the validity of their mating. Her spiritual awareness of the male left no doubt. Not that she had any. If she hadn't felt convinced, she never would have taken him to see her kin. Simple physical involvement never required a trip home to Mother.

A grin and a chuckle left her as she stared out at the landscape from a small ledge above where Speedy, the tryanot, lay curled into a ball to sleep off its kill. He had been gone a long time last night and had returned only a short time earlier in the waning light of the blue moon. The larger moon crawled toward the far horizon even as the daystar's light became a faint sheen over the distant peaks. Soon, she would go inside to sleep for a while.

The increased presence of the larger moon predicted the winter months would soon give way to summer. Daytime travel was barely possible in winter in the area north of the middle of the planet. Soon, that would become impossible. Or just barely possible if one had a wagon full of containers of water protected from evaporation in this quadrant of Estevan. Further south, at the middle of this world, day travel was never possible in summer.

Far to the south, below the middle of Estevan, the Waste had once been a vast body of water with only a small land mass close to that pole. Malada often wondered what had caused the water to dry up. At both the far north and south poles, permanent sheets of ice covered the land. So compacted and dry, even when melted, they gave little moisture.

She knew from her childhood studies that the colonists had tried. Hoping that the melted ice would give them back what Estevan had lost. It was not to be. There was still moisture beneath the land, deep underground.

And in a few sites, it came to the surface in life-giving pools which the Watchers guarded jealously. The people in the city and the port suspected Watchers had such knowledge, but after the first few conflicts had given up trying to wrest that information from them.

What began as an uneasy truce grew into a hands-off policy which both parties honored. All helped by the storms, which made it nearly impossible to use a flyer anywhere on the planet and another odd situation all Watchers knew. Certain tech didn't work in the Waste as it should.

Joun suspected the tech of the dead civilization he had been working to remove from the caverns and take to the big salvage yard as the culprit. Her father's project had generated something which had happened only a few times in their history—a huge meeting of all the kin representatives. Nowhere on Estevan was there sufficient water for all the kin to gather with their tryanots. Instead, each of the families sent one individual to the meeting.

Having just finished her training, Malada attended. Not as a delegate for her family, but as a representative of the Waste itself. It all happened the year before the pirates arrived and parked themselves in the cavern, only to be ousted by SUN later.

The Watchers hadn't agreed to Joun's plan until then. Finding themselves in fear of SUN or the pirates blowing the entire complex to bits, the kin changed their minds. Joun had assured them that the owners of CNY Universal and the huge old salvage yard could be trusted. Malada sensed his assessment to be correct. When she no longer felt any threat from the cavern, representatives from all the kin mounted a clean-up mission. And Joun systematically worked to get what he hoped was the most important tech to CNY.

Below her, Speedy twitched and rose from his nest. The tryanot paced back and forth, uttering what sounded like groans. She stood on the ledge and searched the rough terrain laid out before her in the growing light. Welling up in her from her bones, agitation displaced her earlier peace. Something promising great harm had entered the Waste.

A family of jinge—a female, adult male and two kits—all dashed into a crevice she hadn't noticed before. The small creatures had fluffy fur and large ears and sometimes Watchers kept them as pets. She had one and had never witnessed such behavior before.

Worry for Zet flooded her.

Malada climbed down from the ledge and hurried into the entrance of the cavern, calling for Joun as she ran inside.

His head lifted from the bed, and Joun glared at her. "What are you making so much noise about?"

"I feel a presence in the Waste and Speedy feels it, too."

Leaning on one elbow, Joun's face wore a confused expression. "Speedy?"

"Yes, the tryanot. That's what he wants to be called, but we needn't bother about that right now. The problem is something has changed. It feels much like when the pirates tried to take over the caverns."

That got him out of the nest with eyes wide open. "I thought you no longer had those instincts."

"I still have them but felt it best to not mention it to anyone, as it is now her responsibility. This is different. When even the tryanots and jinges are upset, how can I ignore what they feel? What could be the reason for entering the Waste with bad intent?"

"What I am doing here. We need to pack up and leave. Immediately."

"Where can we go?"

"We must go back to our kinhold and alert everyone. It may be necessary to fight. Where is Zet? Do you know?" Joun asked as he slipped into his outer robe and bent to roll his bedding.

Malada hurried to get her things packed. "I don't know. Not having a way to contact him makes this all much harder."

"Can't you sense anything?" Placing his bundle on his shoulder, Joun reached for hers. "You go behind me and use your covering to brush out my steps and yours. I will find Speedy, as it seems he is now called. Then we will block the opening. That will take the most time."

Removing the robe with the loose, long sleeves all Watchers wore when traveling, she turned her back to Joun and brushed out the marks of their passage. It took her a long time to get it done since she had to move layers of dust from the sides of the corridor to the center. Once, on spotting what she knew to be Zet's tracks, her spirit sank.

If only I could contact him.

Malada put that thought away as she must hurry. Becoming despondent would help nothing.

Joun had the tryanot attached to the cart, and their bundles loaded. As soon as she stepped out of the crevice, he picked up a large, flat rock and turned it so it blocked the fissure at waist height. A few other rocks went on top, with lighter scree tossed into the opening below. When he finished, the crack in the rock looked like nothing more than a den for a wild creature. He led Speedy out to the faint path that curled around the base of the cliff and then upward before turning to retrace his steps back down. Removing his robe, he directed Malada to help him remove all traces of their time at the opening. Garbed again, they started down the trail. Speedy followed them as they walked.

"We have several empty water containers on board, which indicates a long journey. If stopped, we must say we were looking for more crystals for our lights."

"We have none."

With a shrug and a sigh, Joun nodded. "We were unsuccessful. One does not always find what one is looking for. Our crystals are worthless for more than generating light, so no one could want them for anything else. What I really worry about is you. To a slaver, you are a prize."

"Estevan has never allowed slaves on planet."

"True. But the pirates traded slaves. For all we know, the pirates have returned. It's not as if we have an army to stop them. Admin would need to call on SUN or, if they have sufficient credits, hire the Union to help."

"We can fight."

"We can." He nodded. "However, we don't have the weapons pirates have. I doubt we have anything as sophisticated as the ship Zet crews on. We can only hope that what they possess is too technical to work out here."

She had no counter for that argument.

Speedy balked at taking the single-file trail that bordered the deep rift. They hadn't set foot on the narrow trace when a ferocious-looking female strode over the rise that marked the start of the route they must take to get to the kinhold.

"What do we have here?" the female barked out.

When the female's jaw opened wide enough to reveal the second row of teeth, Malada recognized her as a Gossican. A Felskoglander followed and on his heels came a Human. Joun backed Speedy and the cart the way they had come.

"We are Watchers."

"Just who we needed to locate. We have questions for you."

The Gossican's smile set Malada quaking inside. Joun's assumption had been correct. Somehow, they knew about at least one of the caverns. She reached out to stroke Speedy's head.

Joun turned and released the tryanot. "Go!" Joun said as he gave it a hard slap. The creature turned and ran, tail held just off the ground. From various places in the landscape, grunts and groans of various strengths sounded.

The female who had been rushing toward them came to a stop, her hand on something at her belt. "What is that?"

With a shrug, Joun put his hands out, palms up, to show he held no weapons. "Tryanots, I suppose."

Face screwed into an expression of anger, the Gossican regained her composure and darted forward. Joun fell to the ground from the force of her blow. "Why did you loose the thing?"

Her father spit a glob of blood to the side, rose, and stared at the female. "I didn't want him hurt. It seems my reasoning was sound."

Malada watched horrified as the Gossican hit him again.

Chapter 42

His bodily capacity for water topped off, and with several of Tonio's sausages, he left the restaurant. At Tonio's suggestion, he stopped off at Dave's shop. There, he was equipped with a few things, the first of which were combat glasses quickly integrated with his implants. The glasses would allow him to see in visual light wavelengths, then overlay infra-red, ultraviolet, and electronic emissions.

Dave offered him an older exo armor suit he'd taken in trade. Zet thanked him for the thought and explained he had one already tattooed into his skin. The older male cautioned him, saying he didn't know what would or wouldn't work in the Waste. Only the Watchers had any real data, and since city dwellers and spacers alike stayed out of the Waste, he didn't have information to share.

Wishing he'd had more time with Malada and her family, Zet took the weapon Dave offered and the few 6 mm hyper rounds he placed with it, cautioning Zet that they might return to the weapon and do more damage to it and Zet. He couldn't say, having no experience with either the weapon or the ammunition. Estevannians simply didn't mess with the Watchers and the Wastelands. No one had in a century.

He understood fully. The two groups, those in the domed city and the port on the plain, didn't mix with Watchers. Each had carved out their place on the planet and left it at that. Malada's mother's reaction to him had clarified that the Watchers weren't interested in changing the status quo anytime soon.

Which made this entire situation that much more curious. Then he remembered the holo of Keem with the crew of that ship which had lost its captain. How in the seven hells Keem had finagled his way back to Estevan was a mystery.

Discussing Keem with Dave as he tucked the loaded weapon into the hip pouch, they concluded that the crook knew Joun had been bringing items in from the Waste. A flash of something he'd learned had Zet's head popping up. "Funeral boats. Do you think Keem believes there might be one of those on Estevan?"

"By the pit! He might think we have a Yodoran funeral boat out there somewhere. But you know, archeology—lost civilizations and artifacts—is a big business. There are collectors out there who will pay well for a shard of something." The older man stared at the wall for a moment. "There's something out there. I doubt it's Yodoran, but it's old and that's enough for some collectors. Not everyone can afford Yodoran quality. Some are happy to have anything that is old and not easily afforded by the average life form."

"I'll take your word on it. Keem isn't a collector. That bit of slime is a user of anyone and anything he can get his grasping little digits on. Worse, he has a score to settle with the *Demon Lair* and Camat for taking Eldara away from him. Oh, and our engineer, Brown. We stole Brown away as well."

Dave nodded and clapped him on the shoulder. "Be damned careful out there. I hate to see you taking on those three alone. The Gossican and the Felskoglander are formidable separately. Together, they make a tough crew to fight. I'd go with you—"

"No need. Besides which, if you did, I'd need to share my water. I'm better off alone." Zet didn't bother to explain that he fully intended to get help from the tryanots, both wild and domesticated.

"If only communications worked out there."

"I have a means of communication. In a way. There's an old male tryanot, a wild one who stays close to the back of Lady Pia's. If he comes to you, I've got problems out there. Not that you can do much of anything. It will simply be a notification that I'm probably not coming back and to keep a watch for those three, any or all of them. You know, the port really needs a security force of its own. Those three could kill someone and get offplanet without anyone stopping them."

"We know, and we're working on it. First comes making the city admin turn loose of the port and let us act as what we are—a separate entity. Something is in the works, just not soon enough, unfortunately. Please be careful."

"I will." Zet opened the door and left Dave standing in his office, cursing.

He hadn't reached the trailhead when the first grunt sounded a short distance off the trail. Zet understood the wild one he heard meant to warn him of trouble. Determining there was no need to make for the crash site, he adjusted his pace and set off down the trail. Too fast and he would use too much energy and more of his water resource than he should.

Still, worry over Malada and Joun, particularly Malada, threatened to make him lose control. He tucked that away and reached inside to pull out that which he had buried. The training his creators had forced on him. The killing machine they had tried to make him into must come to the fore.

"Emara!"

The voice of Stapen calling her name and the urgency in the tone took her attention from the project on her portable loom. Rising from the stool, she hurried to the entrance of her dwelling. Having worked through the night, and on the verge of retiring for the day, she felt groggy.

Stapen's hand went to one of the telescoping rods which held up the cloth of her much-patched tent. He gasped for breath. *Had he run from somewhere?*

"Joun's tryanot is back... without Joun or Malada. It returned... without the cart. Something is wrong."

Fear for the man she had birthed two children with took hold. Her need to sleep replaced by a surge of adrenaline, she grabbed her son's shoulder. "Have you cared for its needs? We must use it to take us back to their location. And we will need others to accompany us along with two tryanots to carry water."

He took another deep breath before speaking. "Alun and Julz are readying the water bladders and two tryanots to carry them. One of the beasts is Malada's."

"Good thinking. You know how much I hate riding a tryanot, but we must this time. It will be far faster than taking a cart or walking. We dare not wait until night to travel."

"Understood. Nalt is readying climbing gear and the weapons. Shall we take the thing Joun brought back from the cavern? The one that belonged to the pirates?"

Emara squinted up at the edge of the cliff towering on the far side of the small stream that made life here possible. She hated the weapon with a passion. Together, she and Joun had experimented with it far from the haven of this green and productive valley. One of the four water sources they had custody of. Capable of significant damage, she feared its use would harm areas of the Waste for far too many generations. But what if... She blanked that thought from her mind. "Yes. We will take it. But I will manage it. Only me, since I am the only one other than Joun with any knowledge of the thing."

Stapen sighed. "Understood. I wanted no part of it then and remain committed to my negative opinion of the thing. But if something is..." With a shake of his head, the young man stopped speaking.

"What? Why do you think this is more than an accident? If you didn't feel that way, you would never have thought of weapons along with water and climbing gear."

He made a cutting gesture with one hand. "Something feels wrong. What if the pirates have returned and found them in the cavern?"

Her fingers tightened on him, and Stapen winced. "Ah."

Emara released her hold on his shoulder and gave him a pat. "Anything is possible. I asked him to stop going there, but—that one does as he wishes. Still he... they may be only in difficulties. We shall find out. I will ask Illa to go with us. We leave as soon as the tryanots are watered and ready."

"Yes. I will see to the beasts." Stapen turned and left.

"Fool! Stupid, stubborn male. Joun, you had best be alive," Emara whispered as she turned to look for her hand weapons.

Chapter 43

Eldara huddled in a corner in the cleaning unit while he guarded the door of the small room Neelah had put them in. He would have been happier to see his mate angry with Keem. Instead, she was reduced to a terrified lump. For that alone, Camat would feed Keem to the swamp creatures on Greenhouse 2.

How had he maneuvered himself into his present position? The only reason Camat cared was to make sure it never happened again. Keem needed to be hit with a carbonizer and turned to ash so he couldn't resurrect. Worse, Eldara needed to see it take place so she would never have another fearful day.

He hadn't an idea how to make that happen. They only had a few more hours to wait before he could get her off Estevan and into the safety of the *Demon Lair*. Living on the ship brought up an entire galaxy of problems. If she couldn't do what she wished—perform at the restaurant—what then? Camat knew the answer already. Eldara would grow increasingly resentful of the ship and ultimately of him.

Not good for either of them or the crew. Attacking the ship and killing Keem seemed the only solution. A horrendous one. If no one knew why they attacked a vessel reported to be a free trader, it might find them ostracized by other settled worlds. They could find themselves in SUN's line of fire as well. It had been difficult enough overcoming the ship's known background as a pirate before they bought it. Because of the auction and the way the ship came into their possession, nearly everyone in the universe knew about its history.

Without the ship and the rest of his crew, Camat didn't dare stick around to help Zet, much as it bothered him to leave his friend alone with Keem and the other ship's crew. The absence of any kind of security force in the port had never bothered him until now—when he needed one.

He paced the small transient room and worried.

His fifth pass past the open door of the cleaning unit, Camat thought about what he could do and sat on the gelbed. First, he could send a message to the Greenhouse 2 shipyard and get an update on their progress.

Another thought came to him. Might his father have any ideas about what he could do to get Keem permanently removed from Eldara's life? He composed a short message using touch only. He had a feeling Eldara might get angry with him for involving his father. At this moment, his female could take his efforts the wrong way.

Clear thinking got overtaken by her fear of Keem, which angered him. He could keep her safe. *Hadn't he done so until now?* Camat forced the rage he felt for Keem to not take control, as he knew himself well enough to know it could get away from him. He concentrated on getting information on the ship and contacting his father. The male said he wanted to help, now he would get the chance.

Eldara stayed in the cleaning unit while he did his best to find a way out of the situation they had landed in. Camat didn't realize how much time had passed until the tap came on the door. Instantly, he realized it had to be Neelah.

Leaning against the door, Camat made sure the lock would only allow it to open enough to make sure. Standing to the side, away from the slight opening he allowed, he whispered, "Neelah?"

"Yes. The freighter is ready to leave. There hasn't been any movement from the other ship. I have an old gravity luge with shields. Eldara can sit on it, and you guide it. I'll walk alongside, and it will look as if you are the only one getting on the freighter. I'm escorting you to the ship. Not that anyone will ask."

Eldara peeked out of the door to the cleaning unit. "Is it time?"

Camat allowed the door to open all the way, and Neelah entered, pulling the luge behind her. "It is. Let me shut it down long enough for you to get on, and then we'll get the shields activated again. I brought along these other old cases so we can make a wall around you."

While they arranged things, Neelah advised them. "This is the first ship out of port. They have a stop to make before Greenhouse 2 to drop cargo at Nizad. Their timetable estimates planetfall at roughly 192 SUN hours to Greenhouse 2. I suspect they have given themselves extra time in case of delays. I'd guess it's more like 152 SUN hours."

Camat's mind buzzed with the possibilities the instant Nizad left Neelah's tongue. Commander Silver used Nizad as a base since her mating with the shaman of Nizad. If he could have time to talk with her, she might have some ideas for what he could do to get rid of Keem's threat to Eldara for good. Their problem wasn't anything he wanted a record of floating around in space. He absently agreed with Neelah.

The walk across the port to the freighter had him on edge. Curled in a depressingly tiny huddle in the center of the nest they had created, Eldara covered her head with one arm. He didn't take a full breath until the ship made the first jump to Nizad. Only then did Eldara emerge from her self-imposed cocoon of fear.

She didn't argue with his plan. He knew that wouldn't last, but it was a start.

Chapter 44

This must be what it would have been like to have brother warriors with him, the interaction between him and the tryanots. If only—then again, he might not have come to Estevan and met Malada. The empty space inside that his mate filled may well have remained open forever.

Losing her now would leave him shattered beyond belief. They had only just begun the journey of two halves becoming a whole.

The calls of the wild tryanots alerted him to the movements of the others. He received some images from the wild one, but the female with young they had waited the storm out with seemed to project the best. Zet didn't understand how that worked and suspected that kin, genetically modified and brought to life by others, would have been closer still.

He husbanded his resources and crept through the Waste as he knew the wild tryanots did, ever on the alert. Things would change in the cavern if that turned out to be their destination. With almost no place to hide in the entrance, he must be doubly careful.

Finding Joun had to be the goal, as they had turned away from the crash site. That had been a ruse. Someone died in that crash, so he had to assume the pilot was scouting for something.

Joun.

Keem knew about Joun's trading with Lute at CNY. Nothing else explained an interest in the Waste from those on the other ship.

He'd learned about the pirate enclave in the mountains, the one SUN took care of, before Joun explained the history of the old settlement as far as he knew it. Traders gossiped. The stories flew around the restaurant when the evening grew old and liquor freed tongues. Keem thought to exploit what lay in the old city encased in the mountain.

An image of Joun, far clearer than what he had been receiving from the wild tryanots, infiltrated his mind. It came from a creature who knew the Watcher well. *Ah, the one Malada named Speedy.*

Zet rose from the narrow trail used by the wild creatures, one that lay parallel to the path worn by generations of Watchers.

At a higher elevation, he caught sight of a small contingent of Watchers led by the large beast. On four limbs rather than two, he negotiated the slope to the lower trail as quickly as possible with no undue noise and rose to his full height. Speedy rushed to him with a series of grunts.

Behind the tryanot, Malada's female parent twitched aside her face covering. "What do you know?" she hissed out.

After a quick stroke for the tryanot who rumbled as it pushed against him, Zet stepped toward her. Lowering his voice so the sound wouldn't carry, he whispered, "Little other than something is wrong, and I fear for Malada and Joun. Do you know of the crash of the flyer?"

"Someone tried to bring a flyer to the Waste?"

"They did. There is a life form with them, one known to us who crew the *Demon Lair*. That being, Keem, enslaved the captain's mate and spent some time on Estevan before being found by forms he stole from. They took him away, but Keem has returned. I fear he has filled the heads of others with tales of treasure to be found in the cavern of the old ones. There are three others from that ship, and they bypassed the crash entirely to come this way. I believe they are not too far ahead of us, but they may have Joun and Malada."

"This trail angles away from the mountain before turning back again to the pass which crosses over to another area of the Waste. There is—no, was an entrance up there to the venting system of the cavern. SUN blocked it. Joun knows this."

The tryanot's tail brushed against his thigh. "How do you come to have Joun's beast?" he asked Emara.

"He came to us."

"Likely sent to you by Joun to alert you to trouble. There is a Gossican, a Fjellskoglander, and a Human after Joun and Malada and they likely have them by now."

"You meant to go after them alone." She smiled at him. "I think I may have changed my mind about you. How shall we proceed?"

"I have a weapon that uses ammunition untried out here." He gave a shrug.

"I can help you with weapons," she said and then turned to motion to a male behind her.

After the exchange of a few hand signs, Zet found himself in possession of a long blade. Curved, it had a sharp edge that easily pared off a slice of one of his claws. Zet looked up at his mate's parent and grinned. Before he could speak, an image flooded his brain. The beast passed something on from a wild tryanot at the base of what he now knew to be a pass through the mountains. It was a picture of Malada being pushed down, then jerked up again by the Human male while the Gossican and Fjellskoglander took turns thrusting Joun from one to the other. "They are at the pass trying to get Joun to tell them what he knows by toying with Malada."

Emara's hand closed around his forearm. "How do you know this?"

He gestured to the large male tryanot whose head touched his arm. "I can understand them. He has news from a wild brother near there who is spying for me."

"Good enough. I suggest we hurry, although quickening our pace will surely alert them when the dust rises."

"Perhaps not if we send the beast ahead once in sight. They will see him and think he has caused the disturbance."

"A good plan. I know that place. We can get quite close if we stick to the tumble of rocks SUN dislodged after sealing the tunnel mouth. First, we must hydrate. Do you need water?"

"No. I filled every cell and my holding area before leaving the port. I was built for desert warfare. Hurry! I wish to be on the move."

While they took care of that chore, Zet communed with the big tryanot male, giving him instructions which the creature improved on. A second wild tryanot, a yearling male of the female presently spying, would slip back a distance and the large beast would chase it toward the three forms, being sure to let the three see him and the youngster for an instant.

Silently, he congratulated the tryanot on a good plan, turned to glance at the Watchers and took off at a ground-eating pace. If they could keep up, good. If not, he wasn't worried. Engaging with the three if he must, Zet hoped to keep them from harming Malada and Joun. The big male kept pace with him as they hurried down the trail.

Chapter 45

Her father knew the cavern well, but she didn't even know the vent system existed. Malada understood he sought to keep the others from the main entrance while he put them off as long as possible. Speedy would have gone home. His return, alone, would alert the kin that trouble had overtaken them. Someone would follow Speedy back to them. She hoped help arrived before they descended into the mountain.

But it seemed her hopes were no more than dust, scattered on the fierce storms of winter. Then she heard a low rumble. Not repeated, she didn't need to hear it again. Malada smiled. Speedy had arrived and with him would be her mother, surely. Stapen would be in the group along with others.

She hoped no one would suffer a major injury. Turning her head slightly, she took a quick glance at the Fjellskoglander. A formidable male, he and the other two had weapons her family didn't possess. This would not be easy.

A binding of some kind held Joun captive, something that administered pain when he didn't cooperate. The Fjellskoglander hadn't used whatever it was on her. Thankfully. But other than throwing rocks at the male, Malada wondered what she could do to disable him. And the word dust came to mind. Could she blind him with it? Perhaps not.

During a playful tussle with Zet, she discovered something he called exo-armor. It kept her from inflicting so much as a play bite on her mate's body. He told her that others had the same thing. Some warriors used actual armor and others, like Zet, had them tattooed on their skin. Further questions regarding the reason he had it got deflected. Something she intended to remedy... if she got the chance.

Worry for the sleek male she chose drove all else from her mind. She hoped he had taken the freighter to Greenhouse 2, along with his captain. It was enough that her family was in danger.

The attack, when it came, had Speedy at the head of the charge, scrambling up from below. Unexpectedly, her mother and older brother broke from the cover of a pile of rocks only a few meters away and to the right.

When the Fjellskoglander raised his weapon, Malada struck. Using her hands, she flung all the dust and dirt she could grab at the man and didn't stop throwing it at him. He turned toward her and something dark green raced in, separating her from danger.

Zet! Falling to the side, she got out of the way. While scrambling to the side, Malada tried to find her father in the dust cloud she had raised. Scrabbling on hands and knees, she moved toward the rock pile her mother had used as cover where she saw a clear patch of air.

Stapen had a Human male in a wrestling hold, his arm around the other's neck. Julz, beside her brother, worked to tie that one up and take him out of the fight. A short-lived grin lifted her mouth. Julz, for all her small size, could be a terror in a fight.

Both her parents, with help from Alun, fought with the lone female in the group of thieves. When she turned to her left, Zet and the Fjellskoglander traded blows. Great thuds resounded, which would have probably killed her had one landed. The other male had lost the weapon. How she didn't know, her attention having been elsewhere.

Speedy came up behind her and she found herself beneath the beast's bulk, four sturdy legs bracketing her body. Her attention got pulled from the fight between Zet and the Fjellskoglander when something fell to the ground beside her. The weapon the Fjellskoglander had been ready to use on her. The tryanot had somehow gained control of it and brought it to her.

She glanced at it once and thought about using it on its owner, but rejected the idea immediately. She didn't have the first idea of how to even fire it. As most of the dust settled, she noted that the female Gossican had been restrained.

The fight between Zet and the Fjellskoglander went on. The other male tried to knock Zet off his feet, but his thick tail kept her mate upright. When the other male glanced her way and saw the weapon lying beside her, he tried to push Zet out of the way and dive for it. With a roar of anger, Zet grabbed the male's head using his thick claws to form a cage behind the Fjellskoglander's skull, jerked him forward, and smacked his head into the other male's face.

His adversary shook his head as if slightly stunned. Zet lifted a weapon and pointed it at the other male. "Cease! This carries 6 mm rounds and will take your head off. There is no way you can get to a med bed in time to keep from bleeding out. This ends now."

The Fjellskoglander turned and spit a wad of blood to the side. "So it does. Do what you want. We will return and bring reinforcements. Whatever you are hiding here can't be kept secret forever."

"You and these others are stupid as two mating vermin. Too involved to notice if anything is preparing to kill them! I've been trying to tell you, there is no funeral boat here. SUN and a Mercenary's Union ship cleaned out this nest of pirates. Don't you think they would have come back if there was anything worth having in there?"

Zet laughed. "Taken in by Keem, were you? The only thing Keem wants is the woman he once enslaved. The songbird who works in Lady Pia's restaurant. He still thinks to take possession of her and make a fortune from her voice along with giving a little payback to our ship, as she is our captain's mate."

"E'nnty, is this true?" The Fjellskoglander turned his head to stare at the Gossican female.

"How in the seven hells should I know? Keem didn't mention a songbird." The Gossican spat at him from the ground where she sat. "But as soon as I get a chance, I'm getting some damn exo armor."

Lying on his stomach with Julz on top of him, the Human male lifted his head. "How about SUN taking out a pirate nest here? Did you know about it?"

"Fucking no. I hadn't heard that. Keem never said..." The Gossican's reply lost a little of the venom of her first response.

"All you had to do was ask anyone on Estevan and they would have told you. SUN tried hard to block all reporting of the incident. I suspect they didn't want the leader of the pirates to get wind of the cleanup operation. I suppose this Keem entity didn't bother to give you that bit of information." Joun shook his head.

"But you are taking stuff out of there and bringing it into town." E'nnty's vitriol returned, and she struggled against her bindings.

Joun took a step toward her feet and kicked her boot. "Bits and pieces of things like household goods."

Malada knew that to be a lie, but kept silent. They didn't need life forms like them churning up the Waste trying to find whatever a funeral boat was.

"We are only trying to discover more about the people who once inhabited this planet and what caused the ocean to vanish." He waved one hand at the landscape. "This taking of another life form by you is the very thing we hoped to avoid. The very thing. There is nothing of value for you here. Keem sent you off into the Waste while he tries to reclaim what he believes is his property."

"And cost us a crew member," the Human male huffed out. "Was sex with Keem worth it, E'nnty? Was he that good? I mean, every form in the universe knows Gossicans have a thing for Humans. You could have stuck with me and we would be off making money somewhere, not fooling around on a lifeless desert world. There aren't even decent bars on Estevan. The place is a dead loss."

"Yeah. You fucked up, Gossican." The Fjellskoglander threw both hands into the air. "Hey, listen. I'm getting thirsty here. Dehydrated bad. My water bladder is dry and how about we call this a draw, and everyone agrees to stand down?"

"I'm in favor of that," the Human on the ground said.

"We can call it done. But I don't think we can trust you to keep your word, so you all get restrained. We have water and will give you some, but you're going back to port and explain everything to the port authority. It shouldn't be a surprise if you get permanently kicked off Estevan and find the details of this raid made public. No one wants a crew of destroyers on their world."

"Keem is going to pay for this," the Fjellskoglander said as his jaw worked in anger.

"Agreed," the Human male threw in. "And we know exactly where to take him for recompense."

E'nnty sighed. "Yeah. We do. And he fucking deserves all he gets at General Shung's hand. Every fucking little bit."

"So, can we trust you to behave? Of course, we will keep control of the weapons," Emara asked.

"Yes," the Fjellskoglander and the Human replied together. It took a minute more before E'nnty agreed.

Malada crawled out from under Speedy and ran to throw herself against Zet. "How are you even here? I thought you were going to Greenhouse 2."

Chapter 46

Zet lifted her off her feet, and with one arm under her hip, settled Malada against his chest. She hooked an arm around his neck and seemed content to be held. He suspected this would not always be the case. "We learned of Keem's presence and knew at once what he wanted; Eldara."

There was more he would tell her later. No suspicion that Joun had lied could get to the crew of the *Rolatr*.

With just enough truth in the story Joun told to be plausible, Zet thought the entire episode would put the ship and its crew in such a bad light, they would probably work to suppress it. Losing a crew member to an expedition to do the seven hells only knew what on a planet already written off by SUN and the Mercenary's Union would do their reputation no good.

Emara took the small Watcher female's hand and tugged her off the Human, and then bent and released his restraints before glancing at the other two. The Fjellskoglander took a step forward.

"I think we will take this a little at a time." Emara held up one hand. "Walk to that pile of rocks and we will see to rehydrating all of us. That depleted my supply. How you behave will tell me if you intend to hold true to the bargain."

The Fjellskoglander muttered something but complied. With a shake of her shoulders, the Gossican shook off Joun's hand after he helped her up. The female followed with the Human bringing up the rear. The Watchers came behind them, with Zet still carrying Malada next and Speedy last in line.

An overhang of rock gave some shade. The other tryanots lay in the shadow, resting. The Fjellskoglander slid down the dusty wall. One by one, the others followed him. Julz was the first to take a water container to the big male.

A conversation ensued with him giving Julz his name—Uuld. Emara put a stop to more and shooed the young female off to tend to the others.

"I gave my word. I'll not violate it," Uuld told Emara as she backed away and allowed him to get a breath before drinking more.

"Do I know you? Are you someone I can trust? Hardly. I'll be in a more trusting mood when I see your ship powering through the atmosphere away from here. And you have no idea how lucky the three of you were. Had only two of you chosen to make the trip, the vermin would have scented you and attacked."

"Vermin?" he asked after another long swallow.

"Yes. There is nothing left of your friend. Not so much as a bone," Emara replied.

"When we came on them,"—Uuld nodded toward Joun—"it was only the two of them."

"True. But they had a tryanot with them. A large one. He hunts vermin when done with his work. They know this."

"Thank you for the water. It seems you know this land well." Uuld tilted his head back on the rock he lounged against.

"Watchers have lived in this Waste since the days of the first colonists. This is our home." She pointed out over the swell of the land they had climbed to reach the pass. "What do you see out there? Past the cairn of rocks to your left, see the trail? Follow it down to where it disappears below that ridge. Do you see anything scampering over the edge?"

Leaning forward, the Fjellskoglander nodded. "What is that?"

Emara laughed. "A small group of vermin dithering about, wondering if there is any way they can pick one of us out and carry that individual off without being eradicated completely."

"By the fucking seven hells and all the snakes in the pit, I see them." He shuddered. "This is no place for any sentient life form. Ah... forgive me. One not used to it, that is."

"Now you have a tiny inkling of what we Watchers live with to be free to follow our path. It has nothing to do with whatever nonsense you were told. This is not your place. I suggest you never return."

"You have my word on it. I, Uuld, will never set foot on Estevan again. A Fjellskoglander never dishonors his word. I cannot speak for the others, but will tell them all what happened here. Keem is the one who will answer for this debacle."

"If you do it, be sure to use a carbonizer," Zet threw in. "Otherwise, that bit of snake dung will come back to bite you. He thrives on revenge. He must be dead ash to be stopped."

"That might be better than selling his hide to that General Shung." A growl punctuated the Gossican female's words before she went back to taking in water.

"He fucking owes us for all the time lost when we could be making money. Then there's Humbor's family. What do we tell them? This is going to hurt." The Human male lowered the water container and shook his head. "They need recompense."

"Shut it, Etienne," E'nnty said. "You need to be quiet. They knew the risks when Humbor first shipped out. What we really need to think about is lizard-boy's observation. Consider how we came by Keem in the first place. He's been running from Shung all along and whoever took him away from here didn't get him to the general either. That slippery little snake is likely to escape again unless turned into a pile of ash. Another thing to think about, what really happened to Buotch? Did Keem have a hand in that? He may well have."

"Well, you've been involved with him all along," Uuld said. Eyes closed, he leaned his blond head against the rock behind him. "Haven't you been monitoring Keem? How could he get away with something without your noticing? Tell me that."

Zet listened closely, and Malada had to tap him on the chest to get his attention. "Put me down please. There's no real reason for you to continue to hold me."

"Yes, there is," he whispered. "I enjoy it. Would you have me give up something that pleases me?"

Her hand stroked his face, lingering on his jawline as she laughed. "We can continue this later. I really need to rehydrate." Then she giggled. "Rehydrating as you helped that wild female tryanot during the storm does not appeal."

Reluctantly, Zet lowered her and waited until he was sure she stood securely on both feet. With a last pat for him, Malada walked over to give her mother a hug and get a container of water. His mate's female parent stared at him for a moment before turning to look at their captives.

"We will stay here until the daystar sets. Then we will move on toward the port. I suggest you rest. We will take a little known trail not often used because it is rough and difficult. Sleep if you can, as this will be hard work and by daylight I intend to be in the port."

It took the entire night, and dawn found them making their way up the old riverbed. Emara had set a hard pace, one that kept the three from the *Rolatr* too busy staying upright to cause problems.

They tried to stage an escape as they neared the Port Authority building, but Speedy cut them off. Grunting and groaning, the beast with help from Zet herded them to the building. Surrounded, they gave up and went inside.

A tousled Neelah emerged from her living quarters and listened silently until Joun told her of the encounter in the Waste. After hearing that the three from the *Rolatr* had accosted Joun and Malada in the desert, she held up a hand. "Stop! You are all to wait here. I'm contacting Dave, Pia and Tonio, Lute and Sebe. They need to hear what happened. If CoDee is anywhere nearby, I'll ask him to monitor this. I think we have reached the tipping point for a security force in the port. I'll return soon." She pointed at the three captives. "Do not allow them out of here. That's an order."

Hurrying back to her quarters, Neelah left a deep silence in the public office area. No one spoke until she came back in uniform.

"I can't reach CoDee so Lute will act as the CNY representative. This is getting holoed. I'm done with the situation that allowed this to happen. CoDee, as a member of the Union, can provide direction on how to set a force up. This cannot go on."

It wasn't long before Dave Yerks, Lady Pia, and Tonio hurried into Neelah's office, all three looking aggravated. Lute entered a few minutes behind them and Sebe joined electronically from his home.

Joun greeted everyone and began the tale again. The customs official raked her hand through her hair midway through the recital. When Joun finished, she put both hands on her hips. "You thought to steal something from us as poor as we are? You are forever barred from Estevan. I never want to see that ship of yours or your faces on my monitor again. Do you understand me? Never again." She turned to her monitor. "Attorney Sebe, have you any legal information to impart?"

"Only that I concur. However, I would suggest that you withhold taking this public unless they force our hand. If this incident causes any other greedy treasure hunters to flock to Estevan, we will know who sent them. Then we will make the entire incident public, making sure to play up their reprehensible conduct to the fullest."

The Fjellskoglander growled, and the Gossican mumbled something in her language. The Human cursed, fluently. Zet made note of a few of them, ones he'd never heard before. Black hole excrement, Oleratii dropout, it was bad when the most over-the-top, insane, no rules head-case criminals wanted nothing to do with you. Okreth dust collector, Shung shit wipe, snake shit collector, and boat-stealing soaker were all new to Zet. He particularly liked third level recycled reject, meaning the form or the situation wasn't fit for the urine level of a ship's recycler. Camat would certainly want to learn those.

It was almost over. Zet took a step forward. "Keem, who I suspect is hiding in that ship, is the driving force behind this entire mess. What exactly is going to be done about him? As we have no jail, we could take custody of him and turn him loose in the Waste."

"No! I strenuously object. We Watchers do not want him. He's a spacer; let them keep that one." Emara glared at Zet.

"Understood. But if they take him away and Keem escapes, he will be back with bigger and better means of taking what he thinks we have. If he decides to blast Estevan with some weapon, what then?"

"Ah. I suppose you have a valid point." The mother of his mate stopped glaring at him.

"And he got free from the women who took him away last time. I wonder how he managed that?" Dave aimed his question at the Gossican. She understood Dave's inference and looked away while her crewmates joined in the hard stares aimed in her direction.

"Depositing him in the desert will give the vermin a free meal, a large one," Joun said. "I don't want them to get in the habit of attacking travelers in the Waste. It's bad enough as it is. One lone person with a large tryanot is safe—so far."

"I have a suggestion," Malada put in and all heads turned her way. "There is little in the southern sector of Estevan's Waste. Can we somehow get this Keem form transported there?"

Zet thought it over while everyone else discussed how impossible that was since virtually nothing worked properly in the Waste. The loss of the *Rolatr* flyer and crewmember cited as proof of the improbability. "I think there may be a way to manage it."

All talk stopped, and everyone turned his way. "Have the *Rolatr* donate a life pod to us. Put it on the pad, leaving Keem inside and all its propulsion systems disabled. When the *Demon Lair* returns, we can take the pod with Keem inside to the southern sector, fly as low as we can and drop it, with Keen still inside. What he does from there is his problem. But we must make sure it will never fly again."

"Life pods are expensive," E'nnty huffed out. "Why should we give one away?"

"Because you owe us, jinge dropping that you are. We brought you back here when we could have left you restrained for the vermin to make a meal of," Emara said.

"Oh, let the vermin drool go about their business." Lute laughed. "We don't need them or any of their junk. I have a damaged life pod in the salvage yard. I'm positive CoDee and Cat would donate it. As long as they turn him over and keep quiet about this, we can handle it."

"Done!" Neelah slapped a hand on her counter. "Zet, you, Joun and a Watcher take the Gossican over to the ship, get Keem and put him in restraints. Once you are back with him, the other two here are free to board and get the seven hells off our planet. We will deal with Keem from there."

"Agreed." Joun turned to the Gossican. "Come along. Let's get this mess done."

Chapter 47

Keem protested and complained so much that Lute moved the old life pod to a far corner of the CNY salvage yard.

Malada lay in Zet's arms with a smile on her face, remembering how shocked Eldara appeared at learning he'd been imprisoned there. But her new friend had rallied quickly enough and bravely gone with everyone on the *Demon Lair* to deposit him far from the port in the southern sector.

Eldara had the honor of dumping the pod with Keem inside. Built by Tuff-Built, the pod sustained minimal damage when dropped to the bottom of a deep cut in the floor of the old ocean, many meters down.

Their first night in the home they now shared with Eldara and Camat when the males were in port, Malada marveled at the change in her life. A job had materialized in the form of a junior customs agent under Neelah. Something she had never in all her dreams expected.

Lady Pia's old building needing more renovation than it should, the four of them, with materials purchased from Lute, had picked a place away from most of the others and erected a home the four of them could share near the head of the old riverbed that led down to the Waste. She felt more comfortable here, where her family could visit and not need to deal with the noise and bustle of the port.

There, too, changes were underway. CoDee and Cat would make planetfall soon and, working with Sebe, the negotiations with Estevanana would become final. The city admin knew trying to force the port to remain part of their tax base would not work with CNY Universal against it. The company that rose from the ashes of an old junkyard had too much money and power to be ignored. Once Este Port became an entity in its own right, the fledgling security detail being assembled would become a viable force for keeping the peace in the port.

No one wanted a bunch of rules and laws to worry about breaking, but there were some things that must be upheld. Property rights and rights to life being the ones at the top of the list.

Neelah, with urging from Cat, had contacted the Life Foundation for help in assembling and training the new security service. They were promised an officer with experience to help with setting up everything.

Zet's arm tightened around her. "Was I not energetic enough before? Why are you awake?"

"Thinking about things."

"Not the right sort of things, apparently, or you would be paying attention to me."

"You had all my attention earlier."

"I want more now."

She loved the slight hiss his words got when he had mating on his mind. The back of a very sharp claw came out of its covering and bumped her nipple several times before the very tip of that claw traced a delicate line down her body.

"We should be sleeping. There's so much to do before you leave." Her skin tightened and rippled at his touch. Malada had given up wondering how in the entire universe a male who could be kin to a tryanot attracted her. Feeling took precedence with Zet.

"You woke me." His breath drifted across her body, warning her he meant to taste her again. Need for an alien, undefined by race, perhaps engineered, rose, and she surrendered to it.

The feel of the tip of his tail exploring the soft skin inside her thighs—bliss. A fingertip, claw now retracted, stroked her bottom lip and... Zet's body against hers, smooth, tightly muscled and in great need of her.

She relished what came next. All of it.

Epilogue

Itty thought her retreat on Nizad had prepared her for Xigant. Not so. The other female's need for comfort and love hit her again as they met in a corridor. Still, she backed away. How could she open herself to so much emotion? Xigant might overpower her, knock her flat, and drain everything.

Itty fought the pull. Too many others depended on her to care for them.

All the worries she had about Zet vanished the moment she caught sight of her lizard male friend, tall, proud, and glowing almost a pulsing green. When she questioned him, the name Malada got mentioned almost every sentence. Zet had found a mate. How very amazing!

Eldara's presence with Camat had them all guessing until he called everyone into the ready room and explained. By the end of the story, Caran seemed to be nearly in a rage. With good reason. Keem had kept her only partially healed for months as he used Caran's illness to control Eldara. As a healer herself, that snake-cursed tactic infuriated her on first hearing it and nothing had changed. That Eldara would initiate the sequence that would toss the wretch into the middle of the vast southern Waste seemed only just.

The refit of the ship had gone well. Even the AI seemed rejuvenated. The hesitant quality she had sensed getting worse the longer they had to wait to get to the shipyard on Greenhouse 2 no longer tinged the ship's interaction with her. Another good thing.

The *Demon Lair* had come through better than expected for the credits they had available for the work needed. A promise of a contract had appeared through email, and hopefully, Sebe would soon have it. They were to help with setting up a security force for the newly independent Este Port.

The amount of changes which had taken place while she lounged on Nizad had her mind whirling. No problem. They would all cope and get on with life. The best thing that had ever happened to her came the day Bunde brought her to the cellar where the Demons welcomed her. The gang were all her family. Even Xigant.

The thing that surprised them all had been C'entala gift to the ship. He called it a telten, saying it was a gift Camat should have been given when he moved from the nursery. The very first thing they noticed on seeing the ship, they had each gaped in shock at the image now bonded to the hull.

The ship's name seemed to float right below the picture of what C'entala told them was a demon he had searched long and hard to find. A tooth-filled mouth in a green face. Sharp silver tusks and a head holding an intricate gold crown comprised an image of a beast holding a pock-marked world in its claws.

He said he could have it removed if they were unhappy with what he had done. None of them found fault with it. Camat loved it, as did their slightly paranoid AI, the ship having insisted on seeing what C'entala had discovered before the image got etched into the hull.

A demon from old Earth, the product of a long-dead civilization, proudly proclaimed to all who saw it that the newly refurbished ship was the *Demon Lair.*

The End... for now.

About the Author:

Meet award-winning, Best-selling author Cherime MacFarlane. A prolific multi-genre author, she has a broad range of interests that reflect her 'been there, done that' life. Romance, Historical Fiction, Fantasy, Paranormal, many characters and plots evolve from a vivid imagination.

She lives happily in Alaska. A cabin built by her husband and her keeps Cherime and her four-footed friends warm during the cold winters. Occasionally, she makes forays into other parts of the state on picture taking expeditions. Sometimes, she ventures into Canada and down to the Lower 48 but is always ready to come home.

As a reporter for the Copper Valley Views, Cherime MacFarlane received a letter of commendation from the Copper River Native Association for fair and balanced reporting. She was part of a Best Selling in Anthologies and Holidays (twice), and Fantasy Anthologies and Short Stories. The Other Side of Dusk was a finalist in the McGrath house award of 2017. Cherime has been a Best-Selling author four times and has several books that have been Number 1 on various GoodReads Listopia lists.

Other books by the author:

"The Hostage King"[1]

Sci-fi fantasy romance. "He can't leave his world; she won't be tired to a planet again." The shaman-king and the mercenary, a match made by the spirits.

Her ship is her life. She almost sold her soul to get it. The job she took should be an in and out, easy money. Zoom over to planet SW 858, grab a sample of the metal a scout discovered and head home. There's one minor problem. The planet isn't uninhabited. Silver must be careful. The Mercenaries Union doesn't like adverse publicity.

The shaman king knows she's on the way, the spirits warned him. With the Distani discovered, he must plot a course which will bring about their ultimate aim. A secret which could cost them the home they love must remain hidden. He needs the woman, for himself and for the planet he would destroy... if he must.

"A Snake by the Tail"[2]

Pirates abducted her from her planet. The Mercenary Union ship which rescues her may be no better than the pirates. Captain Maden of the Long Sword refuses to take her home.

The Messerian spy tells the captain he is not alone. There are others seeking to eliminate the pirates. He must keep the girl, Dahteste, close. She must not discover she is simply bait in the larger game they play. What gift does the girl have which makes her such a prize?

The predator his ancestors used to be claws it way to the surface around the girl. He wants things he shouldn't. He craves Dahteste.

---

1. https://books2read.com/u/mYAEAw

2.   https://books2read.com/u/4XQ8KL

"Twisted Code"[3]

She's been kidnapped!

Somehow, they disabled her implants. Waking in an antiquated ship with a Gossican captain, Indi has no idea what happened. Can she trust him?

All SUN knows how Gossicans feel about humans. They would do anything for a human partner.

He didn't hurt the female and would have taken her back to her ship... if his rogue AI hadn't interfered. Will she believe him? If not, he could be facing death or life imprisonment.

"The Bloody Stone"[4]

Iliria's clan uncle, Servolt, was a criminal. The introduction into society she expected won't happen. His business partner wants compensation. She goes into a retreat on a backward planet. The delicate female Iskonian is in disgrace and fears being used to recoup Servolt's losses.

Drk feels conflicted. As head of security, his job is to keep the peace, not get tangled up in attraction to beaten-down young females. Two more of her race turn up on Nizad, causing Drk's trouble radar to buzz.

Someone has already paid for Iliria and the buyer wants his modified female. Will she ever be free? Can Drk keep her safe?

"Wave Dancer"[5]

Bantan S'kan is the coder who escaped from the pirates who took Indi and Cenzzy captive. While on the S.U.N. scout ship, the Castner, he learns some things he didn't know about his species. Leisha, a human female from Pacifica teaches him about other things in the back of an escape pod.

Things take a bad turn when they get separated by an appeal from her family while Bantan is out helping free Indi and Cenzzy. He's desperate to find her. But if the pirates discover him, they'll use her to control the coding prodigy. Bantan must hide with Leisha when he can finally get to Pacifica. But how to keep the pirates from finding them?

"A Rookie's Share"[6]

---

3.   https://books2read.com/u/3nEdX9

4.   https://books2read.com/u/4jo8QX

5.   https://books2read.com/u/bQyWW7

6.   https://books2read.com/u/mBw6qk

Bethia, Bet to her friends met Arthan, a Vicillian while in basic. They became partners and fought their way to the top two places in their class. Crewing on the Long Sword is any rookie's dream berth. The gray all over alien interests her until she learns his secret.

His confession doesn't bring her closer, but Arthan felt he must be honest with Bet now that they have a place. He wants the Caletan female, but isn't sure how to attract her. Gray hair, skin and eyes, he's colorless.

Arthan's father is about to cause more trouble. The pirate leader wants what his father promised them and will get it from Arthan any way he can. The plan is to kidnap Bet force Arthan to buy their way free.

Greenhouse 2 becomes a trap for Arthan and Bet when the pirates find them while on leave. Can they get out of the swamp alive?

"Tanu's Vengeance"[7]

The female he was wants revenge through the male he is.

Tanu is Selvian. They spend half their life cycle as female, the rest male. As Tanat she watched her mate brutally murdered. The trauma brought about the change far too soon. Now Tanu, he wants revenge.

The Selvian intrigues Gilda. Stunning now, he must have been a magnificent female. He's in their custody and swears he has vital information about the pirates. Can she keep her distance from the alluring male? The mercenary in her is trying. The female inside wants Tanu.

"His Silver Warrior"[8]

Nic finally finds the woman of his dreams. She takes an instant dislike to him. Nic can't figure out why. He asks a favor of Indi, hack Ivanda's records with the Union. What he finds is a surprise, she lists her sexual preference as pansexual. They'll be on a mission together soon. Along with finding the lost royals of Hocte, he must change her mind about him. A very big challenge. For Ivanda, Nic will take on anything.

---

7.   https://books2read.com/u/3RLavD

8.   https://books2read.com/u/bQPkE6

"Claiming the Songbird"[9]

Captain of a ship with a paranoid AI, a crew of misfit ex-gang members and not a pilot in sight, Camat has his hands full. He's lucked into a few jobs and has a working relationship with two of the most notorious ships to claim membership in the Mercenary's Union. He's dreamed of this all his life.

Still, he's torn. The female he rescued from Keem isn't as grateful or happy to be on the Demon Lair as her sister. Worse, it's not the sister he wants.

Eldara wants to sing, to use her talent where they will acknowledge her as the songbird she is. Staying on the ship with Camat isn't an option.

The desert planet of Estevan is a low budget berth for the ship. When Eldara leaves the Demon Lair for work planetside, Camat fears she will move on to a better venue.

Fate takes a hand, and the male who once owned the sisters surfaces on Estevan. Eldara is in danger.

"Zet – Alien Species Unknown"

Malada is of the Watchers, those who roam the desert. She feels the spirit of the Waste but gives up her role to another—one who needed it more. Malada travels to the port with her father to trade their finds from a vanished civilization. In the chaos of the port, she sees what appears to be a very large lizard on the outside of a ship berthed there. Frightened by something she cannot name, Malada hides behind Joun.

Zet is an alien bred by entities he killed to escape. Taken in by the Demon gang on Calius, he works as hard as any of them to buy their ship. Second Engineer, he combs the ship, looking for anything that needs repair.

On the skin, he catches sight of the Watcher female and feels things he had never experienced before.

Zet is an alien made up of various bits of DNA and formed in a laboratory. Malada is a human female raised in a desert culture generations old, how can it ever work?

"Brain Waves"[10]

CoDee is a brain damaged young man living on a dusty desert world. He is barely functional. He hates it when dead animals get dumped in his junkyard as it "hurts his heart". The world he lives on caters to the older, poorer trading ships.

Someone dumps a large cat in his yard barely alive. CoDee helps her and Cat tries to help him. Memories of the one who injured him reveal the monster is his father.

These two entities from different species brought together on a desert world aren't physically able to bond. Love and respect are another matter.

"Bones of Others"[11]

Cat and CoDee have refitted the Bond and are pursuing their dream of being space traders. Cat only wants to find goods to trade, CoDee yearns to experience and explore. The region of space he longs to investigate has a dark history. Ships vanish.

Cat can't recall the reason this area terrifies and revolts her. Because she can't explain there is no factual basis for resistance when CoDee insists they set a course for that sector.

---

10. https://books2read.com/u/mYG7AY

11.   https://books2read.com/u/mVaKgP

And CoDee has another need. He has discovered how to mimic Cat's physical form when they play. It adds so much more to their playtime and bonding experience.

Samueland is much more than they expected. And there are two other worlds CoDee wants to see, Hunter and Pride. One of them may be their downfall.

"In Pursuit of Cheese"[12]

Cat and CoDee find something on Greenhouse II they never expected. It will change the course of their lives. Short Story

"Planet Crisis"[13]

Cat and CoDee are helping rebuild the planet Caleta after a major disaster. There, they meet Adar Genn who is assigned to train them and work with CoDee. Things don't go as Adar expects.

"Nightwind's Shadow"[14]

It's the "After Times" and a tribe must increase their herds to survive. Easier said than done.

Nightwind, a young hunter, and his dog, Mouse, are expanding their hunting range. But Nightwind finds more than game on the bench land above the head of the canyon. A treasure trove of books... and JoJo.

Nightwind's Shadow is an inter-racial, cross cultural apocalyptic fantasy romance.

"Red Revenge"[15]

---

12.   https://books2read.com/u/mlEWpB

13.   https://books2read.com/u/m0Odk7

14. https://books2read.com/u/3k0WwW

15.   https://books2read.com/u/b5jlVl

The president is a figurehead; the states are split into Red and Blue. Kidnapping across state borders of females able to breed is so bad, some women are having eggs stored and getting hysterectomies. Her grandmother told her to get it done, she didn't. Now she's being delivered to the man who paid to have her kidnapped. Marin is in real trouble.

Tanner Eugene Worthington IV suspects his father may plan to kill him. He's made plans to escape. The woman's kidnapping brings it all to a head.

"Aurora's Song"[16]

The Aurora Borealis has many legends associated with them from the northern peoples who have watched in awe for thousands of years. Not all is benign. Is there something to beware of?

Algen is finally home after spending most of her teen years, and young adulthood in Washington State. She has never been clear on the reason she got sent to live with her father's relatives. Now, she has a job she enjoys and can finally live in the place she loves.

The Aurora Borealis fascinates her; Algen has missed the lights and winter terribly. The Grannies want her to be careful. Should she be wary of the new hire at the native corporation? She's sure if he gets too close, her heart it will be in grave danger. The cultural anthropologist is pursuing her with the single-mindedness of a big predator. Gunrik is too smart, too much of a hunk and far too tempting.

"Encounter"[17]

She never picks berries in the patch behind the cabin. That hollow almost makes her skin crawl. The old cabin has been in her family for

---

16. https://books2read.com/u/38dMJO

17.　　　https://books2read.com/u/4EKPyY

generations. There is a mystery about the place the elders would never discuss. All she knows is many years ago a young couple living there vanished without a trace.

He's not sure what he was hunting. After waking next to the totaled all-terrain vehicle, he doesn't even remember who he is. What he does know is a stand of trees on a ridge is drawing him in that direction. Can he find shelter there or will he die in the Alaska bush? It's stupid, but he is going to make his way to the knoll.

Together they will have an encounter with the past.

"Solitary Hunter"[18]

A lynx shifter is the hardest person to get close to. What makes it worse is being Ken's employee. He's aware of her, more than he'd like. Ken's her boss, his hands are tied. Then the wolverine, a lynx's natural enemy decides to move in.

---

18.   https://books2read.com/u/4AwEg0

Glossary:

Biantan—foolish inexperienced female – Selvian

Maanaca—actual translation part of my body, used as an endearment. – Fantainin

Telten—A gift given when a seed becomes an entity. - Ellaerian

Tiset—small insect which infects Selvian grain fields.

Zeeneet-azet—heart of my body. -Ellaerian